R   Bw

Apache Moon

Also by Jack Bodine
in Large Print:

Beginner's Luck: The Pecos Kid
The Reckoning: The Pecos Kid

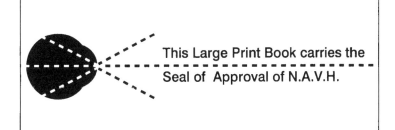

Apache Moon: The Pecos Kid

Book 3

Jack Bodine

Thorndike Press • Waterville, Maine

Published in 2002 by arrangement with
Lowenstein Associates, Inc.

Thorndike Press Large Print Western Series.

The tree indicium is a trademark of Thorndike Press.

The text of this Large Print edition is unabridged.
Other aspects of the book may vary from the original edition.

Set in 16 pt. Plantin by Elena Picard.

Printed in the United States on permanent paper.

Library of Congress Cataloging-in-Publication Data

Bodine, Jack.
     Apache moon / Jack Bodine.
        p. cm. — (The Pecos kid)
     ISBN 0-7862-3832-1 (lg. print : hc : alk. paper)
     1. Braddock, Duane (Fictitious character) — Fiction.
  2. Large type books. I. Title.
  PS3552.O366 A63 2002
     813'.54—dc21   2001058198

Apache Moon

CHAPTER 1

It was dawn, and a chill was on the Texas desert. Duane Braddock opened his eyes; the dark tops of cottonwood trees shivered in the breeze above him. He lay in his bedroll, and his woman was sprawled atop him, her cheek on his chest. The fragrance of her auburn hair filled his nostrils as she slept peacefully, breathing deeply. Duane felt happy to be alive . . . for a few brief moments.

Then he remembered where he was: Apache country. If they caught him, they'd tie him upside down on a wagon wheel, build a fire beneath his head, and perform a little dance as his brains broiled out of his ears. Duane listened for hoofbeats, or the sound of an Apache moccasin on the hard-packed dirt behind him.

He slept with his gun in his right hand, and aimed it into thick cactus and juniper.

"What's wrong?" asked the sleepy voice beside him.

"Thought I heard something."

She yawned and stretched her arms. "Time to get up."

He gazed at her bare shoulder, many shades lighter than her bronzed cheeks. "We can stay in bed a few more minutes."

"Duane . . ."

But they couldn't waste time, because Duane Braddock was wanted for a certain double murder farther north. He and Phyllis Thornton believed that the Fourth Cavalry was hot on their trail, with Apache scouts leading the way. In a small town called Shelby, two men had tried to bushwhack Duane in a general store, but he shot first and then the local cavalry commander arrested him for murder. While he was awaiting trial, Phyllis busted him out of the army camp. That was three days ago, and now they were Romeo and Juliet on the dodge. He'd just turned eighteen, she was sweet sixteen; they planned to get hitched at the earliest opportunity, but couldn't tarry in the bedroll now.

Reluctantly, he separated himself from her and stood naked on the morning desert. A cliff swallow sat atop a fishhook cactus and watched curiously as they dressed, for the bird seldom saw such strange two-legged creatures in that part of the desert. Duane strapped on his Colt and tied the bottom of the holster to his leg, gunfighter style. Then he picked up his Henry rifle, made sure it was locked and loaded, and laid it back down. He wondered whether to chance a small fire. There was dead wood lying around, and a small flame would dissipate smoke quickly in the morning air.

"What are you doing?" she asked as she fastened the buckle of her black jeans.

"Thought I'd make a fire. The meat'll be easier to chew if we cook it."

"Not if there's an arrow in your gullet. Put away the matches, Duane. No fires, please."

Phyllis was far more cautious than he concerning Indians, but she'd been raised on a ranch in Comanche territory and heard about Indian depredations, massacres, rapes, and so on all her life. She wouldn't give an Indian the time of day if she had a watch in every pocket, but Duane had grown up in a Catholic monastery and still wasn't very familiar with the secular world.

Duane was an orphan who'd left the monastery approximately three months ago, because he'd wanted to try life as an ordinary person. He'd studied Saint Thomas Aquinas, sung Gregorian chants, and helped bake bread in the monastery ovens, but since then had gone from one violent confrontation to another with people who tried to push him around or take advantage, like the duo in Shelby. Fortunately, shortly after arriving in the secular world, he'd been taught the tricks of the trade by an old retired gunfighter named Clyde Butterfield. Duane also had been blessed or cursed with an unusually fast hand.

The violence and uncertainties of the real world often baffled his theological mind, and he'd learned the hard way that his best friend was his Colt New Model Army .44. He was adventuresome, rambunctious, usually optimistic, still somewhat pious, nearly six feet tall, wide of shoulder, with white teeth and long black sideburns. His black curve-brimmed cowboy hat was minus its usual silver concho headband, which might attract undue notice in the naked desert. He also wore black jeans, a green shirt, and a red bandanna.

Duane prepared the horses, while Phyllis packed their few belongings. Sometimes she wondered if she'd gone crazy on the night she'd bribed him out of the Fourth Cavalry camp. What am I doing in the middle of Apache territory with a man I know less than a month! But there was no turning back, and she loved Duane passionately, although frequently she entertained reasonable doubts about the events that had overtaken her during the past weeks.

They met at her father's ranch, where Duane had been hired as a cowboy. It was love at first sight, they'd intended to get married, and then came the shootout in the general store. Sometimes Phyllis thought she'd run off with a complete stranger. Although Duane was two years older than she, he seemed immature and naive, perhaps because he'd spent nearly all his life in that peaceful and remote Catholic monastery, while she'd lived on a ranch beset by Indians, rustlers, outlaw gangs, drunken cowboy employees, and bad weather.

But she was no illiterate country bumpkin. Her mother had been a schoolmarm and personally administered a strict, thorough education interspersed with ranch chores. Phyllis Thornton was a true daughter of Texas, ready for anything. As she pulled on her left boot, she heard gunfire in the distance and instantaneously was flat on her belly, Colt in hand, gazing around apprehensively.

Duane lay nearby, holding his rifle tightly, finger on the trigger, trying to figure out how far away the shots were. "Sounds like a small war."

"Good thing you didn't light that fire."

"We'd better stay put until the excitement's over. Might as well have breakfast."

He unwrapped the haunch of antelope

11

meat he'd shot yesterday. It was red, bloody, laced with fat and ligaments. The only thing to do was whip out his Bowie knife, slice off a chunk, and hand it to her.

At that moment, a white head with a black eye poked beneath a cholla cactus. It was Sparky, a mongrel dog that Duane had befriended in Shelby. The dog had a face like a coyote, a body like a beagle, and the hair of a terrier. Whenever there was food, Sparky would make an appearance.

Duane cut off a strip of meat and threw it to the animal, who caught it in his jaws. Then Duane sliced a piece for himself as shooting continued faintly in the distance. They had no salt, plates, or silverware, and he was fascinated by the spectacle of Miss Phyllis Thornton eating raw meat with her hands. Blood dribbled down her chin, but she appeared untroubled. She rode horses, fired guns, wore men's clothing, and gobbled raw meat like an Apache. There was something barbaric about her, and it gave him satisfaction to know that he'd sleep with her every night for the rest of his life. They washed their raw meat down with tepid water.

"I wonder who's winning?" Duane wondered aloud, listening to random shots bouncing off purple mountains and gold mesas.

"I'd give anything for a sourdough biscuit right now, and a cup of coffee."

She'd lived in cow camps with her father and mother, but never on the desert with a person who knew the terrain even less than she. She wished the Bar T ramrod was there to provide advice, but she and Duane only had each other and the grace of God.

He placed his hand on hers. "We'll cross the border in another few days, and then you can have all the biscuits and coffee you want."

"*If* we get through these damned Apaches," she replied.

"We'll get through. This is no time to get discouraged."

He tried to sound cheerful but entertained reasonable doubts himself. They called it a desert because there wasn't much water, and Apaches were bloodthirsty fiends. The Fourth Cavalry might arrive at any moment, but Duane and Phyllis couldn't travel due to the distant shootout.

He gazed at her curvaceous body and let his eyes linger on her upright breasts pressing against the front of her cowboy shirt. The shooting stopped, the desert was silent for several minutes, and birds resumed their serenade.

"I think we should stay here for a while longer," she said. "We don't want to run into whoever won the gunfight."

"You'll get no argument from me." He leaned closer, touched his lips to her ear, and placed his hand on her breast.

Tall, wiry Federal Marshal Dan Stowe rode a lineback dun stallion toward the main house and barn of the Bar T Ranch. His flat-topped, wide-brimmed silverbelly hat was slanted low over his eyes, and he carried a Remington-Rider Double-Action revolver in a hand-tooled leather holster, slung low and tied down. He also sported a long light brown mustache styled in the flamboyant manner of General George Armstrong Custer, under whom he'd served in the great Civil War.

Federal Marshal Dan Stowe climbed down from his horse, threw the reins over the rail, and hitched up his britches. He'd come all the way from San Antone with a warrant for the arrest of Duane Braddock, dead or alive. His face was weather-beaten; he had thin lips and a long pinched nose.

A prosperous spread, Stowe thought as he scanned the barn and outbuildings. He heard wood chopping in the distance, while a cowboy carrying a rifle appeared at the corner of the ranch house. "He'p you, Marshal?"

"I'm lookin' for Big Al Thornton."

The cowboy pointed to the front door of

the main house. "Right through thar."

Stowe climbed the three steps and knocked on the door. It was opened by an attractive matron wearing a gray dress with a white apron. She took one look at the badge and said, "We've been expecting you."

He removed his hat and made a friendly smile. "My name's Stowe, and I'm here to see Al Thornton on official government business."

"I'm Mrs. Thornton — have a seat, Marshal Stowe. Could I get you a cup of coffee?"

"If it's no trouble, ma'am."

He looked her over with the eyes of a whorehouse connoisseur and considered her an attractive sturdy older woman who'd managed not to gain five hundred pounds since getting married. A Navaho blanket decorated the wall above the fireplace, while a painting of Sam Houston hung from the far wall. Stowe dropped onto a chair, crossed his long, lanky legs, and thought of the mission that had brought him to that remote corner of Texas.

A local cavalry commander named Lieutenant Clayton Dawes had arrested an outlaw named Duane Braddock, also known as the Pecos Kid. But the Kid had escaped with the aid of Miss Phyllis Thornton, daughter of the man with whom Stowe was about to speak.

15

The Kid had allegedly shot two people in cold blood, and that was all Stowe knew so far about the violence in Shelby. The accuser, Lieutenant Dawes, was currently on a scout, expected back in a day or two.

Mrs. Thornton returned with the mug of coffee, which she passed to the lawman. "I'll get my husband now." Then she paused. "I hope you don't have bad news."

"Not as far as I know."

She disappeared down the hall as Stowe sipped the coffee, thick and black, cowboy style. Stowe had been a cowboy once and found the work arduous, the pay minuscule, and bunkhouse life a bore. He'd been a lawman for five years and liked the work better than anything so far. You had to outthink your man, and that made the chase interesting.

A powerful-looking, white-haired man appeared, wearing a rawhide vest over a brown shirt with flowing sleeves. "Don't git up, Marshal," he said. "What can I do fer you?"

"I'm afraid I'll have to ask you some questions, Mister Thornton."

Big Al sat on the sofa, leaned forward, and spread his hands. "I know what yer a-gonna ask afore the words're out'n yer mouth. You want to know all about Duane Braddock and my daughter. All right — I'll give it to you

16

straight from the shoulder. Duane Braddock come here from out of nowhere, and it was brandin' season, so I hired him on the spot. Accordin' to the ramrod, he was a hard worker, but he had a firecracker temper and made an enemy of a rancher named Jay Krenshaw, who hired a fast gun called Otis Puckett to kill him. Ever heard of Puckett?"

"He operated out of Laredo, far as I know."

"Duane outdrew him in a fair fight, although there's some that said Duane's dog distracted Puckett, but Puckett was a professional and I don't think he'd let a mutt interfere with a fast draw. Then Krenshaw tried to shoot Duane in the back, but Duane managed to get off the first shot."

Stowe rubbed his lantern jaw thoughtfully. "Sounds like self-defense to me."

"That's what it was. Hell, ask my ramrod. He was thar. So was most of my cowboys. They was a-givin' Duane a party, 'cause he was a-gonna marry my daughter."

Before Stowe could ask another question, Martha Thornton spoke. "Duane doesn't have a bad bone in him. Sure, he's a little hot-headed at times, but so're a lot of other people I could name, like Lieutenant Clayton Dawes. In my opinion, the lieutenant exceeded his authority when he arrested Duane."

"With witnesses like you," said the marshal, "any judge in his right mind would let Braddock off. Why'd Braddock make a run for it?"

Big Al replied, "Put yerself in his mind. He's only a kid, fer chrissakes. They didn't have a stockade, so the lieutenant tied him to a wagon wheel, and Duane was afraid somebody might shoot him in the back, plus there's injuns in the territory. My daughter understood how he felt, so she turned him loose. I reckon they're headed fer Mexico, if'n the Apaches ain't caught 'em yet."

"As far as I'm concerned," Marshal Stowe replied, "they're still at large. What can you tell me about Braddock's background?"

"Accordin' to what he said, he was raised in a Catholic monastery in the Guadalupe Mountains until a few months ago. He went thar when he was one year old, because his parents was dead. His father was an outlaw name of Joe Braddock — ever heard of him?"

"I saw Joe Braddock's name in our files before I left San Antone. He was a real bad egg."

"His mother was a dance-hall girl, and Duane don't even know her name. They wasn't married, and Duane is embarrassed about how he was borned. I wouldn't mention it if'n I was you."

Stowe unbuttoned his shirt and took out

the warrant. "I'll do whatever's necessary to bring him in. I understand that he's also shot men in other jurisdictions."

Mrs. Thornton sighed as she sat beside her husband on the sofa. "Duane's a peaceful boy, but folks won't leave him alone. He was a good hand, and the men in the bunkhouse liked him, but he made an enemy out of Jay Krenshaw, and that's how it started."

Stowe slapped the warrant with the back of his hand. "Of course. If the lieutenant drops the charges, I won't have to go after Braddock. I don't know where that puts your daughter, since she helped him escape."

Mrs. Thornton tried to be brave, but her one and only child was on the dodge. Big Al placed his arm around her shoulder as he said, "I've hired a lawyer in Austin, and he'll git 'em both off. If Duane wasn't guilty in the first place, she had a right to turn him loose."

"I have no warrant for her arrest," Stowe said. "She's a free citizen as far as I'm concerned."

Big Al glanced at his wife. "I'd like to speak with Marshal Stowe alone in my office, if'n you don't mind."

He led the lawman down the corridor to a small room with a desk and an old Confederate flag nailed to the wall. Big Al dropped to his favorite chair and looked into the marshal's eyes. "Let's you and me understand each other. My daughter is the most precious thing in the world to me. If'n you bring her back, I'll give you two thousand dollars, cash on the barrelhead, no questions asked."

Never, in Marshal Stowe's law enforcement career, had he been offered such a fat bribe. It was as much as he earned in two years! Ordinarily he'd turn it down, but *two thousand* dollars? Before he could answer, Big Al raised his right hand and said, "You don't have to break no laws or violate no oaths. All I'm askin' is do yer best to git her out. Here's a hundred for expenses, and you'll git the rest in cash when she's in this house."

Big Al stuffed the cabbage into Marshal Stowe's shirt pocket, the lawman never said a word, and both knew that the deal had been cut. "Give me a description of Braddock," Stowe replied, "and would you have a daguerreotype of your daughter lying around?"

Duane and Phyllis spent the morning in their little hidden spot in the desert. There was nothing to do except be together, and that's how they spent most of the time. Finally, in midafternoon, Duane said, "Maybe we should move out. If we don't find water soon, you know what'll happen."

They broke camp, packed their few belongings, and saddled their horses. Their faces were covered with dust and perspiration, and they hadn't bathed since Shelby. The next few days would be the most difficult and hazardous of their lives. She took off her hat, wiped her forehead with the back of her arm, and said, "My father told me once that if you get into a fight with injuns, make sure you save the last bullet for yourself."

They rode their horses out of the small protected area and encroached on the open desert. In the distance, mountain ranges and lone buttes were silhouetted against the pale blue sky. Sparky ran to the point as Phyllis steered her horse closer to Duane's. She said, "If I don't make it, just remember that I loved you, and I always will, whether I'm in this world or the next."

He grinned. "Hey, cowgirl, don't get morbid on me. Someday we'll tell our grandchildren about how we crossed Apache territory together, when we were young, loco, and running from John Law."

Marshal Dan Stowe made his way toward the bunkhouse, his belly full of beef and potato salad prepared by Martha Thornton. He couldn't stop thinking about what a man could do with two thousand dollars. I'll go to Frisco, or maybe back to Michigan to see the folks. I could buy some nice farmland or a cabin in the woods.

His mind filled with possibilities, for he was a man of many dreams, none of which had come true. One of his fondest long-held ambitions was a trip to England, where his ancestors had lived. A man could have a big time in London on two thousand dollars, or he could invest in stocks and triple his money in a year. Marshal Stowe read newspapers avidly and knew about industries springing up all over America, as towns followed railroads into previous uncharted territory. Fortunes were being made every day, and men like Cornelius Vanderbilt and William Backhouse Astor were richer than most kings.

The bunkhouse was filthy, beds unmade, clothing flung everywhere, cigarette butts on the floor, and pictures of women nailed to the walls. "Anybody here?" he asked.

An old cowboy hat craned around the corner. "Who ya lookin' fer, Marshal?"

"The ramrod."

The cowboy came into view, wearing a dirty blue-and-white-striped apron. "He's on the range with the rest of the crew, but I'm the cook, and I'm the onliest one who stayed behind, outside of the guard. My name's McSweeny, and I ain't wanted fer nawthin', far as I know."

"If you're the cook, then you must know Duane Braddock."

"I knew 'im about as well as you can after a-livin' in this bunkhouse with 'im fer about a month. Braddock kept by himself, and weren't the most talkative person I ever knew."

"Did you see him shoot Otis Puckett?"

"I was a-standin' about as far from Puckett as I am from you right now, and it was self-defense all the way. Puckett braced Duane, not the other way around. If Duane didn't haul iron, he'd be pushin' up daisies right now. Then that no-good skunk Jay Krenshaw tried to shoot Duane in the back, but Duane was aready fer a trick. The Kid's fast — no doubt about it — but he din't start the fracas. I'll swear to it on the Bible, and so will every other man in this bunkhouse, includin' the ramrod."

"If he was innocent, then why'd the lieutenant arrest him?"

McSweeny shrugged. "Because Duane used to go with his wife. If yer know what I'm a-sayin'.

"While she was married to the lieutenant?"

"Afore she met the lieutenant, and most of us think he was jealous of Duane."

"Sounds like all the women in this area went loco over Duane Braddock."

"No tellin' what a woman'll like, but you wouldn't want to rile him, no sir. I've never seen a temper like Duane Braddock's once't he gits a-rollin'. He damn near beat Jay Krenshaw to death about a week afore the shootin'. Never seen nawthin' like it in all my days. Busted his nose, broke his jaw, and knocked out all his front teeth."

"How'd he outdraw Puckett?"

"He was just a leetle bit faster. But that's all it took."

"It's quite a story," the marshal allowed. "Braddock gets out of a monastery and a few months later he's shot all these people? It doesn't add up."

"Things was peaceful afore Duane showed up, but since then we've had two funerals, and God only knows where the boss's daughter is right now."

"What was she like?"

"Sweetest li'l thang in the world," the cook replied, a smile coming to his face. "She set her cap fer Duane Braddock right after he got here, and by gum, she got 'im. They was a-plannin' to git married, and Duane would've ended up with the Bar T someday, but now — God only knows what'll happen to 'em."

Marshal Stowe smiled skeptically. "I still don't get it. Otis Puckett was supposed to be one of the fastest guns alive and an ordinary cowboy outquicked him? I heard something about a dog that bit him."

"Naw, the dog din't bite him. It's just that Duane Braddock has got the talent. It's somethin' a man is borned with, and you can't larn it no matter how many schools you go to. I'll tell you somethin', Mister Marshal. You ever run into young Duane Braddock, you'd better talk real slow. Otherwise, he's liable to shoot yer lights out."

The sun hung like a pan of silver in the clear blue sky, and the desert reflected its shimmering heat. Duane and Phyllis rode through an oven filled with cactus flowers and birds as they scanned for signs of Apaches. The redskins could be anywhere, and one of their favorite tricks was to bury themselves beneath the ground, and you wouldn't see them until they were all over you.

Duane glanced at Phyllis, who sat solidly in her saddle, covered with perspiration, her white cowboy hat held in place with a leather neckstrap. He'd warned her that the journey would be harsh, but she'd come along anyway, for reasons he couldn't completely fathom.

His shirt was plastered to his back, he hadn't shaved since Shelby, and his throat was parched. He hoped they'd hit a water hole soon because less than one canteen of water remained. The sun enervated him, but he didn't dare droop in his saddle. Hunted by the Fourth Cavalry, surrounded by Apaches, low on everything, he didn't want to look bad in the presence of his woman. So he straightened his spine, held his elbows close to his waist, and proceeded erectly across the sage as buzzards circled high in the sky, waiting for them to fall.

The sun sank toward the horizon as Marshal Dan Stowe tethered his horse to the hitching rack in front of Gibson's General Store. He looked to his left and right, then pushed open the door. He found himself in a midsize room with a bar in back and tables everywhere. A few cowboys sat at one of them, playing cards, while a man in an apron washed glasses behind the bar. "Help you?"

"Whiskey."

The bartender filled a glass half full, and Marshal Dan Stowe knocked it back.

"Know where I can find a room for a few nights?"

"I think Mister Gibson's got somethin'. Lemme find 'im fer you."

The bartender disappeared behind the sheet of cloth that was the doorway to the rear of the building. Stowe rolled a cigarette, lit it, and blew smoke out the side of his mouth. Then he turned around, leaned his elbows against the bar, and looked at the interior of the stark saloon. Men had carved their initials into tables, chairs, and unpainted planked walls. Cigarette burns were everywhere, and cuspidors slopped onto the floor. It was the typical little whoop-and-holler, except it didn't have a painting of naked women over the bar.

"Marshal?" asked a short roly-poly man with fluffy white chin whiskers. "My name's Gibson, and I hear yer a-lookin' fer a room. You wanna come this way?"

Stowe tossed the rest of the whiskey down his throat, then followed Gibson into the corridor behind the bar. They came to a parlor furnished with sturdy upholstered chairs, with a picture of Robert E. Lee mounted above the fireplace. At the end of another hall, Gibson opened a door.

It was a small cell with a bed, dresser, chair, and rear window overlooking a backyard with sheds, privies, and piles of wood. They negotiated the price, while the shopkeeper appraised the lean sorrowful-looking marshal. "Reckon I know why yer here," Gibson ventured.

"I have a warrant for Duane Braddock's arrest, if that's what you mean."

"I din't know a man can get arrested for defendin' himself in Texas."

"Were you there the night of the shooting?"

"Saw the whole goddamned thing from beginnin' to end. It was quite a show, let me tell you. I never seen a hand move so fast in my life."

"How'd it start?"

"If'n I'm a-gonna tell ya that, I'll have to go back to the day Jay Krenshaw was borned. He was an ornery cuss all his life, but his daddy owned the second biggest ranch in the territory, and folks put up with him as best they could. Well, one day Duane Braddock showed up, and he waren't the breed what tolerates other people's shit. Jay got a little rough with 'im one day out on the range, and Duane nearly busted Jay's haid open. Jay thought he'd even the score, so he hired Otis Puckett to shoot Duane. One Saturday night Puckett walked into my saloon and told Duane to go for his gun. Everybody thought Duane had come to the end of his road, but he shot Puckett 'twixt the eyes." Gibson placed his forefinger on his forehead, to show the exact spot.

"Why'd Lieutenant Dawes arrest Duane?"

"Good question," replied Gibson mysteriously.

"I understand it had something to do with a woman."

Gibson said nothing and backed toward the door.

"This is an official investigation," the lawman reminded him. "If you withhold information, you can be prosecuted for obstruction of justice."

" 'Course it was over a woman — what else? And she used to live in this very room."

Marshal Stowe looked at the plain unpainted walls and the blue muslin curtain. "What was she doing here?"

"She come to this town with Duane Braddock — she was his woman then. They was supposed to git married, but then Lieutenant Dawes come along, and she married him instead. A few weeks later, the soldiers built her a house on the edge of the army camp, and she and her new husband had fights that you could hear all over this valley. Then she broke up with Dawes, but she's still a-livin' in the house right now. They say her daddy was one of the richest planters in South Carolina afore the war." Mr. Gibson winked lasciviously. "I reckon you'll want to talk with her, Marshal, but you'd better watch yer step. We don't see women like Vanessa Dawes very often in this part of Texas, and yer liable ter fall in love with her, too."

The sun kissed the mountain range in the

distance, casting long shadows across the sage, as Duane and Phyllis approached a circle of heavy foliage. It looked like a water hole, an ideal spot for an Apache bushwhack. Darkness fell rapidly, and one of the horses might break a leg in a gopher hole if they didn't stop soon.

They drew closer to the foliage, and Sparky's head appeared beside a clump of strawberry cactus. He was grinning, which meant that the coast was clear. Duane and Phyllis advanced among the trees, and the temperature dropped perceptibly. Ahead, twinkling in the last light of day, was the water hole. Duane held his Colt in his right hand as he glanced about, to make certain no Apaches were creeping up on him. The horses came to a stop in front of the water and lowered their great heads to drink.

Duane and Phyllis climbed down from their saddles and waited for the horses to finish. It grew darker every moment, and they didn't want to spend the night next to a water hole. They could hear Sparky dashing through nearby underbrush, dutifully scouting the area.

Duane touched his lips to Phyllis's sweaty forehead, and she melted against him. He touched his palm to her glorious rump.

"Don't get any ideas," she said.

"If there are Apaches in the vicinity, I'm sure they would've found us by now." Reluctantly, he removed his hand. "We'll move off a ways."

"Maybe we can take a quick bath."

Just then Sparky exploded into the clearing, obviously agitated about something. His body shook nervously, he licked his lips, and his eyes seemed to say, *Follow me.*

"He's found something," Duane said. "Let's see what it is."

Duane yanked the rifle out of its scabbard, and Phyllis drew her Colt .44. They followed Sparky among Biznaga cactus and Standley rosebushes as the desert grew dark, Venus twinkling impudently in the sky. A coyote yowled in a far-off cave as Sparky plunged ever deeper into the oncoming night.

Duane's legs felt bowed, after long hours in the saddle, and his high boot heels pushed him forward, giving him a cowboy swagger. Phyllis followed, gazing at his long legs. Despite danger, hardship, and Apaches, she wanted to perform certain acts that could probably get her arrested in Texas. Meanwhile, Sparky stopped at the edge of a reddish-purple Krameria shrub and pointed his nose at the lower branches. Something dark and human was lying among the dried leaves. Duane wouldn't have noticed if Sparky

31

hadn't pointed it out. The Pecos Kid and his woman dropped to their knees beside the shrub. They saw long black pigtails and a buckskin dress covered with blood.

"It's an Apache squaw," Duane said. He touched her shoulder and she felt dead. "She must've got hit in the shooting we heard this morning." He rolled her over and his eyes widened at the sight of a little boy in her arms.

Phyllis reached for the child, and his skin was warm. He was approximately three or four, wearing his little breechcloth, moccasin boots, and a red bandanna around his head, and he, too, was covered with blood. She pressed her ear against his chest. "He's alive."

The boy was well formed, brown as a nut, and limp as a noodle, with his eyes closed. There was no discussion about whether or not to help him. Duane picked him up tenderly and carried him toward the water hole. Phyllis paused a moment with the woman and noticed a necklace lying in the dried blood. The boy might want some memory of his mother someday, Phyllis thought. She untied the leather thong that held it together, put it into her pocket, and realized that she was alone.

Duane was out of sight as Phyllis perched beside the dead Apache woman. The victim appeared in her mid-thirties, with a round face and slanted eyes. "May the Lord have mercy upon your soul," Phyllis whispered. Then she turned and ran back toward the water hole.

Marshal Dan Stowe walked down the only street of Shelby, heading toward a house at the edge of town. The night was cool, and he wore his black leather vest over his white canvas shirt, with a blue bandanna wrapped around his neck. A cheroot was stuck in his teeth, and his fingers hooked the front pockets of his jeans.

A blanket of diamonds covered the sky, the moon nearly full. Marshal Dan Stowe thought of distant worlds and the paths of history. Sometimes he felt as if he'd lived two lives: first as an officer in the great Civil War, and the second was his current life. He'd participated in the most massive cavalry battles in the history of the world, and once General George Armstrong Custer had shaken his hand, but now his hand had accepted a bribe like any other crooked lawman, judge, or jurist.

Stowe wanted to return the money, but whenever he reached that decision, he thought about beautiful women with colorful parasols strolling alongside the Thames. All his life he'd wanted to go to the land of Robert

Louis Stevenson, Sir Walter Scott, and Charles Dickens. I'll bring Big Al's daughter back home either way, so it's not as if I'm selling my country down the river, or helping a real criminal to escape.

He approached a lopsided house and re-called the business at hand. Lieutenant Dawes was on a scout, but the lawman hoped to talk with Mrs. Dawes about the ticklish sit-uation that had surfaced in the course of the investigation. According to the testimony of important civilians, it appeared that Duane Braddock was arrested because he'd been planking the lieutenant's wife. The lawman smiled sardonically as he rapped his knuckles on the door.

It was opened by a soldier with a nose like a potato, wearing a white apron, with his sleeves rolled up. The first thing the soldier saw was the badge on Marshal Stowe's vest, and an expression of terror came over his face because he was wanted for armed robbery in Baltimore.

"I'd like to speak with Mrs. Dawes on offi-cial business."

"Yes, sir!"

The soldier turned abruptly and nearly col-lided with a tall, willowy blonde who ap-peared in the vestibule. "Who is it, Private Cruikshank?"

Stowe removed his hat. "Marshal Dan Stowe, and I'm here to ask you a few questions, ma'am."

She looked at him with the eyes of a woman who knew the secrets of managing men. "Right this way, please."

Stowe followed her into a small parlor filled with makeshift furniture. She was slim, with exquisitely carved high cheekbones, her golden hair falling to her shoulders, and nearly as tall as he. Marshal Stowe realized that Mr. Gibson hadn't exaggerated when he described her as a great beauty.

"Have a seat, Marshal," she said. "Can I get you something to drink?" Without waiting for an answer, she poured a glass of whiskey. Then she sat opposite him, crossed her long, lissome legs, and asked, "What can I do for you?"

She spoke with a cultured Southern drawl, and he realized that she was a former belle. "As you've probably guessed, I'm here concerning Duane Braddock."

She smiled faintly. "He's probably in Mexico right now."

"Maybe, but numerous witnesses have told me that he killed Otis Puckett and Jay Krenshaw in self-defense, and your husband had no business arresting him in the first place. I don't want to hurt your feelings, ma'am, and I know this is a delicate matter, but it's been suggested that he arrested Duane out of jealousy over you. Would you care to comment on that?"

"It's perfectly true," she replied without a moment's hesitation. "My husband even admitted it to me, but I'm afraid we're not together anymore. I'm waiting for the lawyers to settle our divorce, and then I'll leave this sorry excuse for a town."

Marshal Stowe looked her over carefully, wondering what her game was. She'd arrived in town with Braddock, then married Dawes, and now was on the loose again. The lawman had seen myriads of women in his life, but never one like this. He was too much of a gentleman to make an improper suggestion, so he said, "Do you think your husband would withdraw the charge?"

"Extremely doubtful, because he's a stubborn ass. Will you go after Duane Braddock?"

"I've got a warrant for his arrest, ma'am."

"I hope it won't be necessary to use force, because I could find you thirty people who'd swear to his innocence. You can arrest him, but no judge would ever convict him."

"I expect that's so, but I've got to bring him in anyway."

The lieutenant's wife fidgeted with her hands, and her cool facade seemed to crack.

Then she looked into the lawman's eyes and said, "Please try to be gentle with him, because he's really just a boy."

She's still in love with him, Marshal Stowe realized, and felt a pang of jealousy. His eyes roved over her once more, then he appraised his own common appearance. Something told him that she'd never sleep with him no matter how much money he had or how many fancy suits. But she willingly gave that long, delicious body to Duane Braddock.

"I'll try to bring him in alive," Marshal Stowe vowed, "but if he puts up resistance, I'll bring him in any way I can."

She smiled reassuringly. "You can reason with him, Marshal. He's not as loco as some say. I'd ask you to spare him for my sake, but we don't even know each other. Yet it would be a shame to kill a man for a crime he didn't commit — don't you agree?"

"It's true that we don't know each other, ma'am, but I'll do my best to spare him for your sake. However, let's make sure we understand each other. If he ever draws on me first, I can't be responsible for the outcome."

"How is he?" Duane asked.

Phyllis pressed her ear against the little boy's chest. "Still alive."

They bathed and wrapped him in one of

Duane's clean shirts while his little breechcloth was drying. He didn't open his eyes while Duane and Phyllis took turns washing themselves. Then they prepared to move toward their campsite for the night. Phyllis climbed into her saddle, and Duane passed her the boy. She cradled him in his arms as Duane led the horses away.

Sometimes Duane wished that he'd never left the monastery in the clouds, but lust for Mexican girls who came to mass on Sundays had drawn him into the secular world. Shortly thereafter he'd met the former Miss Vanessa Fontaine, and everything had gone downhill. Now he was deep in Apache country, the possibility of a posse on his tail, and God only knew what difficulties the child might cause. He spotted a large cottonwood tree standing among a scattering of sage, cactus, and weeds. "This looks like a good spot," he said.

Phyllis gazed tenderly at the Apache boy, and his eyelashes were fluttering. "He's coming to," she said.

The little eyes opened to slits, and an expression of terror came over his face as he glimpsed Phyllis and Duane. Then he closed his eyes and went slack again. Phyllis passed him to Duane, and the Pecos Kid thought he looked like little Jesus in swaddling clothes.

Phyllis climbed down from the horse,

38

pushed up the brim of her hat, and took the baby back. "If he dies, I don't know what I'll do."

"Apaches are hardy people, according to what I've heard. I'm certain he'll survive." But the boy was deathly pale, and Duane wasn't as certain as he tried to sound.

She made the bedroll, while Duane hobbled the horses, removed the saddles, and rubbed the animals down. "Thanks for carrying us so far," he said to them. "If we ever get through this alive, the first thing I'll do is buy both of you some apples."

He returned to the bedroll as Phyllis tucked in the boy. "I wish my mother were here. She'd know what to do."

"Let's pray," Duane replied.

They dropped to their knees on either side of the boy, clasped their hands together, and asked for divine assistance. When they were finished, Phyllis said, "I think we'd better sleep on either side of him and keep him warm with our body heat."

It was a crimp in his plans, but some things were more important than placing his hands upon Phyllis's anatomy. So he pulled off his boots, unbuckled his gun belt, and placed his gun in his right hand. Then he lay against the boy, adjusted the covers, and closed his eyes. He was exhausted and fell asleep quickly. He dreamed about Apache warriors brandishing lances and singing victory songs as they rode across the endless Texas night.

It was nearly ten-thirty in the evening when Marshal Dan Stowe returned to his little room. He peeled off his shirt, washed in the basin, put on a clean red-and-blue-plaid shirt, then sat by the window, where he lit a cheroot.

The room was in the back of the one-story building that contained the saloon and general store, and Marshal Stowe knew that Vanessa Fontaine Dawes had sat in the identical chair on many a night, looking at the sage bathed in silver moonlight. He could feel her emanations and caught a whiff of her perfume.

How strange to find such a woman in a hellhole like Shelby, he thought. She wields charm like a cavalry officer wields his saber, and did everything possible to convince me of Duane Braddock's innocence while still remaining a lady.

But a lady doesn't run off with a young hothead who'd probably end in a noose. What could an eighteen-year-old ex-orphan have that would captivate a woman like that? Marshal Stowe felt jealous of the Pecos Kid, because he'd always coveted beauties like

Vanessa Fontaine, but he was essentially a good-natured fellow, and a drink of whiskey every now and then helped the bitter pills go down.

I could go to London with two thousand dollars — what a hoot! Or I could invest in a railroad, buy a saloon, or start my own ranch. His mind raced with endless possibilities. He could even go to China, India, or Tahiti. Never had he possessed so much money in his life, and he felt a headache coming on from thinking about it so intensely.

He undressed, held the Remington in his right hand, and climbed into bed. The fragrance of Vanessa Fontaine's body arose from the mattress, and it titillated him to think that the golden-tressed beauty had lain in the identical spot. I'll talk to her husband when he returns from the scout and get to the bottom of this mess.

He closed his eyes but couldn't stop thinking about her. Her clothing was immaculate, every hair in place, her skin like unblemished white marble. She reminded him of a reproduction he'd once seen of a painting by Botticelli of Venus rising out of the sea. Evidently she'd been wealthy before the Civil War, but the South had been crushed, and the poor unfortunate woman had fallen a long way. The former Yankee troop commander wanted to save her, but no fire had ignited behind her eyes when she'd gazed upon him. She doesn't care about me in the least, he admitted ruefully, but at least I still have my honor, or do I?

He remembered the hundred dollars in his pants pocket and knew that he wasn't the upstanding lawman and ex-officer that he wanted to be. His innocence had been shattered long ago on vast battlefields covered with blood, gore, and body parts. It's not as if I'm letting an outlaw escape, he tried to convince himself. I've always wanted to go to England, and why shouldn't I? I've been through enough hell in my life, and it's about time I received my reward.

CHAPTER 2

Duane was fast asleep when something suddenly slammed into his chest. He opened his eyes and was horrified to see a painted Apache sitting atop him! Phyllis screamed as warriors held her arms, while other warriors snatched their guns away. Duane was pinned to the earth, and the Apache held a knife to his throat.

Duane gasped as the point of the knife was inserted into the first layer of skin. It had happened so fast, he wasn't certain if it was a nightmare, but he didn't dare move, otherwise the point would pierce his throat easily. His heart thrashed in his breast as he gazed into the face of the Apache warrior leering above him.

The Apache had a red stripe painted horizontally across his nose and cheeks, and wore a buckskin shirt. Around his head was wrapped a red bandanna. Duane heard Apaches speaking their strange guttural language. They rustled around the bedroll, making sounds of concern over the wounded boy.

Duane looked into the eyes of the Apache above him. "We didn't do it," he said. "We just tried to help him."

The Apache warrior spat in Duane's face, and it felt like acid against Duane's skin. He wanted to smash the Apache in the teeth but couldn't move. "Are you all right?" he asked Phyllis.

"That's a knife stuck in your throat, Duane. Just keep your mouth shut, and I'll handle this." She smiled at the array of warriors swarming over the campsite. "Do any of you speak English? I'm the daughter of Big Al Thornton."

A middle-aged Apache with a nose like an eagle stood in front of her. "Who is he?"

"My father, and many times Victorio stopped at his well." She was dropping the name of a famous Apache chief, hoping it would save her and Duane. "My father is a good friend of the Apaches."

The Apache spat at the ground. "No White Eyes is ever a friend of ours. What have you done to this child?"

"We found him, or I should say that our dog found him. We've tried to nurse him back to health."

"I think you steal little boy."

"Little boy belongs with his mother," Phyllis explained. "But his mother is dead. The law is after us, and we don't need a boy to slow us down, but we couldn't leave him behind."

The Apache thought that one over. Meanwhile, other Apaches were examining the boy and could perceive that he'd been given a bath, his wounds were dressed, and he was cared for. The Apaches conversed among themselves while Duane tried to remain calm. The point of the knife stuck into his throat, and a dribble of blood rolled down his neck. Somehow the Apaches had snuck up on them, but why hadn't Sparky warned them? He looked at the face of the Apache warrior pinning him to the ground, and he seemed a creature from another epoch. Duane felt certain that his minutes were numbered and closed his eyes. Hail Mary, full of grace, the Lord is with Thee.

There was a stir as a new group of Apache warriors appeared in Duane's peripheral vision. Another discussion ensued, with much loud talking and hand waving. "What's going on?" Duane asked out of the corner of his mouth.

"Looks like somebody important has arrived," Phyllis replied.

It was a warrior in his mid-twenties, not quite as tall as Duane but with more meat on his bones. He wore a bear's tooth in a thong around his neck, and everyone deferred to him. The young Apache chieftain knelt beside the boy, and tears welled in his eyes. His lips trembled, and for a few moments he had difficulty holding himself under control, but it passed, and his face became expressionless again. He stood, turned toward the Apaches who held Duane and Phyllis, and barked an order. Duane felt the knife recede from his throat. The Apache climbed off him, and Duane could see the full campsite.

Apache warriors were everywhere, wearing war paint, carrying rifles, knives, guns, bows and arrows, lances, and clubs. They had a wild expression in their eyes and appeared more beast than human. Phyllis looked on the verge of apoplexy, while Duane's neck stung from the puncture wound.

The chieftain examined Duane and Phyllis coldly, and Duane couldn't find a trace of humanity on that placid visage. "What are you doing here?" the chieftain asked.

Duane tried to smile. "We're on our way to Mexico. The law is after us."

"What have you done?"

"I shot two men."

The chieftain pointed to the boy on the

blanket, attended by Apache warriors. "That is the grandson of our chief. It appears that you have been kind to him. That is why you are not dead right now."

"Somebody killed his mother," Duane explained. "But it wasn't us. We heard shooting earlier in the day."

The chieftain spat at the ground. "It was Jamata's band of renegades, and they will pay one day. You will come to our camp, and then we will escort you to Mexico, as payment for your kindness to the chief's son."

"You speak English very well."

"I went to one of your schools, and learned how to be stupid."

The rancher's daughter decided that the time had come to observe social proprieties. "My name is Phyllis, and this is Duane," she said to the chieftain. "What is your name?"

"Delgado."

Duane found it increasingly difficult to smile. Apaches were fiendish, diabolical, and maybe, at the camp, he'd be burned at the stake, and Phyllis would be raped to death. Then a new thought occurred to him. "What happened to my dog?"

"He is dead."

Duane was thunderstruck. "How come?"

"He would have warned you that we were coming."

Duane felt a rise of anger but didn't dare let it show. His funny little mutt had become extinct, just like that. He wanted to pulverize the warrior who'd killed Sparky, but the law of the desert was the law of tooth and claw. Duane wished he could bury Sparky and say a little prayer, but the coyotes probably had him now, and he'd spend eternity in dog heaven. A tear came to Duane's eye, and a few of the Apaches chuckled.

Phyllis placed her hand on his shoulder. "Don't worry, you'll get another dog someday."

The warriors burst into laughter, and even Delgado couldn't suppress a smile. "You cry over a dead carrier of fleas, White Eyes? How touching, no?"

Duane heard the sarcasm in his voice and felt like kicking him in the teeth. But Duane wasn't in a small-town saloon and knew that his life hung on a thread. "That dog was my friend," he said simply.

Delgado thought for a few moments, then said something in his language. An Apache warrior carried the little boy toward a horse, and it appeared that they were about to leave the area. Phyllis rolled the blankets, while Duane prepared the horses for the trip. His guns and knife had been taken, and he felt naked. Phyllis tied the bedroll to the back of her saddle and glanced at Duane. "For a moment, I thought you were going to jump Delgado. Keep your hands to yourself, and maybe we'll get out of this alive."

"I'm not looking for trouble," Duane said. "But the sons of bitches killed my dog."

"They don't like white people, as I'm sure you've gathered by now. Please don't provoke them."

"They haven't given our guns back, and that's a bad sign." He touched his fingers to his throat, where blood had coagulated.

"I thought you were a goner," she admitted.

The Apaches climbed onto their horses as Delgado looked back impatiently at Duane and Phyllis. The two White Eyes mounted up and urged their horses forward. The little boy sat on a horse with an older warrior, his eyes closed, still unconscious, wet leaves plastered to the wound on his head.

Delgado shouted an order and the Apache warriors jabbed their heels into their horses' withers. They turned in a westerly direction as warriors coalesced around Duane and Phyllis, placing them in the midst of the formation. Hoofbeats echoed across the desert as they headed for the Apache hideout in the distant hills.

The soldiers returned to Shelby before noon, and Marshal Dan Stowe waited for them to unload their wagons. Then he swallowed the remaining drops of whiskey in his glass, departed Gibson's General Store, and strolled to the camp on the outskirts of town.

The time had come to interview the arresting officer, Lieutenant Clayton Dawes. Stowe had learned that Dawes was a West Pointer, his father a retired general living in Washington, D.C., and evidently there was money in the family. Dawes was estranged from his wife, the former Miss Vanessa Fontaine, whom he'd married approximately a month ago. Dawes also was drinking heavily, according to the scuttlebutt. His signature on a piece of paper had summoned Marshal Dan Stowe from San Antone, with a warrant for the arrest of Duane Braddock, dead or alive.

The lawman approached the canvas tents in neat rows, with soldiers rubbing down horses, cleaning equipment, and recuperating from a scout on the open range. Sometimes Stowe wished that he'd stayed in the army, but it had changed drastically since the war. Then, the men had been average citizens fighting for the Union, but the current crop of soldiers were criminals and failures from all over the world, with the officers frequently worse than the men. Their mission was to subdue Indians, and Stowe could find no honor in that. So he'd resigned his commission, become a common cowboy and then a lawman.

"Halt — who goes there!" The sentry stood before him, carbine at port arms.

"I'm Marshal Dan Stowe, and I want to speak with Lieutenant Dawes."

Stowe was led to the largest tent in the area, whose front and rear flaps were open. He dimly made out the outline of an officer sitting at a desk, presumably writing the report of his scout while it was fresh in his mind. Stowe waited outside the tent while the sentry entered. He heard a muffled conversation, then the sentry returned.

"You can go in now, sir."

Stowe ducked his head as the officer arose behind his desk. Lieutenant Clayton Dawes was in his late twenties, with long dark blond hair and several days' growth of beard. He held out his hand. "I bet I know why you're here."

"I'd like to talk with you about Duane Braddock," the lawman replied.

"Have a seat. I'd offer you something to drink, but unfortunately all I have is water."

Stowe reached into his back pocket, pulled

out a silver flask, and tossed it to the lieutenant, who took a swig. "It's not bad," the West Pointer said, "considering it was made in Fred Gibson's washtub. Have you spoken with that gentleman yet? I'm sure he believes, like all the other fools around here, that Duane Braddock is the victim of my jealousy, right?"

"That's what they all say," the lawman replied laconically, taking out his notebook and pencil. "What's your side of it?"

Lieutenant Dawes's brow wrinkled. "You've probably heard that my wife was once . . . with Braddock, and that's why I arrested him. That's the most vicious insult of my career, because it implies that I'd be petty enough to deprive another man of his liberty, due to my own pathetic jealousy. It has the ring of cheap sentiment, and makes a rather touching story, but it's horseshit. Duane Braddock is a killer, and you can see it in his eyes. But he's got that lost-little-puppy-dog charm and attracts the mother in every woman. I'm sure you've heard his supposedly tragic story by now. He was raised in an orphanage, but he turned out to be a rotten little urchin, and they threw him out. Then he hopped on a stagecoach, rode a few days, and landed in Titusville, where he shot approximately six men. His next stop was this settlement, where he shot two more. And I'm not even mentioning fistfights, barroom brawls, and wrestling matches. He's extremely violent and probably loco, but as I said, he's got a certain charm, and he smiles oh so sweetly. The people around here are rather unsophisticated, and they've been taken in by him. Duane Braddock could shoot a grandmother in the back in broad daylight on the main street of Shelby, and the good citizens would probably say that he was justified, or it was an accident, or the grandmother had evil intentions. Duane Braddock has this town bamboozled, but I'm the local authority and couldn't let him get away with shooting two people."

Marshal Stowe smiled faintly. "I've got thirty witnesses who'll say that Braddock fired in self-defense."

"I don't care what they say. Two men were dead, and I considered it my duty to take him into custody, which I did at great personal risk, by the way. I suppose you've heard that he beat Otis Puckett to the draw? He would've shot me, too, but fortunately I was able to outmaneuver him. Mind if I have another sip of that whiskey?"

The marshal threw the flask, and Dawes plucked it out of the air. He took a few swallows, sucked wind through his teeth, and said,

"If you don't believe me, that's your privilege. All I can do is my duty as I see it, but if you ever run into the so-called Pecos Kid, keep your hand near your gun and watch for a back shot. I wouldn't put anything past him, and he likes to use women to get what he wants. Have you heard that he was about to marry into the richest ranch in the territory?"

"I spoke with Mister Thornton yesterday. He thinks Duane Braddock is innocent, and is anxious to exonerate him."

"Killing is killing no matter how you cut it. If you came here hoping that I'd withdraw my report — forget it."

The sounds of the army camp came to their ears as they stared at each other. Then the marshal placed his left ankle on his right knee and lit a cheroot. "I've spoken with your wife," he said.

Lieutenant Dawes's cheek betrayed a flicker of emotion. "What did the bitch have to say?"

"The same as the others: that you arrested Braddock out of jealousy."

"I don't care what my birdbrained wife says. Braddock is personable and even somewhat charismatic, just like Jesse James, John Wesley Harding, and all the other killers, robbers, and rapists on the loose in the West these days. My best professional judgment is that he's a murderer, and I'm afraid that you'll have to bring him in — if those blood-thirsty Apaches haven't caught him yet."

The column of Apaches came to a stream at the end of a narrow winding canyon. They dismounted, sentries were posted, and they watered their horses. Duane knelt beside his animal, filled his hat full of water, and drank deeply as he regarded the Apaches warily. They moved quickly, brightly, and were extremely athletic, with sinewy arms and legs, deep bronze coloring, and rugged confidence. They continually glanced around, searching for possible danger. Delgado ambled toward Duane, accompanied by three of his warriors. He looked Duane up and down skeptically. "I am afraid that we will have to blindfold the both of you now."

Duane didn't resist as they wrapped the cloth over his eyes. A few feet away Phyllis submitted to the same fate. The world went dark around them, and they were led to their horses. They climbed into their saddles, and the column moved out again, heading in a direction that Duane couldn't discern. He tried to be optimistic, but he knew that Apaches hated white men. Something told him that he probably wouldn't be alive when the sun went down that night.

Marshal Dan Stowe sat at a table in Gibson's General Store, his map spread before him, a glass of whiskey holding down one edge. His guess was the fugitives had gone straight south, in an effort to reach Mexico as soon as possible. The first border town on the route was Morellos, and that was where Stowe hoped to intercept them. Braddock and Phyllis Thornton had a head start, but he knew the territory better than they. In addition, he'd met Apache leaders at treaty signings and powwows over the years and felt that they'd respect his tin badge. They knew damn well that if they killed him, the Fourth Cavalry would chase them to the ends of the earth.

His plan was to travel at night and sleep during the day. The only way to catch your man was just keep on a-comin'. Stowe was relentless in pursuit, and never stopped until he captured his quarry. He thought of the hundred dollars in his jeans, and guilt fell over him yet again, tormenting him endlessly. He tried to convince himself that he wasn't doing something wrong, although he'd accepted a semibribe.

Is Duane Braddock a killer or the victim of jealousy? he wondered. But I'm not the judge, and it's just my job to bring him in — no matter what it takes. And if I can return that girl to her father, so much the better. There's nothing wrong with that, right?

Commands were shouted back and forth as the Apache column came to a stop. "Get down," said the voice of an Apache warrior.

Duane lowered himself to the ground. The Apache came up behind him and untied the blindfold. The bright sunlight knifed into Duane's head. A narrow craggy incline lay straight ahead. Duane turned to Phyllis, whose blindfold was also being removed. They moved toward each other and embraced.

"Come," said the Apache warrior. "No time for that now."

Other Apaches laughed as they tugged their horses up the impossible path. Duane couldn't understand how they could traverse those jagged teeth. If he were riding by, he'd never dream that men could use it for an avenue of escape.

"What is the delay?"

It was Delgado striding toward them, a scowl on his face. "White Eyes, we know that you are weak, but please do not slow us down too much. We are anxious to return to our camp, see our wives, and mourn for our dead."

"We'll keep up," Duane vowed. "We're not as weak as we look."

Delgado placed his hands on his hips and said arrogantly, "White Eyes are pathetic, but you are stealing all our land. It is — how you say — a cont . . . cont . . ."

"Contradiction?" Phyllis asked.

Delgado turned to her and looked her over. "Thank you," he said coolly. Then he moved off with the sure movements of a mountain cat, and Phyllis wondered how many people he'd killed in order to become a leader of Apache warriors. She shuddered as he issued the command for the warriors to proceed.

Duane held the reins of his horse as he prepared for the task that lay ahead. He was determined to demonstrate that a white man could climb as fast as they, even though they'd probably kill him later. I can't slow down no matter how tired and thirsty I get.

The column advanced up the mountain, and Duane looked for the next spot to put his foot. He had to pick and feel his way around sharp boulders that were hell on boots. He looked at the moccasins that the Apaches wore, and they appeared little more than deerskin stockings, not much protection from sharp edges. They must have feet like iron, he mused as he searched for the next toehold. They were amid steep cliffs, rock escarpments, and vast plateaus. Duane turned to look at his horse, which he'd met on the night that Phyllis had sprung him out of the army camp. She'd said it was one of her father's best, and his name was Steve, while Phyllis's horse was Suzie. Duane glanced at his woman and saw that she was climbing steadily, her hat covering her face as she examined the trail before her.

He figured that he'd be tortured to death while the warriors turned Phyllis into a slave. Apaches liked to stake white people to anthills and pour honey over their faces. Or wrap rawhide thongs around a white man's head, and when the thongs dried, they crushed his skull.

If any of them lays a hand on Phyllis, I'll go for his throat, and I don't care what they do to me. He swallowed hard, because death would be nothing compared to what could happen to Phyllis. He flashed on the monastery in the clouds, where every day was like the last, full of prayers, books, and bread baked in the monastery ovens.

I'm here because of animal lust, he confessed to himself. Then he recalled Proverbs 6:27: *Can a man take fire in his bosom, and his clothes not be burned?*

He glanced ahead at the convoluted passageway, and the climb had only just begun.

Just keep going, he told himself. You can't be delicate in front of these damned injuns.

Marshal Dan Stowe examined his equipment one last time, as potbellied Mr. Gibson puffed a Pittsburgh stogie. They were standing at the hitching rail in front of Gibson's General Store, and the lawman made certain the cinches weren't too tight on his riding horse or the load unevenly distributed on his packhorse, a sad-faced creature with long ears always in motion, listening for news.

"What'll you do if you run into Apaches?" Mr. Gibson asked, flicking an ash off his stogie.

"The trick is not to run into them in the first place."

"They say they got eyes in the backs of their heads."

"So do I." Marshal Stowe placed his boot toe into the stirrup and raised himself into the saddle. "If any letters come for me, hold them till I get back. And if I don't get back, forward them to the U.S. Marshal's office, San Antone." The lawman touched his forefinger to the brim of his hat as the horses pulled into the street. He settled into the saddle, adjusted his hat low over his eyes, and rode toward the edge of town, rocking in the saddle with the motion of his horse's hooves.

He'd gone on many man-hunting expeditions, and it was a matter of simple persistence, unless the Apaches had found Braddock and Miss Thornton first. At the edge of town, a door opened in front of a familiar house and a tall blonde wearing a purple ankle-length dress appeared. Marshal Stowe pulled back his reins and the horses came to a halt beside Mrs. Vanessa Dawes. She looked at him solemnly and said, "I understand that you've spoken to my husband."

"He refused to withdraw his charges, ma'am. I'm sorry."

"That bastard!" she said bitterly. Then she tried to smile. "Just promise me one thing. *Please* don't shoot first and ask questions afterward. And *please* be gentle with him. I know that you have no reason to trust me, but Duane really is a decent boy. I can look you straight in the eye and tell you that he isn't a murderer."

Marshal Stowe couldn't help grinning at the fervor of her plea. "What about all the people he shot, and the ones he punched in the mouth?"

"There's always some bully who wants to pick a fight with him. Is he supposed to lie down and let them do it?"

He placed his arm on the pommel and leaned toward her. "Mrs. Dawes — if it will help your beautiful head to rest more easily at night, I promise that I'll be extremely reasonable with Duane Braddock, and I won't rattle him in any way."

"God bless you," she replied with a sigh of relief.

He touched his spurs to the belly of his horse, tipped his hat, and the animals plodded on to the darkening sage.

CHAPTER 3

Small, dark huts were scattered over a hilltop in the midst of ravines and steep gorges. A waterfall in the distance made a constant dull roaring, and sentries were posted high on the ridges, watching for the approach of enemies. If Duane hadn't come here himself, he wouldn't have believed that people could live in such a remote godforsaken spot.

The huts were as tall as an Apache, constructed of branches and animal skins. The entrances all faced east, and they were small hovels with no windows, quite different from tepees of the Plains Indians or hogans of the Navaho. Duane, Phyllis, and the warriors advanced toward the camp, while Apaches of both sexes and all ages emerged from the huts. The women wore buckskin skirts and blouses, while the men had on white breechcloths, moccasin boots, and red bandannas. They jabbered excitedly to each other as Duane maneuvered his horse alongside Phyllis's. The Pecos Kid and the rancher's daughter looked into each other's eyes significantly. Both knew that they might be torn from limb to limb in the minutes to come. He reached out his hand and grabbed hers, for that last bit of warmth. They squeezed, and she made a brave smile. "We'll be just fine," she said, trying to convince both of them.

Apaches swarmed around Delgado, asking questions in their rasping language. The chieftain replied, and a woman began to wail. The wounded boy was lowered to the arms of another woman. The villagers appeared disturbed and a few glowered accusingly at Duane and Phyllis.

"If they come for us," he said out of the corner of his mouth, "just fight them until they kill you. It's the easiest way, according to what the old cowboys say."

Phyllis set her mouth in a grim line. It looked like Apache women were about to attack, and she wished that her fingernails were longer. "They'll never take me alive," she said evenly.

One group of Apaches made a circle around the boy, and the rest surrounded Duane and Phyllis. Delgado alighted from his horse and broke through the crowd. He looked up at Duane and said, "Get down."

Duane and Phyllis lowered themselves to the ground, and the Apaches inched closer. Duane and Phyllis tensed, waiting for the first knife thrust. Then Delgado launched into an Apache speech while the others listened intently. Duane's flesh crawled at the sight of so many vicious savages. He gazed into their eyes and saw bottomless incomprehensibility. He'd heard stories of white men being skinned alive, or tied to cactus plants with rawhide, and as the rawhide shrank, it pulled you slowly into death from a thousand sharp needles. He gritted his teeth and tried to hold himself together.

Next to him, Phyllis was pale as the wisp of a cloud floating across the sky. She'd lived a pampered life and had never been on her own before. But she swore that she wouldn't whimper and cry, even if they burned her at the stake. She was Big Al Thornton's daughter, and she'd fight them till her dying breath. Women wailed and shrieked at the edge of the crowd. It was bizarre, and Phyllis's hair stood on end. Then Delgado turned toward Duane.

"Follow me."

Duane looked in his eyes for the lie, couldn't find it, but that didn't mean it wasn't there. You couldn't trust Apaches, and it appeared that the worst was yet to come. Delgado waded into the crowd, and the Apaches made a path for him. Duane tried to orient himself but had no point of reference. They could be anywhere, and possibly even in Mexico. He followed Delgado through a sea of faces, some expressionless, others openly hostile. Duane was certain that a hatchet would fall on his head at any moment.

His hand found Phyllis's, and they squeezed tightly. He looked at her, and her jaw was set firmly. She was ready to go down fighting, and his heart swelled with pride for the courage of his woman. "If I have to die," he told her, "I'd rather do it with you than anybody else."

"Thanks, Duane," she replied dryly, for she wasn't eager to die under any circumstances.

Delgado led them closer to the huts, and Duane examined pots, baskets, and bones lying on the ground. The children were naked except for breechcloths and red bandannas, jumping around like monkeys. A screech arose from the far side of the camp, and Duane shivered at the inhuman sound. Stew simmered in pots atop small fires that emitted no smoke, and the food didn't smell bad to two Texans who hadn't eaten all day. It appeared that they were headed for a hut in the midst of the others.

"Wait here," said Delgado. Then he ducked and disappeared into the hut. Grunts and murmurs could be heard from within, while Duane and Phyllis held each other's hands tightly and tried to be hopeful. They'd arrived at the residence of somebody important, who presumably would pass judgment.

A flap of antelope skin at the door to the hut was pushed to the side. Delgado emerged and stood respectfully to the side, like a guard at Buckingham Palace. Duane's eyes were drawn to the tent flap, from which a great personage would doubtless come forth. A gnarled brown hand appeared, the flap exploded, and a tall, husky Apache came into view, with the face of a cruel old man, the corners of his mouth turned down. He wore the standard knee-high moccasin boots and white breechcloth, with a blue cavalry officer's shirt and a belt that supported a knife and a pistol of strange manufacture. He peered intently at Duane, who braced himself for the worst.

The old man opened his semitoothed mouth and delivered an oration in his exotic tongue. Duane didn't know whether it was a welcome to Apache Land or a death sentence. It went on for some time, and Duane glanced at Delgado, to catch a hint of what was being said, but Delgado was expressionless, like a statue carved from mahogany.

Then the old chief reached forward, and Duane realized with a jolt that he wanted to shake hands. Duane expected a sneaky Apache trick, but all he could do was reciprocate. The old chief clasped Duane's hand warmly in both of his and muttered something unintelligible.

Delgado interpreted the statement. "He thanks you for saving the life of his grandson, and wants to give you five horses. He is Pinotay, our chief."

Duane had no need of five horses, but all he could say was "Tell him that we thank him for his generosity."

Delgado relayed the message, and the chief smiled. Then he launched into another oration as the crowd listened devoutly. Once again Delgado interpreted. "He says that you and your woman can stay here as his guest, until the posse stops looking for you. Then you can go on your way."

"Do you think we could have our guns back?"

Delgado spoke with the chief, who issued orders. The warrior who'd jabbed his knife into Duane's throat stepped forward, with Duane's Colt jammed into his belt. He drew the gun and protested vigorously. An argument ensued among several warriors, the chief, and Delgado. It appeared that the warrior didn't want to give up the gun.

Duane looked at Delgado. "What does he say?"

"That is Gootch, and he says that the gun is rightfully his, since he won it from you."

"But he didn't win it from me," Duane protested. "He stole it from me while I was asleep."

Delgado relayed the message, and Gootch jumped up and down furiously, slammed his fist into his palm, glowered at Duane, and issued a statement in a bloodcurdling voice.

"He says that you have insulted him," Delgado interpreted. "If you want the gun, you will have to fight him for it."

Duane looked at Gootch, who was two inches shorter than he, but with thick corded arms and a barrel chest. He appeared as though he could break Duane in half, but Duane had fought bigger men before and knew that you had to maintain your distance, pick your shots, and systematically beat them down. But fighting an Apache wouldn't be a mere barroom brawl. Apaches were said to be even worse than Comanches.

"Don't even think about it," Phyllis cautioned. "You wouldn't stand a chance."

Duane felt more like a coward every moment. He looked at Gootch and imagined blood dripping from his fangs. This is the kind of Apache who burns people upside down on wagon wheels. Duane wasn't afraid of white men, because white men had a certain code that he understood, but an Apache was unknowable. He wanted to back down but couldn't say the words.

Then the chief spoke again and proceeded to deliver another major statement. It went on at some length, and Duane wondered what he was saying. It was like President Grant delivering his State of the Union Address. Finally the chief completed his statement and turned toward Delgado for interpretation.

Delgado smiled faintly. "This chief has said that a White Eyes cannot be expected to fight a warrior from the People, because White Eyes are so much more frail than the People. So no disgrace will come to you if you do not fight Gootch, who is an experienced warrior and has killed many enemies in the past."

Apaches looked at Duane with pity in their eyes, while others were openly contemptuous. "What about my gun?" Duane asked.

"This chief will give you one of his."

"I want my own gun."

"I am sorry, but Gootch will not give it up."

Duane turned toward Gootch, who smiled triumphantly and murmured something that sounded like an insult.

"What did he say?" Duane asked, a deadly edge to his voice.

Delgado coughed. "I did not hear."

"What was it?"

Delgado sighed. "White Eyes, why don't you keep quiet while you are ahead?"

"My name is Braddock, and I want to know what he said."

"Duane," Phyllis said, "this is no time for a temper tantrum."

The Pecos Kid ignored her as he glowered at Delgado. "I'll ask you once more — what did he say?"

"He said that . . . you remind him of a girl he knew once."

It felt like a slap in the face, and the old familiar rage and shame ignited in the orphan's belly. Gootch winked and made another remark.

"What did he say that time?" Duane asked.

Delgado frowned. "White Eyes, you've had a long day. Why don't you lie down and rest for a while?"

"I asked what he said."

"He said that it would be a disgrace for a warrior such as himself to fight a puny White Eyes like you, but perhaps you might want to fight his wife for the gun?"

A silence came over the gathering, and Duane was aware that the chief was peering at him intently. Maybe I can punch Gootch into submission, but if he ever catches me in his arms, he'll crush my ribs.

"I think it's time for you to be sensible," Phyllis offered. "Why don't we lie down for a while?"

"I'm not tired," Duane said, his eyes fixed on Gootch.

Gootch burst into laughter at the mere thought that a feeble White Eyes would want to fight him, but the orphan was extremely sensitive, and derisive laughter was the cruelest insult he knew.

"I'll fight him for the gun," he said.

Delgado smiled and raised his hands in supplication. "Do not be a fool, White Eyes. You are listening to the evil ones."

Duane's blood rose, and he'd left caution behind long ago. "If he doesn't give my gun back, I'll beat the piss out of him. Tell him what I said."

"But, White Eyes . . ."

"I told you that my name was Braddock."

The chief requested interpretation, and Delgado responded at length. Then Delgado delivered Duane's challenge to Gootch, and the warrior's mouth became a thin grim line. He replied in a low throaty utterance.

"He said that he would not dirty his hands on the White Eyes."

Duane's spine stiffened involuntarily. He knew that a wise man would make a polite remark, but he didn't feel polite. He stared at Gootch and said to himself: There stands a man who thinks he's better than I.

"Let me handle this," Phyllis cautioned.

Duane ignored her. "Mister Delgado, tell him that if he doesn't give my gun back, I'll break his neck."

Delgado smiled diplomatically. "White Eyes, you are at the brink of death, whether you know it or not."

"Please convey my message."

"I am afraid I cannot, because you will be dead an instant later."

The warriors, women, and children were all looking at Duane, and he knew that they saw him as an inferior creature. The orphan was outraged, while the theology student tried to assert himself. Fighting is wicked, but a man who seeks to humiliate another can't be permitted to get away with it.

Before Duane knew what he was doing, he found himself rushing toward Gootch. He reached out his fingers for Gootch's throat and dived into the air, tensing for the inevitable collision. Gootch appeared unaware that danger was about to descend upon him, when suddenly he moved, and that was all Duane saw. Duane was plucked harshly out of the air and unceremoniously thrown to the ground. Stunned, he looked up to see Gootch pinning him down, holding the knife to his throat. Their faces were only inches apart, and Duane could smell Gootch's fetid breath. The point of the knife pierced Duane's throat in the identical spot as before, and Duane realized that he was going to die. Holy Mary, Mother of God, pray for us sinners now and at the hour of our death.

"No!" hollered Phyllis.

Her onrushing boots could be heard, and then came the sound of a scuffle.

"Let me go!" she hollered.

The knife sliced deeper into Duane's throat as Gootch grinned fiendishly above him. The Apache warrior murmured something in his feral language, and Duane heard his funeral oration. Glory be to the Father, the Son, and the Holy Ghost.

Suddenly Gootch pulled back and rose to his feet. Duane raised himself on his elbows and saw a group of Apache warriors holding Phyllis's arms. Gootch raised two of his fingers and made a brusque statement in his language.

"He said," Delgado interpreted, "that he has given you your life two times, but next time you will not be so lucky."

Blood oozed out of the hole in Duane's

throat and dripped to his shirt. He was shaken by the experience, because his own speed and skill usually won fights. He couldn't help feeling humiliated.

The warriors turned Phyllis loose. She ran toward Duane and he caught her in his arms. They hugged, kissed, and she tried to comfort him, for she'd never seen such an expression on his face.

Gootch stormed away and disappeared into the crowd. The chief approached, held out his arms, and delivered another speech. He'd never use one word when fifteen would do, but Delgado supplied a terse interpretation. "A wickiup is being provided for you. The chief invites you to have supper tonight at his fire."

Duane nodded, for he had no words for the experience that he'd just endured. A knife had been a fraction from severing his jugular vein, blood trickled down his chest, and he'd just received a dinner invitation! The sun disappeared behind the mountains, and the wickiup huts cast grotesque shadows over the camp. He felt Phyllis's breasts jutting into his chest, and realized that he was still alive. The crowd dispersed, leaving Duane and Phyllis alone. He held her tightly, and wasn't sure if he were comforting her or she were comforting him.

"The only reason he didn't kill you," she said, "was he didn't want to offend the chief."

"But he didn't give our guns back either."

"Maybe you can trade your new horses for them."

Duane scratched his head. "Why didn't I think of that?"

"You'd rather fight than think. It's what's wrong with you."

The Apaches retreated toward their wickiups, except one old man. He appeared to be seventy, average height, with one eye half-closed, and deep leathery lines on his face. He studied Duane, and Duane felt two beams of light pass through him. Then the old man limped away, and Duane thought perhaps he was an Apache lunatic. Night came to the encampment as the women lit fires. Duane and Phyllis sat cross-legged on the ground near the chief's wickiup and faced each other. Duane tried to grin bravely, but it came out crooked and uncertain.

Phyllis spat on her handkerchief and pressed it against Duane's throat. "For a moment, I thought I was a widow, and we're not even married yet. Christ said that we should turn the other cheek, remember? It looks like you forgot everything you learned in that monastery."

"I'm not Christ."

She pressed the handkerchief against his throat. "He insulted you pretty bad."

"He threw me around like a rag doll, and there wasn't a damned thing I could do about it."

"We don't want to insult our hosts, but in a couple of days, after the posse gets tired of chasing us, we'll ask to leave. And if the old chief says no" — Phyllis made her own tough smile — "I guess we'll have to be Apaches for a while."

Approximately sixty miles to the north, Marshal Dan Stowe rode his lineback dun across the night desert. The moon was bright, and he could make out the forms of prickly pear cactuses. The lawman was wide awake, poised, and vigilant. Apaches didn't generally attack in the night, but a bear, rattlesnake, or hungry wildcat might be lurking in the vicinity. The desert was a place where creatures killed and ate each other constantly, and he could smell the sweet perfume of death in the air.

Sometimes he wondered why he'd never settled for a normal life, with a wife and kids, a normal home life, and all the accoutrements that most men desire. Occasionally he suspected there was something wrong with him, as if he were incomplete, malformed, and demented.

He'd been raised in a family of four boys and three girls in a small Michigan town. His home life had been a tangle of conflicting alliances, verbal cruelty, and continual competition among his brothers and sisters for nothing of consequence. He was overjoyed when the war broke out, because it provided the chance to leave the domestic catastrophe into which he'd been born.

War was the most profound experience of his life, and to his amazement, he'd been good at it. He'd enlisted as a private in the First Michigan Volunteer Cavalry, worked his way up the ranks, and had been awarded a battlefield commission for "gallantry in the face of the enemy" at Gettysburg. Marshal Dan Stowe didn't appear heroic, but he'd participated in numerous cavalry charges, cut down countless Confederate soldiers with his cavalry saber, shot them with his service pistol, and strangled a few with his bare hands. General Custer himself had congratulated him after Brandy Station, and he'd participated in the Grand Review in Washington, D.C., on May 23, 1865, to commemorate the penultimate victory. With the rest of the U.S. Army, Captain Dan Stowe had ridden down Pennsylvania Avenue at the head of old Troop B, passing in front of the White House and saluting President Johnson, distinguished senators, famous generals, and wealthy industrialists from New York, Boston, and Philadelphia.

The Grand Review had been the pinnacle of his life, and his situation had deteriorated ever since. Captain Stowe mustered out of the army, roamed the frontier like a vagabond, then an officer friend with connections in Washington had secured the appointment as federal marshal. Stowe had been earning his daily bread stalking outlaws since they'd pinned the tin badge on his shirt.

He lived in hotels, boarding houses, and frequently slept under the stars. He drank fairly heavily, out of boredom and loneliness, and if it really got bad, there were always whores of one stripe or another, not to mention rambunctious wives, old maids, and the occasional squaw. He didn't know what a family would do for him, except make him miserable.

His thoughts turned to Vanessa Dawes, whose marriage was currently in the hands of lawyers and judges. Although Marshal Stowe had slept with many varieties of female, there weren't any Vanessa Dawes in his repertoire. She was the ideal woman who ordinarily became the wife of a wealthy financier or a U.S. senator, but instead she'd run off with an eighteen-year-old hard case known as the Pecos Kid.

It didn't make sense, but the world often presented discordant notes to a man whose trade was the underbelly of life. The marshal had met child murderers, jewel thieves, counterfeiters, cutthroats, bank robbers, rapists, assassins, and madmen. Nothing was strange or unusual to him, and sometimes he thought *that* was why he'd become a lawman, because the darker shadows of life contained iridescent glimmers that he found appealing.

He'd sensed perversity beneath Vanessa Dawes's cool outward reserve, but he'd never sip from that delicious well. The expression in her eyes had been unmistakable. She doesn't find me attractive, and there's not a fucking thing that I can do about it.

He chewed a cheroot in frustration but didn't dare light it. What is it that I lack, he wondered, and how can I get it? Charm isn't something you buy at Gibson's General Store, and I guess you have to be born with it, like Duane Braddock.

Marshal Stowe wasn't bitter about the Pecos Kid's romantic advantages, because a man has to play the hand he's dealt. If I bring Duane Braddock back alive, perhaps Mrs. Dawes will reward me. And with two thousand dollars in my pocket, she might even go to London with me. He turned down the corners of his mouth as he rocked backward and forward on the saddle. Sure she will, Marshal. Don't hold your breath.

The haunch of an animal roasted over the fire, sending savory fragrances spattering into the air. Duane and Phyllis approached as Delgado rose to greet them. "I hope you don't mind horse meat," said the Apache, a twinkle in his eye.

Duane and Phyllis sat among warriors, women, and mischievous children. The chief wasn't there yet, but Duane spotted, on the far side of the circle, the old crippled man who'd scrutinized him earlier. He sported a scar from his hairline to his chin, evidently struck in the face with a cavalry saber, half closing his left eye permanently. His features were kindly as he nodded to Duane.

Duane nodded back. It was a treacherous world, and he was trying to feel his way. The warriors were silent, and he'd never before felt so alien among other human beings. But were Apaches really human? He turned toward Delgado, who didn't become the leader of the savages because he was reluctant to kill white people.

Delgado grinned, and a beam of firelight glinted off a tooth. "Don't worry, White Eyes. We will not poison you tonight."

Did he read my mind? Duane wondered, a

chill passing up his back. There was some-thing superhuman about them, as though they lived in worlds beyond his comprehen-sion. He placed a protective arm around Phyllis's shoulder, although he couldn't de-fend her from Apaches. These people can do anything to us they want.

The wickiup flap was pushed aside sud-denly, and the old chief appeared, wearing his U.S. Cavalry blue shirt with the gold leaf insignia of a major on the shoulder straps. Everyone rose to greet the chief, who noncha-lantly sat at the fire next to the old man with the scarred face and crippled leg.

Duane found himself wondering what had happened to the major, because the Apache chief didn't buy the shirt at a rummage sale. Apaches weren't farmers and owned no facto-ries. If Apaches wanted guns, saddles, or army shirts — they stole them.

An old woman emerged from the tent, wearing the same two-piece buckskin billow-ing blouse and skirt as the other women. Her hair was medium gray, tied with a red ban-danna, and she wore a blue bead necklace. Duane thought her picturesque, and she moved with immense grace as she cut slices from the dead horse. No plates, silverware, or napkins were provided, and the table was nonexistent. They're nomads and travel light,

Duane realized. That's why the Fourth Cavalry can't catch them. He looked at stars glittering overhead, and the moon appeared to be laughing at him. They roam this beautiful land, and their main problem is us.

Duane held up his hands as a hot slab of meat was handed to him. He nearly dropped it, and a strange succulent odor wafted to his nostrils. He tried to think friendly thoughts, but it was difficult with so many armed savages in attendance. He glanced at Phyllis and caught her looking at Delgado. She noticed Duane's sudden interest, and a guilty expression came to her features, then she smiled. Duane felt jealous as he turned toward Delgado. If an ordinary warrior like Gootch could knife me in a second, what could a leader like Delgado do? Absentmindedly, Duane touched the handkerchief covering the scab on his throat. It hurt every time he moved his head.

He continued to examine Delgado, who calmly gnawed horse meat. There was something vaguely Oriental about him. What a strange hybrid he must be. "Why'd you go to an American school, Delgado?" he inquired.

"Many years ago, when the White Eyes first came to this land, they made treaties with us, and we didn't understand. It was decided that we must learn their language, so some of us went to their schools."

"There's something that I want to talk with you about. I'd like to trade Gootch five horses for the guns and rifles that he took from me. Could you be the go-between?"

"Two horses should be enough."

The meal continued, and Phyllis became aware that Delgado kept glancing at her. Attention from men was no novelty, but she'd discovered that it could backfire. She knew that Apaches married young and wondered who Delgado's wife was.

A woman with a small boy approached the fire, and it looked like the child whom they'd found beneath the bush. A red bandanna covered the wound on his head as he toddled toward the chief, his grandfather, who clasped him tightly.

Phyllis heard Duane's voice. "Is that the same one?"

"Looks like him."

Delgado raised his eyes. "It is the same boy."

"I'm surprised he's up and around so soon."

"That is because he has not been seen yet by White Eyes doctors."

The boy seemed steady on his feet but wasn't as sprightly as others his age. The boy whispered something into his grandfather's ear, and the old chief turned him loose. Phyllis watched with mounting curiosity as the boy walked in a direct line toward her. He stopped a few feet away and said something in a child's soft voice.

Delgado provided the translation. "He says he remembers when you were holding him in his arms, like his mother."

Phyllis reached into her pocket, took out the necklace, and draped it around his neck. He touched the blue stones with his tiny fingers and tears came to his eyes. Then he turned and ran to his grandfather.

A cruel expression came over Delgado's face. "My sister was killed by evil renegades from this tribe. We will find them soon, and that will be the end of them."

Duane sank his teeth into the slab of meat in his hands, and was hungry enough to eat a horse's hooves. It was tender as beef but tasted the way horses smelled. He sipped sour fermented liquor from a cup, but he'd drunk worse in saloons, "What's this stuff called?" he asked Delgado.

"*Tizwin*. It is made from corn."

One of the Apaches jumped to his feet, pointed at Duane, and began an angry tirade. Duane couldn't comprehend the language, but it was clear that the Apache didn't like his dinner companions. The angry Apache turned away abruptly, stormed into the night, and Duane took the cue. "It might be better," he said to Delgado, "if my woman and I ate by ourselves."

"You are the guests of our chief. You cannot leave."

"We didn't kill those people today," Phyllis explained. "Why was that man so angry?"

"The White Eyes are our enemies," Delgado replied.

"But we must try to live together in peace."

"The People can never live in peace with the White Eyes, unless the People live on reservations and become slaves to the White Eyes."

"Why don't you become farmers and ranchers? There's plenty of land for all of us."

"You have your lifeway, and we have ours. Why do birds fly, and the rivers flow? The White Eyes goes to church on Sunday, gets down on his knees, and prays for beautiful things. Then the rest of the week he cheats, steals, and makes trouble."

"Didn't Apache renegades kill those women today?"

Delgado glanced away angrily, and Phyllis decided to let the matter drop. Meanwhile, Duane took another swallow of *tizwin* and was starting to feel floaty. The huts looked like immense beetles in the light of the moon as stars blazed across the sky. It reminded him of his cowboy job, when they'd sit around a campfire every night, pass the bottle, and talk about horses, war, and the gals they left behind. But the Apaches lived in the open year-round, traveling with the seasons, and the White Eyes threatened their lifeway. These people aren't giving up without a fight, he realized. There'll be blood all over this desert before they're subdued.

The warriors muttered among themselves, and occasionally a woman would add a comment. Several heated remarks were made, and an argument broke out on the far side of the fire. Duane looked at Phyllis daintily placing a piece of horse meat into her mouth. He realized that the *tizwin* was altering his perceptions, because she looked like the cowgirl madonna, with a golden halo behind her head.

The *tizwin* produced a different effect from the rotgut whiskey that he'd been drinking since leaving the monastery in the clouds. Lights flashed inside his eyeballs, and Phyllis's body melted into a conglomeration of geometrical shapes. I've drunk too much of this stuff, he realized. I'm really getting plowed under. He felt the need to move his legs, for they were turning into the trunks of trees. "Anybody mind if I take a walk?"

"Do not wander too far away, White Eyes," Delgado cautioned. "Bears, mountain cats, and rattlesnakes live here, too."

Duane's feet barely touched the ground as he staggered from the fire. His head felt as though it were disintegrating, and his hands were globules of jelly. I guess you're not supposed to drink *tizwin* like water, he said to himself. He made his way beyond the perimeter of wickiups and examined the ground for snakes, scorpions, and lizards. Then he sat cross-legged and gazed at jagged outlines of mountain ranges in the distance. The Apaches were on a collision course with civilization and their lifeway would be eradicated soon. Regardless of how hard they fought, there wasn't enough of them to stop America.

Duane couldn't help admiring the indomitable spirit of the Apaches, and if they committed atrocities, so did the White Eyes. Duane had read the story of the famous massacre at the Santa Rita Mine, where white men invited the Apaches to a banquet, and while the Indians were dining, the civilized gentlemen opened fire with cannon at close range, killing men, women, and babies. Bloodshed had increased on both sides ever since. If I were an Apache, Duane thought, I'd fight back, too. At the monastery, he'd spent his life analyzing God's creation from every conceivable view. There were worlds beyond worlds, and then came the Apaches, the most ferocious Indians in North America according to the soldiers who fought them. Duane became aware of a presence behind him and saw the old man with the half-closed eye standing behind him. Duane rose, reaching for his empty holster, alarmed by the sudden appearance.

"Sit," the old man said.

Duane did as he was told, and the old man dropped opposite him, gazing into his eyes. Two rays of light penetrated Duane's mind, making him dizzy. He waited for the old man to speak.

"You have a warrior's heart," the Apache said in a deep voice. "But you are dumb. I am a di-yin, and my name is Cucharo. Was your grandfather Apache?"

Duane was taken aback by the question. "I was an orphan, and I don't know anything about my grandparents. What's a *di-yin?*"

"A medicine man."

The old man's belly was flat as a young warrior's, his limbs were sinewy, and Duane had never seen such a vital-looking old man.

"You do not know how to fight," Cucharo said sadly, shaking his head slowly in disapproval. "You make big noise and run straight at your enemy. He has plenty time to get ready and then you jump on him. It is a miracle Gootch did not kill you." Cucharo stretched his bony fingers forward and pinched Duane's arm. "You are not healthy, but I will help you. The mountain spirits have sent you to me — I do not know why. They say that I must teach you to be a warrior."

Duane was astonished by the declaration. "Who are the mountain spirits?"

"They are everywhere, but we cannot see them. You have come to me in a dream. Tomorrow at dawn, you be at my wickiup. I will tell you everything."

The old man limped away, and Duane pondered his words. Am I part Apache? he wondered.

He had vague recollections of his mother, who'd had blond curls and liked to cuddle him. His father had worn a black mustache and smelled of whiskey and tobacco. Duane recalled playing with his father's gun, but he'd arrived at the monastery when he was approximately one year old, so how much had he imagined?

Duane knew little about his background but now had something new to contemplate. Maybe my father was part Apache, and that's why I feel an affinity for these people. The medicine man saw me in a dream? A shiver ran up his spine at the mere thought of the old man with the scarred face. He's probably killed a hundred White Eyes, and maybe I'm next on his list.

Duane heard another step behind him. It was Phyllis, approaching with her cup of *tizwin*. "I think they've put something in my drink."

"It's their whiskey. Have a seat."

She dropped to the ground beside him, and he placed his arm around her shoulders. "I'll bet you never realized, when you first met me, that we'd end up at an Apache camp."

"I feel strange, Duane. There's something about these people."

"The old man with the scar said he's been dreaming about me, and he's going to teach me to be a warrior. He thinks I'm part Apache."

She looked at him in the moonlight, and he had the same straight jet-black hair as they, with high cheekbones and almond eyes. "Come to think of it, you *do* look kind of Apache. I hope you don't intend to spend a lot of time here."

"Only be a few days, like the chief said. There's nothing to worry about, I hope."

"Have you ever thought that they're playing with us, like cats and mice?"

"Don't let your imagination run away with you. I think they've been good hosts so far."

She imagined Duane wearing a breech-cloth, with a red line painted across his nose and a red bandanna on his head. "That Delgado scares me half to death. I never saw a more shifty-eyed injun in my life."

"He seems friendly enough to me."

"I think they're all acting and they're getting ready to massacre us."

"Maybe you drank too much of that *tizwin*. I know that I did. Jesus, it's a beautiful night. I can't help envying these people, Phyllis. They're not worried about owning houses, herding cattle, or buying beans. They run free, like a herd of mustangs, without a worry in the world."

"Apaches have been killing Mexicans, Americans, and other Indians for hundreds of years. Have you forgotten what happened to your throat?"

Duane touched his finger to the wound. "If I knew how to fight like an Apache, he wouldn't've defeated me so easily."

"They look down on us," Phyllis complained. "When the time comes, they'll kill us without a qualm."

Delgado materialized behind them. "I've brought your guns."

They wondered how long he'd been standing behind them and how much he'd overheard. He sat opposite them and laid the pistols, rifles, and saddlebags on the ground.

Duane and Phyllis strapped on their Colts, and Delgado watched them curiously. Duane opened the saddlebags, and his extra cartridges were intact. None of his personal belongings were missing, and he didn't feel quite so naked anymore. "I was talking with Cucharo before. He thinks I'm part Apache. What do you think of that, Delgado?"

"Cucharo is a famous medicine man among us. If he says you are part Apache, he is probably right. But Apache is not what we call ourselves. We are the People, and the White Eyes are trying to snuff us out. There will be much blood on this land, I am certain of it."

"We must make peace together, before things get that far."

"It is already too late, White Eyes."

"But Jesus Christ said that we must love each other."

"Is that the one who rose from the dead? How can anyone believe such a thing?"

"It's no stranger than your mountain spirits."

Delgado suddenly appeared angry. He leaned toward Duane, pointed at his nose, and said, "You best be careful what you say about the mountain spirits. We owe everything to them, and to Yusn."

"Who is Yusn?"

"He is the Great Spirit."

"Where did he come from?"

Delgado shook his head impatiently. "No one knows these things."

Phyllis said to Delgado, "Why is it that you act as if I'm not even here?"

"Because you are his woman."

"Does that mean I don't exist?"

"It is not good to look at another man's woman. The People are not the White Eyes. It is getting late, and I will take you to your wickiup."

Duane and Phyllis slung their saddlebags over their shoulders and followed Delgado across the camp. Little children ran among the campfires as their elders sat eating, drinking, and plotting the destruction of the renegades.

Delgado approached a wickiup near the center of the camp. "This is yours."

"We don't want to take somebody's home," Phyllis protested. "We can . . ."

Delgado didn't pay any attention to her. He looked pointedly at Duane and said, "Good night."

Then the Apache warrior walked off, leaving Duane and Phyllis in front of their new home. Duane dropped to his knees and peeked inside the door. It was pitch-black, so he lit a match. No lantern or candle was inside, animal skins lay over the dirt floor, and it smelled leathery, with the faint odor of tobacco in the air. He crawled all the way in, and Phyllis followed on her hands and knees. They could see the stars through a smoke hole in the curved roof.

"I'm afraid of these people," Phyllis said as she pulled off her boots. "My father told me a story once about a bunch of Apaches who became friendly with some Mexicans, and when the Mexicans relaxed, the Apaches slaughtered them."

Duane tossed his hat on top of the saddlebags, yanked off his boots, and unstrapped his holster. Then he formed a pillow out of the saddlebags, placed his gun close at hand, and grabbed for his future wife.

They sank into the animal fur, grasping at each other's bodies. He unbuttoned her blouse, while she reached for his belt. They rolled naked over the fur, making wild scratching love. The fierce spirit of the Apaches inspired the White Eyes, as life renewed itself high in the mountains of Texas.

Lieutenant Dawes strode across his little post, showing himself to the troopers. At West Point they'd taught him that discipline

was maintained when the men saw their officers sharing the same hardships as they. It was
dark, and the men were preparing for Taps.
Some washed pots and pans, others repaired
harnesses, a few cleaned their carbines, and a
special detail tended the horses. Four guards
were posted, to make sure Indians didn't steal
anything. The moment you dropped your
guard, that's when they attacked.

A group of troopers hammered a broken
wheel and laughed as Dawes passed. The
lieutenant suspected that they were making a
joke at his expense, but he realized that he'd
behaved stupidly when he'd met the former
Miss Vanessa Fontaine one day, married her
a week later, and split apart from her approximately ten days after that. He'd probably
laugh if someone had told him the same story
about another officer.

Lieutenant Dawes felt humiliated by what
he'd done. He came from a distinguished old
army family, but he had behaved like a
madman. The former Miss Vanessa Fontaine
had appeared when he'd been lonely, and in
his deluded vanity, he'd thought he swept her
off her feet. But now he knew that it was the
other way around. Basically, she'd figured he
was the best ticket in town.

Lieutenant Dawes passed a smirking
trooper polishing his boots, and he looked

vaguely like a Gypsy. The frontier army got all the world's rejects who couldn't or wouldn't find ordinary careers. It was rumored that a substantial number were wanted for committing crimes. Lieutenant Dawes believed that he was losing his grip on them. *They don't respect me, soon they'll defy me, and possibly one of them will try to shoot me — all because I married that crazy woman.*

He felt as though he should exact vengeance, although he knew that she hadn't done anything wrong except act in her own self-interest. *I should've been more sensible, but I was unhappy and she was so lovely.* He remembered burning nights in her arms, with her elegant legs wrapped around him. They'd got on fairly well in their ordinary domestic life, except she wouldn't stop praising a certain sadistic little killer. That was when Lieutenant Dawes had realized that his golden goddess had feet of clay. *How could she not see through the facade of the Pecos Kid?* Dawes had disliked Duane Braddock from the moment they'd first met, but every woman wanted to mother him, and older men tried to play big brother, choosing not to see his destructive spiteful nature.

But Braddock was still on the loose, as dangerous to the citizens of Texas as the Apaches. *Maybe I should take the men out on* a scout and see if we can track the little bastard down. The odds are that the Apaches have killed him, but maybe not. I'd love to see the look on Vanessa's face if I could bring back Duane Braddock in shackles and chains.

He altered his direction and made his way toward the tent of Sergeant Mahoney. That gentleman, a former resident of the notorious Five Points neighborhood in New York City, reclined near his fire, smoking his corncob pipe. He had a thick, drooping red mustache, a red nose, and a chin like the prow of a ship. Upon hearing footsteps, he raised himself to a sitting position.

"You don't have to get up," said Dawes, dropping to one knee beside him. "We're going out on a scout tomorrow morning after mess. Bring enough food and supplies for an indefinite period."

"But we just came back from a scout, sir!"

"And now we're going on another one. I've just given you a direct order, Sergeant."

Sergeant Mahoney grimaced as he puffed on his pipe. "Sir, there's somethin' that you don't understand. You been a-pushin' the men pretty hard, and there ain't a damn thing to do in Shelby 'cept get drunk. I think you oughtta let 'em rest awhile, otherwise yer liable to have a problem on yer hands."

Lieutenant Dawes raised his eyebrows.

"Rest?" he inquired. "This is the Fourth Cavalry, not a resort. Our mission is to keep the Apaches under control, and the best way to do that is to go where they are and let them know that we're not tolerating their foolishness."

"But, sir," Sergeant Mahoney pleaded, "even soldiers got to sleep, refit, and let the horses fatten a little. Mark my words — if you take the men on another scout so soon, you'll have a rebellion on your hands."

"I'm still in command here, Sergeant. See that you carry my orders out, unless you're ready to give up those stripes."

Lieutenant Dawes walked back toward his tent, hands clasped firmly behind his back. He dominated thirty-odd men through the authority of his shoulder straps and the strength of his will, with no one to back him up except Sergeant Mahoney. But Lieutenant Dawes was big, strong, skilled in the use of weapons, and relatively fearless. He believed that he'd prevail in the end because that's what they'd taught him at West Point.

He arrived at his tent, lit the lamp, and spread out his map. The Pecos Kid and Phyllis Thornton would go straight through Apache territory to Mexico. If I swing far east and then turn due west, maybe I can cut their trail, he pondered. Or maybe they'll be holed up somewhere, surrounded by Apaches, and be glad to see the Fourth Cavalry riding toward them. It's worth a try.

Lieutenant Dawes's lamp burned long into the night as he studied his map and plotted the capture of the man who'd destroyed his marriage.

Marshal Dan Stowe sat erectly in his saddle, peering into shadows for signs of danger as he rode through the endless sprawling night. He was determined that nothing and no one would take him by surprise, for he'd learned during the war that alertness spells the difference between victory and defeat.

Hunting outlaws was the most exciting civilian pastime he knew, because outlaws shot back, providing special ironies. He speculated that one day he'd find an outlaw just a little smarter than he, or the Apaches would get him and gouge out his eyes. It's my job to bring in the Pecos Kid — that's all I know. And if I find that girl, so much the better.

In his drowsy dreamlike state, he saw the castles of Northumbria rising out of the sea, with knights on horseback and ladies wearing long veils. I'll go to Stonehenge and pray with wizards of antiquity, and maybe I'll sail a boat to the Isle of Wight, or visit Glasgow, Shetland, and Sussex. My dreams'll come true when I get that two thousand dollars, and to hell with everything else.

Vanessa Dawes sat in her parlor, sipping whiskey diluted with water, while staring out the window at the open range basking in moonlight. Boring day followed boring day, and she was becoming restless, particularly at night when she was alone. With her defenses down, she contemplated possibilities that she was able to avoid during the day, when she had to present a bright face to the world.

Vanessa Dawes appeared elegant, sophisticated, and cultured to the tip of her toes, but she was deeply troubled beneath her fashionable shell. I'm thirty-one, alone, virtually penniless, and relying on a divorce settlement to spring me out of this damned town.

She hated Shelby and all that it stood for, which wasn't much in her estimation. Everybody knew everybody's business, and she'd become the notorious woman because she'd arrived in town with Duane Braddock, married Lieutenant Dawes a week later, and now was filing for divorce. It was difficult for the provincials to understand, and she wasn't sure that *she* understood.

This is what happens to a woman who listens to her heart instead of her mind, she lectured herself. If I ever marry again, it'll be for dollars. I'll go where rich men congregate — Austin, San Francisco, or even New York — and find one for myself, the older and sicker the better, and when he dies, I'll become a merry widow. Or maybe I'll just give it all to Duane Braddock, if he'll come back to me.

Vanessa Dawes was obsessed with money, because a woman with no resources could end up a prostitute in the Last Chance Saloon. She'd been raised in opulence, the only daughter of a wealthy planter, but then the War of Northern Aggression broke out, her brother was killed in action at Antietam, the family plantation was destroyed, her father died of the catarrh, and her mother of sorrow shortly thereafter.

South Carolina had been taken over by carpetbaggers and scalawags, she had no home, and all she could do was drift west, singing songs of old Dixie in saloons and taverns where Confederate veterans congregated. It hadn't been much of a living, and several men had taken advantage of her susceptibilities during her travels, but finally she'd ended up in Texas, and that's where she'd met Duane Braddock.

She'd committed certain indiscretions with Duane, but he'd been too beautiful to resist. The initial passion wore off when she realized that he was as impoverished as she, with no decent prospects, and their life together would be hardscrabble poverty. Shortly thereafter, she'd met Lieutenant Dawes. He'd looked splendid in a uniform, and his prospects were excellent, but he was the jealous type, and she soon grew tired of being persecuted.

The West Pointer had been a flash in the pan, but the Pecos Kid often came to mind in the dark of night as she prepared for bed. He'd been fun and helped her forget the misfortunes of the moment. A woman can't expect more than that from a man, she deduced.

But you're nothing without money, she reminded herself, and Lieutenant Dawes had offered the life of an officer's wife, far better than the poverty of a common cowboy like Duane Braddock. She'd made the determination with her mind, not her heart, which always would belong to Duane Braddock.

I'm getter older every minute, she reminded herself, and it's time to make use of whatever ammunition I have left. I don't want to be a toothless old crone begging for nickels in dark alleyways. She shuddered at the mere thought and hugged herself. As soon as I receive my divorce settlement, my hunt shall commence. I'll never marry again save for money, and when the old son of a bitch dies, *then* I'll buy myself anything I want, including maybe Duane Braddock.

Dawn appeared through the smoke hole as Duane opened his eyes. He smelled animal skins, heard a dog bark, and felt naked Phyllis snuggle against him. Wind rustled the outer branches of the wickiup as she stirred. "Where are you going?" she asked sleepily.

"I have to see Cucharo. He's going to teach me how to be an Apache warrior."

She rubbed her eyes as he dressed in the darkness. "Fighting is all you care about," she complained. "You wouldn't get into so much trouble if you were more peaceful."

"If I let people push me around, you'd leave me for sure."

"No, I wouldn't. If there's one thing in life that you can rely on, that's me."

He didn't say anything, because the former Vanessa Fontaine had made the identical remark before running off with the overzealous Lieutenant Dawes. Duane strapped on his gun, then leaned forward and kissed her right nipple. "Stay out of trouble," he whispered.

Then he was out the door and nearly bumped into Cucharo sitting before the wickiup, "You are late," the medicine man intoned.

Duane stared at him in disbelief as the first sliver of sun appeared over the mountains. How'd this arthritic old fogy get so close without me hearing him?

"Follow me," said Cucharo.

Duane pulled his hat tightly on his head and walked beside the medicine man. They soon found themselves on the open land, moving away from the camp. Duane realized that the old man was spry and limber as he dodged Spanish bayonet cactus plants. It was all Duane could do to keep up as sharp thorns tore his pants and shirt. The sun rose higher in the sky as Duane and Cucharo proceeded toward a steep-cliffed canyon. A roadrunner cut in front of them like a gentleman in a suit hurrying to his office, while a flock of bob-white quails flew overhead.

Cucharo stopped suddenly. "You are so slow," he said reproachfully.

"I generally ride a horse," Duane alibied.

"You must keep your body strong, because someday you might not have a horse. Are you hungry?"

"We should've brought food with us, and I'm getting thirsty, too."

Cucharo pulled a plant out of the ground, dusted off the bulbous root, and took a bite. Then he handed the plant to Duane, who looked at it suspiciously. It tasted remotely like a potato. Cucharo dusted the spines off a yucca fruit and handed it to Duane. Then the medicine man dug a hole in the dry sand. At the depth of approximately one foot, cloudy water appeared at the bottom.

"The White Eyes want to tell us how to live, but we know more than them." Cucharo gathered more food, while Duane munched on his impromptu breakfast. He'd never realized that food was available in such abundance in the desert. What's so great about living in a house when you can roam through the mountains like an Apache?

Cucharo sat opposite him, and they dined as the sun cleared away the morning clouds. A hummingbird floated in front of a yellow cactus blossom and sipped nectar. The peace and silence reminded Duane of the monastery in the clouds.

"Yusn has given us everything we need," Cucharo said. "Look up — do you see the stars?"

Duane pushed back the wide brim of his cowboy hat and looked at the blue sky. "You can't see stars during the day."

"The warrior trains his eyes by looking at stars during the daytime. Go ahead — try."

Duane stared at the sky, saw dots before his eyes, but they weren't stars. He exerted his vision and felt a headache coming on. "It's impossible to see stars during the day."

"What the White Eyes can't do himself, he thinks is impossible. The White Eyes has such small spirit."

"Maybe we can't see the stars during the day, but we have our own education."

Cucharo shrugged his shoulders dismissively. "What education?"

Duane darted to the side, spun around, and went for his Colt. The thunder of gunfire rolled across the desert, and Cucharo dived toward the ground. Duane shot the arm off a cholla cactus, the flower off a dumpling cactus, the fruit off a prickly pear cactus, and drilled a hole in the middle of a golden rainbow cactus.

The air filled with gunsmoke as the shots echoed off the mountains. Cucharo raised himself, eyes like saucers. Duane reloaded his Colt, waiting for a compliment from Cucharo, but the medicine man said nothing. Instead he sat down and continued his breakfast.

They completed the meal in silence. Duane

believed that Cucharo and the other Apaches had contempt for him, and he was determined to prove himself. When the food was gone, Cucharo rose. "Come with me."

Duane followed him deeper into the valley, with sharp cliffs and ridges on both sides. A raven flew overhead, searching for carrion, while the sun reflected off light sand, making colors extremely vivid. The desert pulsated with radiance, and Duane wondered if last night's *tizwin* was coming back to haunt him.

Cucharo stopped suddenly again. "What do you see?"

"Dirt, plants, the usual stuff."

Cucharo smiled haughtily, then clapped his hands once. Duane jumped two feet in the air and reached for his gun as creatures erupted from the ground all around him. Cucharo grabbed Duane's gun hand, and the Pecos Kid blinked in astonishment at seventeen Apache children covered with dirt. They'd buried themselves in the ground, waiting for Cucharo's signal.

"You are blind," Cucharo said, "but I must do what the mountain spirits say. Before you can be a warrior, you must strengthen your body. We start when we are young, so I will leave you with the children. I hope you can keep up with them."

Cucharo stepped backward, a crooked

smile on his face, then he dodged behind a thicket and was gone. Duane found himself with Apache boys from five to fourteen, wearing breechcloths, knee-high moccasins, covered with dirt, and grinning at the success of their trick. A little boy said to Duane, "Come with us, White Eyes."

They turned and began to walk. Duane joined them, confident that he could keep up with mere children, Apaches or not. Then the boys broke into a trot, and Duane stretched his legs. The children darted among cactus plants, laughing and shouting to each other. Duane took deep breaths as he marveled at the vigor in the children's legs. He'd spent his childhood studying theology, whereas they ran wild like coyotes.

The floor of the valley inclined as Duane and the boys headed up the side of a mountain. Duane gasped heavily through his mouth but didn't dare fall behind. It was one thing to be humiliated by a mature warrior and another to be bested by children. The mountain became steeper, and Duane's tongue hung out as he struggled to maintain the pace. The boys taunted, laughed, and ridiculed him. If they can do it, so can I, he told himself grimly. If this is what I have to do to be as strong as an Apache, I'll give it my best.

The boot of his toe found a gopher hole, he

lost his balance and raised his hands to prevent his face from crashing into the ground. As soon as he landed, little hands plucked at his clothes, helping him to his feet, and little eyes danced with delight. Duane righted himself as the children ran off again, heading toward the summit. *No matter what happens, I can't let them outrun me,* he thought to himself. Taking a deep breath, he trudged after them. The children ascended the mountain rapidly, their laughter riding the breeze, while the White Eyes rampaged behind them like a tired old buffalo.

Phyllis slept after Duane left and was awakened an hour later by children talking loudly near her wickiup. Other sounds of the Apache camp came to her, and she opened her eyes. *My first full day with the People,* she realized. She still felt sleepy, but curiosity got the better of her. She put on her cowboy clothes, pulled on her riding boots, adjusted her range rider's hat, and poked her head outside. A little boy was standing there, and he held out his hand. "Come with me."

Phyllis emerged from the tent. Women nearby rubbed a gooey substance into antelope hides, while more women cooked in pots. Some of the women carried babies in cradleboards tied to their backs. One warrior glued feathers to an arrow, while another chewed a length of sinew. The campsite was the scene of many activities as the boy led her to the old chief's campfire.

"Sit," the boy said.

Phyllis dropped to the ground, wondering what would happen next. She wished Duane hadn't left her alone among warriors who looked as though they were removing her clothing with their eyes. Her gun gave her a feeling of security as her stomach rumbled with hunger.

A young Apache woman emerged from a nearby wickiup, carrying a wicker bowl. She placed the bowl before Phyllis and said, "Eat."

The bowl contained roots and other vegetable matter that Phyllis had never seen before. She picked up something that looked like a radish and sniffed it tentatively.

The Apache woman smiled coolly. "Do not worry, White Eyes girl. We will not poison you."

How do I know that? Phyllis wondered as she sank her teeth into the root. The Apache woman was approximately twenty-five, with high cheekbones and Oriental eyes. Her hair was wavy, parted in the middle, flowing to her shoulders, and held in place with a red bandanna.

"My name is Huera," she said. "I am the third wife of Delgado."

Third wife? Phyllis asked herself. "How many wives does he have altogether?"

"Four."

"Don't you get jealous of each other?"

Huera smiled. "What for?"

"Don't you want him all to yourself?"

"The more wives, the less work. But only a rich warrior can have many wives. Most warriors have only one wife. But you do not have to do any work while you are here, White Eyes girl. We will take care of you."

"I don't mind work," Phyllis said. "I've been working all my life. What do women do?"

"We build the wickiups, cook the food, make the baskets and jugs, work the skins of animals, take care of the children, and make the clothes."

"What do the men do?"

"Hunt, fight, go on raids, and make their weapons."

Phyllis could understand better why additional wives would be welcome in a wickiup. It sounded like hard work from dawn to dusk, not unlike ranch wives. Americans were permitted one wife per household, but a wealthy man could hire maids. Was it that different from the Apache lifeway? "Don't you get jealous when your husband sleeps with his other wives?"

Huera waved her hand dismissively. "What for?"

Phyllis wondered how a person could say such a thing. If Duane slept with someone else, it would be the most terrible betrayal imaginable. Is it possible for a man to love four wives? Phyllis wondered. She remembered the previous night, when she and Duane had languished in each other's arms. She'd been a virgin until a week ago, but now it was a new world.

Delgado loomed before her, wearing only his breechcloth, moccasin boots, and headband, muscles rippling in the sun. He peered intently at her, and his energy spiked her brain. She was certain that he knew what she'd been thinking. Delgado turned away, grabbed Huera's arm, and muttered a command in Apache.

Huera didn't resist as she let Delgado pull her toward a wickiup. He pushed her inside and then he looked significantly at Phyllis. He entered the wickiup as Phyllis bit into a sweet and sour prickly fruit. He's trying to tell me something, and I think I know what it is.

She sipped water from a jug as the sun warmed her clothes. She wished she could take a bath and wondered what had happened to Duane. She'd been warned about Apaches all her life and now was living among them. Somehow they didn't seem so bad . . . yet.

She looked around the encampment, where women and men performed their specialized tasks and small children ran about like happy puppies. These are people who massacre white folks every chance they get, she realized.

Phyllis heard an ominous moan issue from the wickiup where Delgado had dragged Huera, and Phyllis's ears turned red as she realized what Delgado and Huera were doing. Delgado had grabbed Huera as if she were his personal property, and Phyllis felt revolted by the sounds issuing from the wickiup, yet somehow it stimulated her lurid imagination. She imagined handsome Delgado dragging her into a wickiup, and it didn't seem like such a bad idea. Her hand trembled as she bit another root. Don't even think about it, she counseled herself. It can only lead to trouble, and I'm a good Christian girl, or am I?

The cavalry detachment was lined in two ranks before Lieutenant Dawes, with two wagons of supplies to the right. The men sat erectly in their saddles, campaign hats slanted low over their eyes. They'd barely returned from their last scout but now were going out again. Hatred for their commanding officer radiated from their beings as they awaited his orders.

Lieutenant Dawes inspected them coolly from beneath the brim of his campaign hat. They weren't the best soldiers in the world, but they were all he had. He'd fought Indians in the past with such men, and they seemed to do best when their lives were in the most danger.

Sergeant Mahoney rode closer, the front of his campaign hat turned up for better vision. He saluted smartly and said, "The detachment is ready to move out, sir."

Lieutenant Dawes returned the salute. "Detachment — right face! Forward hoooooo!"

War equipment jangled, and horses' hooves thudded as the detachment moved toward the open range. Lieutenant Dawes touched his spurs to the flanks of his horse, and the animal trotted toward the front of the formation. He took his position as leader of the detachment, his horse slowed, and he bounced up and down in the saddle.

He'd planned a longer scout than usual, but the men didn't know it yet. Just the thing to toughen them up, he told himself. He expected complaints and resistance as the days wore on but felt certain that he could handle them. They'll respect me more when this is over, because my endurance usually is outstanding.

In the recent past, whenever he went on a scout, his wife, Vanessa, had come to see him off. She and the children of the town had applauded as the soldiers passed, but now Vanessa spent her days in their former house, waiting for the divorce to become final, and the children had become bored with the Fourth Cavalry.

Lieutenant Dawes led the detachment in a southwesterly direction as he reflected upon his former wife. She was extraordinary on the outside but vain, selfish, argumentative, and impractical on the inside. There has to be something wrong with a woman of thirty-one who'd run off with an eighteen-year-old killer.

Lieutenant Dawes remembered the first time he'd met Braddock. It had been in Gibson's General Store, and the Kid had just found out that Vanessa was going to marry the U.S. Army officer. Dawes had thought Braddock was going to shoot him in cold blood, but instead the Pecos Kid had stormed away without drawing his Colt. He obviously was afraid of me, Lieutenant Dawes figured.

I know he's out there somewhere, probably lost, with an arrow sticking out of his ass. If he's alive, I'll find him, and if he's not, at least the troopers will get some practical experience in desert living. As the old sergeants say, the men aren't happy unless they're complaining.

Dizzy with fatigue, Duane staggered to the top of the hill. The little boys pointed their fingers at him, laughing gleefully. Coughing, spitting, he tripped over his boots and dropped heavily to the ground, gulping air. He had pain in his chest, the heat was making him delirious, and he felt nauseous.

The little boys pulled him to his feet. "No rest now," one said. "Come on, weak White Eyes. Do not let the mountain lion get you."

They punched him with little hands and kicked him with tiny feet. Duane felt ashamed to be in such terrible physical condition, so he forced himself to his feet. The children were already speeding down the hill, jumping over obstacles, giggling happily.

Duane unbuttoned his shirt, then loosened the bandanna around his neck. His black cowboy hat attracted sunlight, perspiration dripped down his cheeks, and he struggled to follow the little boys. I'm going to die, he thought, gulping air frantically. I'll never be an Apache or anything else, but I hope they give me a decent burial.

★ ★ ★

Phyllis wondered what to do with herself after breakfast. The other women seemed unwilling to come close, although they continuously shot glances in her direction, not all friendly. Phyllis felt as if she were unwelcome, useless, and pointless.

It annoyed her that Duane had left her alone, but she couldn't expect him to be her father. The Apache camp was outlandish, and she didn't know what was expected of her. She decided to sit tight and wait until something happened. The exuberant mating ritual had long since subsided in the nearby wickiup, and Phyllis wondered what was going on now. Delgado had four wives, and whenever he wanted one, evidently he just dragged her into the nearest wickiup. It was the strangest thing that Phyllis had ever seen, but no one seemed to think it unusual, although everyone could hear what had transpired.

Phyllis realized that she knew little about Indians, although she'd been hearing about them all her life. I should study them, and if I ever get out of here, I can teach Americans about how Apaches live, what they eat, what they wear, and how they treat their wives.

A figure appeared in the entrance of the wickiup: Huera coming outside. She walked toward Phyllis with a certain loose gait, and her face glowed with an inner light. She appeared pleased with herself as she sat beside Phyllis. "Have you enough to eat?"

Phyllis stared at the young Apache woman in confusion, for she seemed to show no shame for what she'd done. The walls of a wickiup were just antelope skins and a few sticks, and sound carried easily from one end of the camp to another. "I'm not hungry anymore, but isn't there something I can do to help out?"

"Today we are fixing skins, but the work might be too hard for a White Eyes girl."

There it was again, the Apache condescension that was getting on Phyllis's nerves. "If you can do it, I can do it," she declared.

"Stay here, and I will bring you a skin."

Huera walked toward the side of the wickiup, where animal skins were stacked. She selected one, filled a pot with goop, and carried both to Phyllis. Then she sat, poured some of the goop on the smooth side of the hide, and worked it with her fingers. "This is how we do it," she explained.

"What's in the pot?"

"Brains mixed with fat."

The mixture looked disgusting, its fragrance bordered on horrific, and Phyllis nearly gagged.

"If you don't want to do it, you don't have to," Huera said.

Phyllis rolled up her sleeves and wondered whose brains they were. Then she took a deep breath, plunged her hands into the pot, scooped up some of the substance, and dumped it onto the skin, which she proceeded to massage. The substance was slimy and stinky, and Phyllis wondered who had dreamed up the Apache method of curing skins. Perspiration soaked her shirt as she remembered the line from Genesis: *Ye shall earn thy bread by the sweat of thy brow.*

"Delgado told me that he likes you," Huera said playfully. "He said he liked to think of you, while he was with me."

Phyllis was astonished by this tidbit of news, and all she could say was "I'll bet that made you feel real good."

"The more wives, the less work."

"I don't believe you, because I don't think we're *that* different, Huera. I'll bet you must be a little jealous."

"Men go from one woman to another like dogs. You cannot expect much from them."

Would Duane be unfaithful to me? Phyllis wondered. But Duane had been raised in a monastery and possessed high moral values, although he'd lived with the former Miss Vanessa Fontaine, and God only knew how many others. Phyllis even had speculated occasionally about her own father, when he returned from business trips with the smell of whiskey about him. He and Phyllis's mother would argue for days afterward. "I guess you can never be sure of any man," Phyllis admitted.

"How long have you been with yours?" Huera asked, her eyes twinkling with mischief.

"I've known him for about a month."

"He is very handsome, but Gootch nearly killed him yesterday. I do not think he will make a good husband, because he has no strength in his arms."

"Never underestimate a cowboy."

Huera spat into the dirt. "Cowboys ride on horses all day and think it's work. But he is very pretty. Almost like a girl."

"It sounds as if you're interested in him."

"I do not think that your man could feed two people, but maybe he is a good crook."

"Why do Apaches take things that don't belong to them? It's not very nice."

"I could say the same thing about the White Eyes, for you are stealing our land. If you were not protected by our chief, you would be Delgado's slave right now, and your man would be food for the buzzards. Delgado could do whatever he wanted with you, and you would love it. You do not fool me one bit, White Eyes girl. I have seen the way you look at Delgado. You want him, but you won't admit it."

"You're jealous, but you won't admit that. Well, don't worry about it. I'm not interested in your husband."

Phyllis would have difficulty explaining what happened next. One moment she was arguing with Huera and the next moment she was on her back, her left arm pinned by Huera's right hand, her right arm held down by Huera's knee, and a knife pressed against her throat. "This is not the White Eyes world," Huera hissed through her teeth. "Be careful what you say or I will kill you."

Huera let Phyllis up, and Phyllis was shocked. Never had she been involved in physical violence before. The attack had been sudden, vicious, and had incapacitated her instantly. She looked at Huera, who calmly rubbed brains into the hide that lay before her. Phyllis was tempted to whip out her Colt and blow Huera's head off. I'll be ready for you next time, Phyllis thought. You'll never take me by surprise again.

Duane and the boys returned to the camp at noon. The boys were tired but still happy, while Duane stumbled over his feet as he made his way to his wickiup. He crawled inside, rolled onto his back, and closed his eyes.

He'd never been so drained in his life. It was as though weights were fastened to his arms and legs, holding him to the earth. His chest heaved, and he thought he was going to die. Now he knew why seventy-year-old Cucharo had so much vitality. Apaches spent their lives running up and down mountains.

Phyllis entered the wickiup and looked with concern at his face. "Are you all right?"

His green features and wheezing respirations told the story.

She took his hand. "You'd better eat something. Come to the fire."

"Let me die in peace."

"The Apaches say we're inferior, and now you're proving it."

Duane groaned as he rolled to his knees. He followed Phyllis out of the wickiup and made his way to the fire, where Delgado sat with his four wives and numerous children, some of whom had been running Duane ragged all morning. He collapsed near the fire as Phyllis whipped out her Bowie knife. She cut a chunk of meat off the mule deer roasting on a spit and handed it to Duane. He dug his teeth in, feeling like a cross between a wolf and a wildcat. Phyllis passed him a canteen of water; he drank deeply, then cut the next strip himself and stuffed it into his mouth. A tremendous desert hunger yawned inside him, which he had to satiate.

Delgado and his wives held a conversation among themselves, glancing at Phyllis and Duane and chuckling. Phyllis was tired of being ridiculed by the Apaches, and Duane had taught her the classic fast draw, not to mention a few other neat gun tricks. But she couldn't defeat them all. Apache gratitude was wearing off, and the savages were becoming more openly contemptuous of them.

Huera sat at the right of Delgado and whispered something into his ear. Delgado glanced at Phyllis, then averted his eyes quickly. Something amused him, and he smiled. Phyllis found his manner presumptuous, as if he thought he could drag her into a wickiup and she'd thank him afterward. You ever lay a hand on me, my fine Apache friend, and I'll put one right between your eyes.

Duane and Phyllis returned to their wickiup and sat on animal skins beneath the circular column of light admitted by the smoke hole. Duane's strength returned, and he wanted to play with Phyllis until the medicine man came, but she appeared out of sorts. He frequently experienced difficulty deci-

phering her moods, for she could be happy
one moment and cranky the next, whereas he
was more even-tempered, or so he thought.
"Are you all right?"

"I don't trust these people," she replied.
"No matter how you look at it, we're enemies.
I wish we could leave today."

"We just arrived, and it wouldn't be good
to hurt the chief's feelings. As long as we're
under his protection, no one will harm you."

"The men look like murderers, and the
women are even worse."

He placed his hand on her shoulder and
gazed into her eyes. "We'll get out of this if we
remain calm. In a few days, I'll talk to the
chief. I'm sure he'll let us go."

Phyllis rubbed her arms nervously. "I'm
afraid of them."

He was about to unbutton her blouse when
he heard a sound outside the wickiup. "It's
Cucharo, and I've got to be going. Don't
worry so much. Everything'll work out fine."

He crawled out of the wickiup, leaving her
fidgeting in the dimness, the feel of his lips
still on her throat. He had interesting places
to go, while she remained amid the hostility of
the women. Phyllis recalled the moans of lust
emitting from Delgado's wickiup and felt terrible forebodings. The rancher's daughter
found herself in a strange new world and

126

wasn't sure how to proceed.

She thought of that grand old desperado, her father, swaggering about the Bar T, his big, white rancher hat slanted low over his eyes, a cigar sticking out of the corner of his mouth. He wouldn't take crap from anybody, and certainly wouldn't hide inside a wickiup all day.

Phyllis crawled outside, and Duane had disappeared. She adjusted her holster, then sauntered toward Delgado's fire, as if she didn't give a damn about anything. Delgado's wives were gathered, working on animal skins, and their eyes raised as Phyllis approached. She knelt among them, dipped her hands into the mixture of fat and brains, and resumed rubbing it into the antelope hide.

Huera glanced at her skeptically. "You were so tired — I did not think you'd come back."

"What does a woman do if she needs to take a bath, or don't you take baths?"

"We will go to the river later in the day. You can come with us. If you are not afraid." Huera's eyes twinkled with mischief. "A mountain lion may eat you."

From her kneeling position, Phyllis performed the classic fast draw, took aim at a branch sticking out of the top of Delgado's wickiup, and pulled the trigger. The camp rocked with the gunshot and the branch split in two. The wives stared at Phyllis in alarm, and warriors poked their heads out of their wickiups, weapons in their hands. She calmly blew smoke off the end of her gun barrel and dropped it into her holster. Then she resumed working on her antelope, and the women were more respectful.

CHAPTER 5

Marshal Dan Stowe rode into Morellos on a hot Wednesday afternoon. He was bearded, cadaverous, hollow-eyed, his tin badge covered with mud, and no one noticed that he was a lawman. Morellos was a typical medium-sized border town on the edge of the desert, remote from the Mexican and American armies, and infested with every stripe of desperado, bandito, outlaw, cutthroat, and traitor. Stowe had visited before, and law enforcement was erratic at best, totally corrupt at worst. A man's life wasn't worth a plugged nickel when the sun went down over the streets of Morellos.

Two oxen approached, pulling a wagon covered with animal skins, and the lawman wondered what was being smuggled beneath the pile. One-story adobe buildings with flat roofs and small windows lined the street, and the largest contained hotels, shops, saloons, and stores. Marshal Stowe turned onto Main Street, headed for the best hotel in town. He wanted to take a bath, have a drink of whiskey, and change clothes, for the tension had been terrific in Apache country. He'd had the feeling that they were watching his every move, and the only reason they hadn't attacked was he kept one finger on the trigger of his Remington twenty-four hours a day. Now at last he could get some real sleep.

He left his horses at the stable, then walked across the dusty street to the McAllister Hotel. In the lobby, old upholstered furniture crowded together, while sooty lamps hung from the walls. A Mexican with a long mustache sat behind the counter, reading a six-month-old newspaper.

"Room for the night," Stowe said. "And a bath."

The clerk winked. "How about a woman?"

"Maybe later." Stowe leaned over the counter and looked into his eyes. "You got anybody in this hotel named Braddock?"

The clerk adjusted his glasses as he glanced through the registration book. "I do not see that name, sir."

Stowe took the book from his hands and read the names. Most were illegible, but he couldn't find Braddock or Thornton, not that people always used their real names. "Ever heard of the Pecos Kid?"

The clerk scratched his nose. "Didn't he shoot somebody famous?"

"Duane Braddock is about six feet tall, eighteen years old, and has got a bad temper."

"That would describe half the men in this town, senor."

"I'd like to take the bath right away. And send a steak and potatoes to my room."

Stowe slipped a coin to the clerk, and the clerk winked as he passed Stowe the key. Stowe traversed a maze of narrow, crooked corridors, found his room, and unlocked the door. A rickety chair and bed with a cavern in the middle comprised the decor. He pulled aside the stained burlap curtain and examined the outbuildings in the backyard. Then he sat on the bed and rolled a cigarette.

It was good to have a roof over his head again, but the room felt cramped and dingy compared to clean nights under the open sky. Texas would be a great place if it weren't for the damned Apaches, he thought. He drank from his canteen, puffed the cigarette, and wondered if Duane Braddock was in town with his ladylove. There was a knock on the door, and the marshal pulled out his Remington. "Who's there?"

The door opened, and two Mexican women entered, carrying a wooden washtub.

They were followed by Mexican men carrying buckets of hot water, which they poured into the tub. Stowe pulled off his boots and a terrible stench filled the room. One of the women opened the window wider. Finally the tub was filled. The women left a torn towel and a misshapen lump of soap. Stowe latched the door behind them, removed his clothes, and slipped into the hot water, puffing on the cheroot.

I wonder if Braddock and the girl were smart enough to get through the Apaches? he asked himself. I'll talk to the sheriff first thing in the morning, and he'll tell me who's in town. If the Kid's here, I'll arrest him. If not, it means the Apaches got him, but they don't kill women. It's possible that my two-thousand-dollar reward is sitting in an Apache rancheria right now, and she's probably scared half to death.

Duane had been running with the little boys for nearly a week, and his muscles had become thicker, his breath smoother, and his legs steel springs that propelled him steadily onward. The children played tag as Duane went up the side of the mountain like an antelope wearing a cowboy hat.

The life agreed with him, and he felt better than ever as he leapt over a boulder. The old medicine man had hinted that he intended to impart special warrior knowledge, but thus far all Duane did was run up and down mountains every day in the company of frisky little boys.

They dashed over ground where horses couldn't go as they learned how to elude the Fourth Cavalry. Duane realized that the boys were warriors in training, strengthening their bodies as they studied the terrain on foot. He had to admit that it was more fun than studying Saint Thomas Aquinas in the monastery scriptorium. The freewheeling Apache lifeway made sense to him, but Duane knew that nothing was free, and Apaches weren't known for philanthropy. *The old di-yin wants something, and I wonder what it is.* He skirted around a cactus, and his jaw dropped at the sight of Cucharo sitting cross-legged stolidly in front of him! Duane tried to stop, tripped over his feet, and landed on his hands and knees. He looked up, but Cucharo had disappeared.

The children plucked at his sleeves. "Come, White Eyes. Or we will leave you here."

"I just saw Cucharo," he replied.

"He is back there." The little boy pointed in the direction of the camp. "Why are you so slow?"

Duane rose to his feet, and they leapt away from him, headed toward the crest. Duane ran behind them, slapping the dirt off his hands. *Did I see Cucharo, or am I going loco?* The former cowboy felt light-headed, wild, and expansive. *Cucharo's a clever old fox, but he doesn't* really *have magical powers, does he?*

Phyllis was harvesting mescal with the other women. They dug out the cabbagelike clusters of leaves at the hearts of the plants and tossed them into big burlap bags. The mescal would be cooked at the camp later that day.

"We go where the food is," Huera explained, working alongside Phyllis. "In the season of Many Leaves, we are here with the mescal. In Large Leaves, we go after the wild onions and locust flowers. In Thick With Fruit, we gather the pinyon nuts in the northern mountains."

"What about winter?"

"We eat what we have saved, and if we run out, the men go hunting or on a raid. The Mexicans and Americans have more than they need anyway."

Phyllis pondered the significance of Huera's statement and concluded that Apaches stole not because they were inherently wicked but only for basic survival. They're a proud people, she realized, and they're not giving up easy. She was about to dig up another cactus plant when she noticed an Apache woman working several feet away. The woman, in her mid-thirties, had a grotesque gnarled scar where her nose was supposed to be, and she hacked mightily at the base of a mescal plant. Phyllis tried to imagine what terrible fate had befallen the unfortunate woman.

They swept across the desert, accompanied by several warriors deployed as bodyguards, and one was Delgado carrying his rifle cradled in his arms. He and Phyllis were polite with each other, but tension bubbled barely beneath the surface.

Phyllis knew that he wouldn't dare rape her, for he was too devious for that. But she had to admit that despite everything, he was an attractive man swaggering around half naked. She evaluated him with the eyes of a woman and concluded that he had much to offer. Duane was a mere good-natured boy compared to the Apache warrior.

But she was a good Christian and couldn't admit the sentiments to anybody. It was a wonder that she admitted them even to herself. No one will ever know, and I'll never actually do anything, she swore. But the thought vexed her, and sometimes at night she thought of

Delgado when she lay in Duane's arms.

She wiped her forehead with the back of her hand. I'm not in love with that Apache murderer. Why, he's barely one step above an insensate beast. I wish Duane and I could leave today, but that damned old medicine man has got Duane under his thumb. Days pass, and we're still here.

It wasn't that she didn't like Apache life. In fact, she preferred working outdoors, and the wickiup was a cozy place to sleep at night. Maybe people don't need as much room as they think, she figured. She wasn't accustomed to having other women for company, unlike the Bar T where it had been she and her mother against fifteen men.

The Apache women had stopped insulting her since the shooting demonstration. But Phyllis never relaxed her vigilance, and if she heard an unfamiliar sound, she went for her gun. The women also carried weapons — long, gleaming knives. They listened and watched, too, ever alert for enemies.

Phyllis faced another mescal plant, and her eyes fell once more on the woman without a nose. The woman's eyes were sad, and she looked like a monster. Phyllis searched for Huera and saw her twenty yards away, behind a cholla cactus.

Phyllis walked toward her and whispered in

her ear, "What happened to that woman over there — the one without a nose?"

"Her husband cut it off."

Phyllis stared at her. "Why?"

"Because she cheat on him."

"Is this a custom of yours?"

Huera nodded.

"What happened to the man she cheated with?"

"He is dead."

The sheriff's office was next door to the El Sombrero Saloon, on the main street of Morellos. Marshal Dan Stowe found the local lawman sitting at his desk, looking at a stack of wanted posters recently arrived by stage from Austin.

"Well, I'll be a cotton-mouthed water moccasin!" Sheriff Abner Tillman declared as he rose behind his desk.

The two lawmen shook hands. "Looking for your own picture?" Stowe replied. "I know you're wanted somewhere — a crazy son of a bitch like you."

"To tell you the truth, I was a-lookin' fer you!" Sheriff Tillman wore a black beard that grew nearly as high as his eyes. A Bible sat on his desk beneath a book of Texas statutes, laws, regulations, and directives. "What brings you to town?"

"I'm looking for two people, and I figure they arrived within the past several days. One's an eighteen-year-old man, medium weight, black hair, and the other's a sixteen-year-old girl, also black hair, cute as a button I'm told. Seen them around?"

Tillman rubbed his chin thoughtfully. "We got a few gals like that, but they been here awhile. As fer the man, he could be anybody. What've they done?"

"His name's Duane Braddock, and he shot two men in Shelby. The girl's name is Phyllis Thornton, and she sprang him out of the army camp where he was being held. They cut out from Shelby and headed due south. I figure they had to come here, unless the Apaches got them."

Sheriff Tillman snorted. " 'At's probably what happened. The damned redskins fed Braddock to the coyotes and took the girl for a slave."

Stowe looked from side to side, to make sure no one was around. Then he leaned toward Tillman and said, "There are traders who do business with the Apaches. Can you give me a name?"

"They might not want to talk to you, 'cause yer the law and most of 'em sell whiskey to the injuns."

"I asked for a name."

"You can't trust 'em as far as you can throw 'em. They're liable to take one look at that badge on yer shirt, shoot first, and ask questions later."

"Name?"

Tillman sighed in defeat. "Halfway down the block you'll see a saloon named the Black Cat. Ask for Miguelito and tell him I sent you."

Lieutenant Clayton Dawes sat cross-legged beneath a mesquite tree, studying his map. He wore a scraggly beard, his clothes were filthy and tattered, skin peeled from his cheeks, and he wondered where in hell he was.

He and his men had been on the scout for nearly two weeks, and all they'd found were rattlesnakes, gophers, and armadillos, while a medley of buzzards circled overhead. They'd run out of water once but found a hole before anybody dropped out of the saddle.

Lieutenant Dawes's eyes were hollow and staring from so much sunlight, while his perspiration-soaked uniform hung loosely on his frame. But he wasn't one to give up easily. What kind of country would America be if outlaws committed crimes without fear of retribution?

He hadn't seen any Apaches, but smoke

signals had risen from the mountains every day. The red devils were tracking his progress, and he wished they'd come into the open, so he could talk with them. He was becoming increasingly certain that Duane Braddock and Phyllis Thornton had been captured or killed by Apaches. Even seasoned desert riders were stopped by Apaches, so how could two dumb children get through?

He heard footsteps and raised his eyes. Sergeant Mahoney approached with his campaign hat low over his eyes and a scowl on his face. "Request permission to speak to the detachment commander, sir?"

"Pull up a chair and sit down, Sergeant. What's on your so-called mind?"

Sergeant Mahoney sat cross-legged opposite Lieutenant Dawes, while a group of men and horses gathered about thirty yards away. The doughty sergeant leaned forward and asked, "Do you have any idea of what yer a-doin', sir? This is the longest scout we been on, and it looks like we're a-goin' around in circles."

"We're not riding in circles, Sergeant. I'm keeping track of our progress with my map and compass. We're right here." He pointed confidently to a likely spot on the map, although he had no idea of their present location.

Sergeant Mahoney narrowed one eye. "Don't you think it's time we headed back to Shelby, sir? I mean, what the hell do you think yer a-doin' out here?"

"Sergeant Mahoney, let me remind you of an important fact. I ask the questions and you answer them. Not the other way around."

"The men're gittin' riled, sir. They don't mind fightin' Apaches, and they can live on thirteen dollars a month, but they don't like to scout day after day fer no good reason. Git my drift?"

"This is still the army, Sergeant. The men will follow my commands, or I'll place them under arrest. We're on official government business, and don't let the men forget it."

Sergeant Mahoney spat tobacco juice into the dirt. "What's the official government business? You know what the men say? They think yer a-lookin' fer Duane Braddock 'cause he screwed yer wife."

Color drained from Lieutenant Dawes's face. Never had he been so insulted by an enlisted man, but he was a West Point graduate and his self-discipline remained impeccable. "Duane Braddock escaped because of the men themselves. He's a fugitive, and I'll damn sure arrest him if he passes by, but he's not why we're here. You've been in the army long enough to know better, but I guess I'll have to spell it out for you. It's important to scout Apache territory, so the redskins'll learn that they don't have a free hand here."

"That ain't what the men say 'cuzz . . ."

Lieutenant Dawes interrupted him. "I don't care what the men say as long as they don't say it to me."

Sergeant Mahoney observed madness flickering in the murky pupils of Lieutenant Dawes's eyes and decided to back off. "What should I tell the men, sir?"

"They'd better keep their eyes peeled and their mouths shut. And if any of them thinks they're big enough to shoot me, they're welcome to try."

The sign said BLACK CAT SALOON. A crude black cat was painted next to the bat-wing doors, which Marshal Dan Stowe pushed open. He stepped out of the backlight and stood with his hand near his gun, ready to draw and fire.

The saloon was filled with Mexicans, Americans, and half-breeds of every type, speaking to each other in low tones, playing cards, and drinking whiskey. Stowe figured that half were wanted, with the rest plotting future crimes. The border was a good place to do business, in case fast disappearances were required.

Everyone looked at the tin badge as the federal marshal threaded among the tables, his hand near his Remington. The bartender muttered something, and a group of customers made way. "What can I do fer ya, Marshal?"

"Whiskey."

The bartender filled a glass to the halfway mark, and Stowe threw a few coins on the counter. "I'm looking for Miguelito."

"Who's Miguelito?"

Marshal Stowe reached forward and grabbed a fistful of the bartender's shirt. "Sheriff Tillman sent me to talk with him."

The bartender went pale. "Over there."

A dark-skinned midget with a nose like a fist sat at a table, reading a newspaper and drinking whiskey. Marshal Stowe carried his glass across the floor as gamblers and desperadoes watched his progress. Miguelito saw him coming and lowered his hand toward his gun.

"Mind if I sit down?" Stowe asked. Miguelito didn't dare protest as Stowe eased himself onto the opposite chair. "Sheriff Tillman sent me."

Miguelito was a hunchback, his chest lopsided. "What d'ya want?"

"They say that you trade with the Apaches."

"What if I do?"

"I'm looking for two Americans, a man and a woman, eighteen and sixteen. I have reason to believe that your people might've got them, and I want them back."

"If my people found 'em, they're dead."

"Don't Apaches take women for slaves?"

"If she's young and pretty . . ."

"I'm sure she'd fit the bill. Can you find out where she is and then let me know?"

The hunchback grinned, showing a gold tooth. "If a federal marshal is lookin' for her, she must be pretty important, no? How about twenty dollars, half in advance?"

"I'll give you five dollars now and the rest when I get her out."

Stowe flipped a coin into the air, and the midget snatched it up. "What if she's dead?"

"We'll cross that river when we come to it. I think you'd better get started right now."

"I have other things to do, Marshal. Do you think you are the only business that I have?"

Stowe reached over the table and grabbed the midget by the throat. "How'd you like to go to jail right now and stay there for the rest of your life?"

Delgado sat in his wickiup, smoking his clay pipe. He felt confused and wanted to speak with Cucharo, but Cucharo was spending most of his time with Duane

Braddock, for a reason that Delgado couldn't determine.

Chief Pinotay was becoming more feeble every day, and soon another chief would be chosen. There were no ballot boxes, and the best warriors would battle for the high office. Delgado wanted to consult with Cucharo about the matter, but Cucharo was always gone with the White Eyes man.

Delgado lived in two worlds, one Apache and the other American. He'd seen many of the White Eyes' wonderful machines, big homes, and plentiful food, but he still preferred the holy Apache lifeway. If you had a dollar in your pocket, there were twenty-five other White Eyes men who wanted to put their hands upon it.

Delgado was better educated than he let on, but he couldn't discuss intellectual matters with other Apaches. Sometimes Delgado thought that his soul had been polluted by education. Occasionally he suspected that his Apache brethren were ignorant and simpleminded. He hated his American education yet was fascinated by what he'd learned.

He was a man of many conflicts, and if that wasn't enough, his thoughts often turned to Phyllis Thornton, the pretty White Eyes girl with the big bosom. He confessed to himself that he was in love with her, or possibly in lust with her, he wasn't sure. He could kill Braddock easily but that would be a disgrace, for Duane was a paltry White Eyes boy. Delgado steadfastly refrained from flirting with Phyllis because Apaches were prudes. If Phyllis left Duane, then I could get her, but I don't think she has the courage to leave him.

He knew that she was interested in him and yearned to have him place his bronzed hands on her smooth white flesh. He'd show her the other side of the moon, but she was afraid, and so was he. Delgado didn't want to behave like a fool, and the best way to avoid embarrassment was to live according to the ancient lifeway. But if Duane fell off the side of a mountain, Delgado would shed no tears.

He heard footsteps, and a voice called, "Delgado."

"Come in."

The animal flap wiggled, and a slim Apache named Akul appeared. "We have seen bluecoat soldiers, and they got many horses, with much weapons and ammunition. They appear lost, and their guard is not vigilant." Akul smiled greedily. "I think that we should take the horses from the bluecoat soldiers."

Delgado puffed on his pipe thoughtfully. "Keep your eyes on them, but look for the renegades, too. Sooner or later evil Jamata will have to go out and then we will catch him."

Akul departed as Delgado meditated upon the lack of news about Jamata's renegades. Delgado's beloved older sister had been killed by them, and the renegades had demonstrated their contempt for the People, the lifeway, the chief, and Delgado. The dead must be avenged, and I will skin Jamata alive someday, he swore. Delgado's warriors were scouring the mountains, searching for the renegades, but they'd found a lost wandering detachment of cavalry instead.

Horses represented wealth to an Apache, and that didn't include guns, ammunition, and other valuable articles. But what were the bluecoats doing in such an obscure corner of the desert? They are crazy, but soon they will learn the lesson of the desert, he thought.

It was sunset when Duane and the boys returned to the camp. He entered his wickiup; the skins and furs smelled like home, and he reclined, closing his eyes and smiling with satisfaction. His lessons were going well, and he thought that he'd found the Garden of Eden in the mountains of southwest Texas. The children had taught him how to trap small animals for food, an arcane skill more valuable than anything he'd learned in the monastery in the clouds. Then Cucharo had shown him the subtle points of tracking, and now Duane could describe everything that had happened on the ground during the past twenty-four hours. I'm not leaving this place until I know everything the Apaches know. Then I'll never have to worry about dying in the desert.

The animal flap was thrust to the side, and Phyllis crawled into the wickiup. Her clothing had become shredded like his, and her legs could be seen through tears in her jeans. Her skin was deeply tanned, she wore an Apache headband and looked tawny wild. "I keep telling you that I want to leave," she began, "and you keep putting me off. We've been with the Apaches for nearly a month, and I think it's time that we set a date for hitting the trail. We're Americans — remember?"

"But I love this life, and you've never looked better. C'mere."

She pushed him away. "If you loved me, you'd take me out of here."

Leaving had become her favorite subject, and she sang the same tune over and over. "I guess the work is too hard for you."

"It goes deeper than work. You're seeing these Apaches as something that they're not. Don't forget that war and killing is their way of life, and they can be extremely brutal. Yesterday I saw a woman with her nose cut off because she was unfaithful to her husband. Huera told me that if a woman has twins, her husband has to kill one of them because that's what their beautiful holy lifeway commands them to do."

"I never said they were angels, but things aren't so great in the White Eyes world either. I've read in newspapers that babies are killed by rats in big cities, or poisoned with milk from cows that're fed garbage. What's worse?"

She looked him in the eye. "If I had twins, would you kill one of them?"

Duane didn't like the tone of her voice. His beautiful desert princess was becoming a nag, and it wasn't so long ago that she'd loved him without question. "I could never kill my twin son or daughter, and I certainly sympathize with any woman who had her nose cut off, but I'm learning interesting new things from the Apaches, I feel better than ever, and tomorrow Cucharo is taking me into the mountains for a few days of special teaching."

Phyllis scowled as she sensed another betrayal. "In other words, our stay with the Apaches has just been extended. Sometimes I think you love that old man more than me. Well, I'm an American, and I want to get the hell out of here!"

"Perhaps you can go home without me, and I'll follow when things settle down."

"Maybe I should've left you tied to that

wheel. Your mind is open to every stupid idea that comes along. I'm afraid that something terrible will happen if we stay here. What if the chief dies? Apaches aren't the best hosts in the world for White Eyes."

He kissed her cheek. "Nothing's going to happen because that old chief is probably healthier than we. I'll bet we're safer here than at the Bar T."

She gazed meaningfully into his eyes. "Just remember one thing, Duane. When the trouble starts, don't say you weren't warned."

It was pitch-black in the desert as clouds obscured the moon and stars. The soldiers huddled around their bonfire, chewing on a family of javelinas that they'd shot before the sun went down. Tents were pitched and horses tethered to the picket line, guarded by four troopers at each corner of the compass.

Lieutenant Dawes sat by himself, studying his map in the light of the fire. He knew that he was somewhere south of the Pecos, deep in Apache territory, and his men were rebellious.

They were tired of living in the open, worried constantly about the next water hole. But Lieutenant Dawes was drawing a map based on his observations, with special marks for water holes. He'd send a copy to Colonel

MacKenzie at Fort Richardson, to show what an intelligent and diligent officer he was. Perhaps I should write about local flora and fauna for scientific journals. A desert isn't just sand but a symphony of life and colors. Every day he saw more smoke signals on the mountaintops as his movements were transmitted from tribe to tribe.

The Apaches knew where he was, but he didn't know where they were. Lieutenant Dawes gnawed on a chunk of wild pig as he conceived new tactics for fighting Apaches. Special detachments would be trained to live like Indians in small roving bands. Their job would be to hunt redskins relentlessly and force them out of Texas. Then the land could be opened for commerce and towns would grow around water holes that now sit alone in the desert.

Land in southwest Texas is cheap, Lieutenant Dawes speculated, but if the Apaches were driven out, it would rise in value. Fortunes are being made every day in the new postwar America, and if I plan now, I can be a rich man someday. He'd already inherited a substantial sum from his grandfather, who'd been a banker, and it was being invested in stocks and bonds by a Wall Street brokerage firm. But land is the best investment of all, he figured. One day Texas will be covered with cattle, cities, and roads. Nothing can stop America now.

He heard footsteps as Sergeant Mahoney approached, his rusty beard dotted with bits of wild pig. Mahoney didn't bother saluting as he dropped to one knee beside Lieutenant Dawes. "The men told me to tell you that they want to return to camp, sir."

Lieutenant Dawes folded the map. "I don't care what they want. They *will* obey my lawful orders."

Sergeant Mahoney leaned closer and said in a low voice, "Sir, I don't think you know what's a-goin' on here. They're a-gittin' mad as hornets, and they all got guns."

"America wouldn't have much of an army if soldiers told their officers what to do."

"There's a time to go by the book, and a time to use some common sense, sir. You been in the sun too long."

Lieutenant Dawes narrowed his eyes. "Are you saying that I've gone loco?"

"I've been a soldier fer eighteen years, and I ain't never seen a scout like this. But I warned you about the men, and that's the best I can do. From now on, I ain't responsible."

It was midnight when Marshal Stowe returned semi-inebriated to his hotel. The lobby was bathed in the golden effulgence of oil lamps, illuminating the clerk and a few drunks passed out on sofas and chairs. The lawman shambled toward the clerk, rested his elbow on the counter, and said in a low voice, "I'm ready for one of the gals."

"I'll send her to your room, Marshal."

"Want to pick her myself, if you don't mind."

"Right this way."

The clerk led him down a corridor, across a hall, and to a dark door without a number. The clerk knocked, the door opened, and a woman with a garishly painted face stood in the crack.

"A customer," the clerk said.

The door opened wide, and the woman grabbed Marshal Stowe's sleeve. "Come on in, cowboy. Don't be afraid."

Then she saw the tin badge, and her confidence faltered. Marshal Stowe figured that she'd probably spent time behind bars during her career, but he smiled genially as he followed her into a crowd of women drinking coffee, smoking cigarettes, and waiting for the next customer. Some were American, others Mexican, with a few in between.

"Which one you want?" the madam asked.

"I like to take my time."

"Juanita, get the marshal a glass of whiskey."

The marshal dropped into a chair and felt suddenly dispirited. Why'm I always sleeping with whores? he asked himself. He recalled lovely, graceful Vanessa Dawes, practically a different species from the women before him.

They looked as if life had used them hard, and they used it in the same way. They earned their daily bread selling their bodies to the highest bidder, and when they grew too old to attract customers, they begged on the streets. Disease was the plague of their lives, and frequently they were shot or knifed by irate customers. It was difficult for the marshal to feel romantic, but he considered abstinence unhealthy.

So he looked for one who wasn't too fat, skinny, or old, without a broken nose, and not completely toothless. He noticed such a whore sitting in the corner, somehow sad beneath her thick layers of cosmetics. He raised his finger and pointed. "Her."

"That is Teresa. You have made a wise choice, Marshal. Go to your room, and she will be right there."

Marshal Stowe clomped down the maze of corridors and became disoriented midway. Finally, after walking into a few walls, he arrived at his door, drew his gun, listened, and then stepped into the small enclosed space. He searched for a bushwhacker beneath the bed, locked the door, took off his hat, lay in bed, and closed his eyes. The Remington remained in his right hand.

He thought of the hunchback midget half-breed Miguelito. If the freak could locate Phyllis Thornton — what a bonanza. It would be nice to see Trafalgar Square at dawn, or watch the sun set over the white cliffs of Folkestone. All my dreams will come true if I can find Phyllis Thornton.

But he didn't trust Miguelito. The half-breed had shifty eyes, and what could you say about a man who sold whiskey and guns to the Apaches? I shouldn't have anything to do with people like that, the lawman told himself, but it's the only way to get to England.

He didn't dare let his guard down with Miguelito because the half-breed would betray him for horses, guns, and the shirt on his back. But if Miguelito can find Phyllis Thornton, I'll play his game. Life's greatest blessings never come easy.

There was a knock on the door.

"Come in."

Teresa entered the room, fluttering her eyelashes ridiculously, evidently inexperienced at her work, but it didn't matter to the lonely lawman. "Wash that shit off your face," he ordered. "Then take off your clothes and come to bed."

CHAPTER 6

Duane couldn't sleep much that night as he anticipated his trip to the desert with Cucharo. It would be for an indefinite period, and they'd bring weapons but no food or water. Cucharo had implied that something significant would be imparted, and Duane wondered what it possibly could be. He hadn't told Phyllis the full story because she'd spoil everything with another tantrum about Apache life. His sweet little Texas flower was becoming a double-barreled shrew.

He gazed at her profile outlined by moonlight slanting through the hole in the roof. Her beauty bloomed more every day as her body toughened and firmed. But wickiup life didn't interest her because she'd been princess of the Bar T. Her main tasks had been office work, and horseback courier between her father and cowboys riding the range. Working animal skins, digging mescal, and gathering prickly pear fruit wasn't her notion of gracious living. She was a daughter of Texas, not an Apache squaw.

The sky became lighter as Duane dressed silently in the darkness, tied his holster to his leg, and stuffed his pockets full of bullets. A man could run into anything on the desert, including man-eating bears, Apache renegades, or rattlesnakes that you wouldn't notice until they sank their fangs into your leg.

Duane pecked his beloved wife-to-be lightly on the cheek, for he didn't want to awaken her and start another fight. Then he put on his cowboy hat, crawled out of his home, and silently made his way toward Cucharo's wickiup. The camp appeared deserted, but he knew that guards were about, watching for enemies in all approaches to the mountaintop. Apaches were the most suspicious and watchful people Duane had ever known. They see you, but you never see them.

He came to Cucharo's tent, sat cross-legged in front of the door, and waited for his master to appear. He had a mild headache from inadequate sleep, his stomach was an empty cavern, and he dozed as the leather door twitched. Cucharo poked his nose out, and Duane jumped to his feet, watching his mentor sniff the air, as if the old *di-yin* could divine truth from the smell of the desert. "Follow me," the medicine man croaked.

They headed for the valley, and neither spoke as dawn broadened on the horizon. Cucharo appeared to be heading toward one of the taller mountains, its summit a cap of purple rock. The old *di-yin* ascended the foothills swiftly and Duane followed close at his heels. A buzzard sat on the branch of a juniper tree, watching them hungrily. They climbed higher, and Duane viewed huge tracts of desert spread beneath him, with smoke signals in the distance. Cirrus clouds streaked the sky, and a river wound like a gleaming silver snake near the horizon. It was shortly before noon when they reached the summit.

"Sit," said Cucharo.

Duane dropped to a cross-legged position on top of the mountain. He could make out settlements, cattle, and buildings like dots in the distant wastes. Cucharo sat opposite him, examined his face, and said, "You think I have brought you here to teach you important things, but only Yusn can teach them. This mountain is a place of power, and I will leave you here. If you are smart, you will learn. If you are dumb, you will die. Give me your gun."

"What do you want my gun for?"

"You must be without any weapons except your knife."

Duane wondered if it was an Apache trick. Is Cucharo trying to steal my gun?

"If I wanted to steal it," Cucharo replied wearily, "I could've done so long ago."

"Can you read my mind?"

"If you do not trust me, I do not care. We can go back to the camp, and you can leave with your woman. Apache warriors will escort you to the Mexican border, and you will be free."

Duane wanted to continue his Apache education, as curiosity outweighed caution yet again. He unstrapped his gun belt and passed it to Cucharo, who said, "I am going to leave you now, and we may not see each other again for a long time. Open your heart to Yusn, and you will become a warrior." Cucharo looked over Duane's shoulder. "Is that a snake?"

Duane pulled his knife from the scabbard in back of his belt, but there was no snake. He turned toward Cucharo, but the medicine man had disappeared. The mountaintop was barren, a gust of wind blew over the crest, and Duane felt vulnerable without his gun. Incredible distances stretched before him, and an eagle flew high in the sky.

He paced back and forth, wondering what to do. The sun hammered him. His clothes became soaked with perspiration, his hat drooped over his ears, and his mouth went dry. He walked down the mountain to the line where vegetation began, then selected the fattest barrel cactus available, drew his knife, and sliced off the top. He cut out chunks of wet pulp, sat beside the cactus, and chewed. The sweet sap rolled over his tongue as he spotted mescal plants nearby. At least I won't starve, he said to himself optimistically.

He'd never been alone in the desert and felt jittery. He pulled his knife out of its scabbard and ran his finger along the ten-inch blade. It was sharp, but he wished it were sharper. The wood handle was attached with rivets and had seen much use.

He heard a sound behind him and spun around. The blank desert looked back at him. He wondered whether Apache renegades were sneaking up on him, to cut off his head. Wild animals lived in the area, and he didn't want to step on a sleeping poisonous spider. Maybe I should've listened to Phyllis and gone to Mexico.

The desert was a brilliantly colored panorama, while the air filled with the perfume of flowers. This place was here long before I arrived in the world and will be here long after I'm gone, he realized. He sat beside the barrel cactus, chewed pulp, and gazed at the lowlands. He'd read that southwest Texas had once been a vast sea and imagined monster fishes hurtling through endless centuries, while he was a mere speck in the flow of time.

He glanced behind him, to make sure no hungry sharp-toothed creatures were sneaking up on him. But no one was there, and he felt strangely isolated from the rest of humanity. There was nothing to do, and he hadn't slept well the previous night. He stretched out on the ground, covered his face with his hat, placed his head on the palms of his hands, and closed his eyes. He heard the rush of wind and soon fell into deep slumber.

Miguelito sat on his saddle, stirrups adjusted for his short legs, as he rode through a forest of cottonwood trees. He examined them carefully, to make sure they concealed no robbers. Miguelito sometimes carried substantial money and was a tempting target. But he was part Apache, and his wariness never flagged.

He was born of a Mexican mother captured by Apaches, while his father had been a prominent warrior. Miguelito was raised by Apaches until he was twelve, when he and his mother were repatriated by the Mexican army.

The Mexicans treated him like an oddity;

he grew up with virtually no friends, and as soon as he was old enough, he returned to the Apaches. But he didn't feel at home among them either, because he'd picked up too many White Eyes habits. So he became the ideal middle man and kept his money buried in an iron box in a secret desert spot. Someday he planned to do something with it but didn't know quite what.

A raspberry bush moved at the side of the trail, and an Apache guard arose behind it. "Miguelito, have you brought firewater?"

"Not today, but maybe next time."

The warrior waved him onward, for Miguelito was every Apache's friend and they treated him like a noble emissary from the outer world. He dismounted at the beginning of the narrow defile and proceeded to climb its sharp-toothed path. He knew that they'd be eager to see him, for he was their main link with the cornucopia of goods produced by the White Eyes.

It was a tough climb, but he soon came to the top of the mountain. He'd visited three other camps since speaking with the marshal, but hadn't found the American girl yet. He approached the gathering of wickiups. Smoke arose from fires, and children chased each other though the alleys. A baby bawled her eyes out in a cradleboard hanging from a bush but was ignored because Apaches believed that babies should never be coddled.

Children gathered on both sides of Miguelito, and he tossed them rock candy. Ahead, a group of women dug a hole for roasting mescal, and poker-faced Miguelito observed their hindquarters as they scooped dirt out of the earth with their hands. Then his eyes widened at the sight of a woman in American cowboy clothes. Her skin was deeply tanned, but her facial characteristics were distinctly American. That's her! he thought jubilantly. He steered his horse toward the chief's wickiup as a smile spread over his face. It looks like I've just made twenty dollars. He dismounted in front of the chief's wickiup, reached into a saddlebag, and pulled out a bottle of white lightning.

The chief appeared at the entrance, and a grin appeared on his face. "I am so happy to see you again, Miguelito."

Miguelito handed him the bottle of whiskey, and the chief led him into the wickiup. The fire was out, but the faint trace of woodsmoke was in the air. Miguelito filled his corncob pipe with tobacco, lit it, and passed it to the chief, who sucked the stem until his eyes popped out.

"I am here to learn what you need,"

163

Miguelito said. "Soon I will return with my wagon, and we will trade. Do you have horses?"

"Soon we will have many, do not worry about that. I will call a council tonight, to find out what you should bring us. Do you have any news?"

"Yes," Miguelito replied. "The White Eyes are looking for the woman that you have captured."

The chief was taken aback. "She is not a captive and can leave whenever she wants. Her man is here, too." The chief explained the bloody and tragic events that had brought the two White Eyes to their camp, and Miguelito listened carefully.

"The renegades must be wiped out," Miguelito declared, "but why don't the White Eyes return to their people?"

"Because the man likes us, and Cucharo says he is part Apache."

Miguelito didn't mention the White Eyes again because he didn't want to arouse suspicion. The old chief sipped white lightning as Miguelito reflected upon the reward. I can buy a load of whiskey, water it down, and quadruple my money in thirty days. I knew I'd find the White Eyes girl before long. The marshal will be happy, but I wonder what's in this for him?

★ ★ ★

Duane heard a sound behind him as he awakened in the darkness. He reached for his Bowie knife; a hawk cried in the distance, and the full moon hung in the sky.

He could spot no hungry creature sneaking up on him and wasn't sure of what day it was. His mouth was dry, stomach hollow, and fingers tingled. He felt eerie and peculiar in the moonlight, and it was difficult to see clearly. Nocturnal hunters had emerged from their dens, while bats flitted across the sky. "Cucharo?"

There was no answer. Duane made his way toward the barrel cactus that he'd cut open earlier in the day. The pulp had dried, and flies buzzed around. He cut in deeper, for moist sweet flesh. Then he sat cross-legged and chewed the liquid out of it.

He reckoned that it was the middle of the night. I wonder how long I'll have to stay here? He missed Phyllis and realized that he was neglecting her, but it wasn't every day that a man could learn the Apache lifeway. Absentmindedly he touched his fingers to the scar on his throat.

Something growled behind him, his hair stood on end, and he turned around. A mountain lion stood there, glowing in the light of the moon. Duane was on his feet in a second, poised, the Bowie knife in his right hand. The lion dropped into a crouch, ready to spring, and its claws were enormous.

Duane struggled to shift from his meditative pose to the dripping fangs before him. It looked like down and dirty to the bitter end with one of the most dangerous beasts of the desert. He held the Bowie knife in his right fist, dug in his heels, and his heart pounded wildly as he prepared for the gory encounter that loomed before him.

The lion sprang, its claws reaching for Duane's face, while Duane slashed at the great cat's belly. The animal floated closer, as if in slow motion, and moonlight glinted off its sharp claws, while its eyes sparkled like obsidian. Duane could smell the beast's rotten-meat breath as he rammed the knife in to the hilt.

His hand met no resistance, and he passed through the lion's body. As Duane spun around, the lion disappeared. Then Duane looked from side to side, wondering what had happened to the ferocious creature. He dropped to his knees and searched for tracks, but there were none where the lion had been.

Duane became afraid for the first time since Cucharo had left him. A bizarre event had occurred, and he didn't know what to make of it. He knew that he hadn't dreamed the lion because no dream could be that vivid. Or could it?

What the hell is real? He looked around, trying to understand. Am I awake or asleep? He no longer felt in control, and it terrified him. Maybe I should go back to the camp, and to hell with this Apache business. I don't want to be a warrior *that* bad. But then he thought of Cucharo's disapproval, and even Phyllis would be contemptuous, for she was becoming an Apache against her will, with the same harsh code.

Hallucinating a lion isn't so terrible, he tried to persuade himself. Be thankful that it wasn't real. Duane felt the need to pray and dropped to his knees. "I've always tried to be a good Christian," he explained to God. "It's not as though I was a horse thief or a murderer."

An eel crawled up his back, because he realized that he'd committed many sins in his life, from drunken brawls to fornication with prostitutes, and he'd coveted a few wives, too. He'd even shot some people, though it was in self-defense. I'm no angel, he realized, and maybe the time has come for me to pay for my sins.

He had the disquieting sensation that something was occurring behind him. He was afraid to look, but afraid not to. He took a deep breath, reversed position slowly, and held the knife in his right hand. He perceived a faint ghostly glow at the top of the mountain. Narrowing his eyes, he tried to make out what it was. Are my eyes playing tricks again? The moon and stars pulsated rhythmically as insects sang Gregorian chants. He wondered what had been in that barrel cactus as his eyes returned to the top of the mountain. The truth finally dawned upon him. It's Cucharo, and he's lit a fire!

Duane ran up the hill like a bull charging the red cape. His legs worked like pistons, his lungs sucked wind, and the glow became brighter as a figure stood in its midst. "Cucharo — am I glad to see you!"

Duane drew closer and realized that it wasn't Cucharo at all. To his amazement, an Apache woman came into view, wearing a dyed white buckskin dress, as golden effulgence emanated from her being. She wore white moccasins decorated with tiny red beads, and her hair was jet-black, bound with a white linen headband.

Duane stopped cold in his tracks and struggled to understand. This evidently is a visitation of the Virgin Mary, he told himself. I'm having a religious experience, and it's nothing to go loco about. He pinched himself, but it hurt. All he could do was drop to his knees and bow his head before the radiance of the ghostly apparition.

"Come closer," she said.

He wanted to run, but she held her arms out to him tenderly. The music of the desert swelled in his ears as he arose. A silver thread pulled him toward her, and her eyes filled with bottomless compassion. Flower petals rained upon him from the sky, she wrapped her arms around him, and he filled with delicious sweetness. Tears of joy welled up in his eyes as she kissed his forehead.

He'd never felt so protected, warm, and cozy. He closed his eyes as she lowered him gently to the ground. He was deeply asleep as soon as he touched down, and she covered him with a white blanket. Then she sat beside him, strummed a lutelike instrument, and hummed an Apache melody into the night.

Phyllis sat bolt upright in the wickiup, covered with cold sweat. Her heart beat swiftly; she felt menaced and reached for Duane. But he was on the desert with the strange old medicine man, and God only knew what was happening to him.

She returned to her animal skins and searched for a comfortable spot on the ground. She was worried about Duane, because he wasn't a real Apache warrior and the desert was full of danger at night. She wondered what would happen if he were killed. Will they let me leave, or will a warrior claim me as his woman? She imagined seminaked Apaches fighting for her virtue, and she'd have to go with the winner or else. Apaches lived according to their own codes; they left their old ones to die and killed babies due to superstition and ignorance. The unforgiving desert had produced an unforgiving people.

In the cozy warmth beneath her animal skins, she entertained certain naughty thoughts concerning Delgado, the Apache aristocrat sleeping with one of his royal consorts. She couldn't help wondering what it was like to make love with a savage, compared to a civilized man like Duane. Am I missing something? she asked herself as she hugged the animal skins closer. But I'd never actually do it, I really don't think. I'm not that loco, or am I?

The sun seared Duane's eyes; it was midday, and he felt as if he'd slept for a long time. The woman in white was gone, and he figured she'd been a dream. Must be something in the air up here, he thought. He was hungry, so he walked down the hill to the vegetation line, dug roots out of the ground, and plucked fruit from cactus plants. Then he carried his lunch to the top of the mountain, sat, and proceeded to dine.

His head felt clear, and his ears could discern a bird singing like a flute in the distance. The food disappeared rapidly as natural juices satiated his thirst. He thought of his strange dreams and wondered what they meant. He'd been certain that the lion would kill him, and the Apache woman had felt real. The mountain experience was unsettling him, and he wanted to return to the village but hated to be a quitter. He wondered how much longer he'd have to stay there, exposed to the elements. Clouds scudded across the sky, and it looked like rain. Duane was restless and decided to build a shelter.

Somebody hollered suddenly, and Duane jumped three inches into the air. He saw an Apache climbing the mountain, and Duane had never seen him before. Duane was alarmed by the knife in his hand, an angry expression on his face. Duane realized that the Apache was going to attack!

Duane jumped to his feet, yanked out his Bowie knife, and prepared to defend himself. Is this a dream, too? he asked himself as the Apache warrior lunged. Duane danced nimbly to the side as the Apache rushed past him. Then Duane charged, while the Apache spun around. They confronted each other, not more than six feet apart. The Apache was taller than Duane, more heavily muscled, but older, with a scar on his chin. The Apache feinted with his knife, and Duane took a step backward. He wanted to run for his life, but the Apache would get him in the back. "I haven't done anything to you!" Duane blurted. "Are you sure that you don't have me mixed up with somebody else?"

The Apache shouted something unintelligible and rammed his knife toward Duane's gut. Duane grabbed the Apache's wrist while driving his own knife toward the Apache's heart. But the Apache's free hand stopped his thrust in midair. They were locked together, grappling frenziedly, trying to gain an advantage. Their faces were inches apart, and Duane could see flames burning behind the Apache's eyes. They heaved, but each was unmovable.

Duane snaked his leg around the Apache, pushed, and the Apache dropped backward. Duane found himself off balance, lost his footing, and toppled over the Apache. Next thing Duane knew, he was falling head over heels down the steep side of the mountain. It was covered with rocks, twigs, and ridges; he landed on his left shoulder, rolled over, bounced around, and then his head struck a boulder, opening a two-inch gash, while his left arm hit the branch of a tree, nearly snapping off his wrist. He fell past a small cave, in which a bear lay sleeping, and the sound caused the creature to open its eyes and snarl.

Duane continued plummeting down the side of the mountain. He grasped a sapling, pulled it out by the roots, tossed over, tumbled about, his face scratched by branches, his shirt flayed. He saw the solid trunk of a ponderosa pine, reached out wildly, and tackled it, nearly shattering his shoulder.

He'd terminated his fall but was dazed, more dead than alive. He'd never relinquished his knife from his grip, however, and swung it around, expecting the Apache to jump on top of him.

But the Apache hadn't followed him down. Is this a dream, too? he wondered. I wish I could wake up. His clothes had become rags, he was covered with contusions and abrasions, and the sole was torn off his left boot. For the first time it occurred to him that he might not survive his trip to the desert.

He continued to search for the Apache and spotted a cave cut into a rock wall. He limped toward it, peered inside, and saw that it was tall enough for him to stand. His eyes fell on something lying in the middle of the floor, and he readied his knife as he approached cautiously. It was a white breechcloth, deerskin moccasins, and a red headband. "Cucharo?" he asked.

There was no answer as his voice reverberated through deep caverns. Duane touched his hand to the fabric and wondered how it got there. Then he removed his torn clothing and put on the breechcloth, tying it with the belt that held his knife. The moccasins fit perfectly, and he wrapped the red headband around his head. A tiny clay pot sat before him, filled with vermillion paste. He stuck his finger into it and ran it across his nose and cheeks.

Then he stood and noticed a shimmer in the back of the cave. Holding the point of the knife before him, he advanced toward it. The closer he came, the lower his jaw dropped in amazement. The rear of the cave was a solid gold wall! He picked up a nugget as big as his thumb. It gleamed and glittered within its depths, but something told him to leave it alone. Cucharo had told him that yellow metal was sacred to the People because it belonged to the mountain spirits. He dropped the nugget as if it were a hot coal and backed toward the entrance of the cave.

Clouds covered the sky as he swiftly climbed the side of the mountain. His skin felt electrified without the restrictions of clothing, and the leather soles of the moccasins gripped the rocks better than his cowboy boots. Up the crags he went, enjoying the exercise. When he arrived at the summit, a bolt of lightning rent the heavens.

He stood with his legs spread, fists resting on his hips, and watched storm clouds boil and rumble in the sky. In the distance jags of lightning flew to the ground like iridescent Apache lances. The mountain shook with pealing cannonades of thunder as swirling mists gathered closer. Duane bowed his head to the power of Yusn as the holy water baptized him, cleansing his wounds and washing away his sins.

"Sir — wake up!"

Lieutenant Dawes lay in his bedroll as rain lashed him and the heavens roared. Sergeant Mahoney's face was distorted with fury. "Apaches got the horses!"

Dawes jumped out of his bedroll, drew his service revolver, and ran toward the picket line in his stocking feet. Hatless, his heart pounded thickly; the rain was so heavy he couldn't see anything. In the distance he heard shouting, gunfire, confusion. Suddenly a figure materialized out of the night, lying on the ground before him. It was a trooper stripped of every article of clothing, his equipment gone and his throat cut from ear to ear.

"They got all the horses!" Sergeant Mahoney said bitterly. "I knowed this'd happen, you goddamned idiot!"

The truth struck Dawes with full force. He staggered toward the picket line, and the lines were cut, every horse stolen. The men crowded around in the pouring rain as the full implications sank in. Gaunt, grizzled, bedraggled, with water dripping from their campaign hats, they were stranded in Apache territory, and the odds were that they wouldn't survive! Corporal Hazelwood came running out of the storm. "The guards're all dead!"

Lieutenant Dawes wasn't prepared for the dilemma, but all he could do was rely upon his West Point training. "They're dead because they were asleep!" he bellowed angrily. "They let the Apaches sneak up on them! Hereafter, I'll expect my guards to stay awake, otherwise they'll get the firing squad!"

They looked at him as if he'd gone mad. Then Private Cruikshank snickered. "I'm a-gittin' sick of this son of a bitch!"

Lieutenant Dawes yanked out his service pistol, and every man in the vicinity followed suit. They all aimed their weapons at each other in the midst of the pounding storm, and he realized that he'd finally gone around the bend. With a nervous smile, he returned his pistol to his holster. Rainwater dripped off the end of his nose as he said, "Let me remind you that I'm still in command, and not one of you has been relieved of your duties. We've got to pull together and get the hell out of here."

Private Cruikshank snarled, "We'll never get out of here, you goddamned horse's ass! We're miles from the nearest settlement, and the Apaches're all around us!"

"They didn't get our guns and ammunition," Lieutenant Dawes replied as rain soaked his clothing and filled his boots. "We can fight them off if we hold together like soldiers. We know where the last water hole is, and there's wild game everywhere. There's no cause for panic."

"He's right," agreed Sergeant Mahoney, aiming his U.S. Army Colt at Cruikshank. "He's the rankin' officer, and this is still the Fourth Cavalry. I'll tolerate no more back talk, gripin', or horseshit. What're yer orders, sir?"

Lieutenant Dawes had no idea what to say. One moment he'd been sleeping peacefully and now had been plunged into the most terrible predicament of his career. He remembered a line from the famous war manual written by the Prussian General Karl von Clausewitz:

The most important component of field command is the ability to remain calm, and make rational decisions in the face of the most overwhelming reversals.

Lieutenant Dawes pulled back his shoulders, set his jaw, and said, "When the storm stops, we'll head north. Post four more guards, Sergeant Mahoney. I intend to check them personally during the night, and if I catch anybody sleeping, I'll shoot him on the spot. Now let's get out of the rain."

The heavens pealed with the cymbals of Yusn as sheets of water whipped them. They tramped back to the campsite, and Lieutenant Dawes was pleased with the way he'd handled the emergency. He knew that an officer must present a facade of strength and resolution to his men, regardless of what terror he was feeling. Lieutenant Dawes had studied the lessons of modern warfare, but how can you defeat an enemy whom you can't see?

The campsite came into view through pouring curtains of rain. The firepit was there, brimming with water, but bedrolls, wagons, tents, ammunition, pots and pans were all gone! The Apaches had plundered the camp while the White Eyes were arguing about the horses. Lieutenant Dawes struggled to make a rational decision in the face of total catastrophe.

"The goddamned son-of-a-bitch Apaches got everythin'!" Private Cruikshank said angrily.

Corporal Hazelwood turned to Lieutenant Dawes, his soaking wet uniform shining in the light of the moon. "Now we're really in a fix, and the onliest reason we're here is becuzz yer wife was a-screwin' Duane Braddock, and everybody knows it!"

Lieutcnant Dawes stiffened. "Watch your lip, soldier!"

"We're all a-gonna die fer that bitch you married!"

Lieutenant Dawes stared him in the eye. "You enlisted in the army, and nobody told you that you'd win every battle. If you say one more insubordinate word to me, I'll place you under arrest, and if you resist, I'll personally subdue you. Is that clear?"

Corporal Hazelwood measured Lieutenant Dawes, who was eight inches taller and approximately seventy-five pounds heavier. "Yes, sir," he said sullenly.

Lieutenant Dawes balled his fists as he looked at them disdainfully. "Are you soldiers or little girls? If you wanted a soft life, you should've stayed home with your mothers. Hereafter, half of us will be on guard, while the other half sleeps. And if any of you think you're smart enough to shoot me in the back, you'd better be accurate, because the next shot will be mine. Sergeant Mahoney — post the guard!"

The troopers looked at each other expectantly, but no one had the guts to make the first move. Sergeant Mahoney barked orders, as army tradition returned to the beleaguered detachment. Lieutenant Dawes looked for shelter, but there were few trees, none offering significant protection. He sat upon a boulder as rain streamed down his cheeks. We'll get out of this somehow, won't we?

Duane came to consciousness atop the mountain. He lay belly down as rain pelted him. His first thought was that something had gone wrong, for his rear legs felt shorter, he'd grown paws with claws and possessed a tail! He looked at himself, and growled in astonishment. Somehow he'd become a mountain lion!

He didn't want to be trapped in a lion's body, but there was nothing he could do about it. He rose on all fours, swished his tail, licked his chops, and wondered what to do next. This is only another dream, he tried to console himself. When I wake up, I'll be Duane Braddock again, won't I? He wasn't so sure but noticed that his sense of smell had become more acute, and he could detect rabbits and gophers farther down the hill. His lungs filled with the musty fume of earth and vegetation, and he felt as though he could leap incredible distances, while his powerful jaws could crack the backbone of an antelope.

He bared his fangs and roared proudly. What's wrong with being a lion? I have ten claws that can tear enemies to shreds, and I'm very strong. Rivulets of water ran down his fur but didn't penetrate to his skin. He felt limber, alert, and invincible. He opened his maw wide and yowled at the heavens.

Then he heard a snarl behind him, and the hair stiffened on his neck. Turning apprehensively, he was horrified to see a black bear eight feet tall, with immense arms, long claws, and significant fangs. Duane stepped backward as the bear approached, its eyes filled with rage. It was as though it were challenging Duane for domination of the mountain, and Duane's lion's pride wouldn't let him retreat with his tail between his legs. He growled at the bear, which became more incensed. The bear arose on its back legs and raised its front paws in the air, as if proclaiming itself champion.

Duane knew that if he tangled with the bear, he'd be bloodied and maimed for life. But a lion doesn't run like a rat, a coyote, or a man. He reared back on his hind legs, extended his claws, and showed his fangs.

The gesture inflamed the bear further, for it, too, had pride. With a bellow that drowned out the thunder, it charged. Duane crouched for maximum springing power as he waited for the bear to come within range. His sinews tightened and then he leapt into the air.

The bear braced itself for the inevitable collision, they crashed into each other, and Duane dug his claws into the bear's fur as he sank his teeth into the bear's throat. But the bear's hide was like iron, and the bear's great arms wrapped around Duane. The bear squeezed with such force that Duane felt his eyes bulge in their sockets. But meanwhile he sank his teeth deeper into the bear's throat, and musky blood burst onto his tongue. Duane and the bear were locked together in an embrace of death as the bear staggered beneath Duane's weight.

Duane felt his bones snapping as bear blood flooded his mouth. He feared that he'd die, but he'd die as a lion and not a rat. If you kill me, bear, you'll carry my scars to your dying day. Duane worked his jaws furiously as his fangs cut deeper into the bear's jugular.

Blood gushed down Duane's throat, and the bear loosened his hold. Duane concentrated his jaw muscles on the point of contact, then the bear's lifeline snapped. The gigantic animal staggered, blood foamed from his mouth, and his eyes went glassy. Then the bear sighed, fell to the ground, and Duane leapt out of the way.

Rain soaked Duane's fur, he gasped for air and gazed at his dead adversary. He felt broken inside, while gigantic bolts of lightning smacked into the mountaintop. Weary, battered, bleeding, he lay beside the bear, closed his eyes, and drifted into unconsciousness.

Phyllis was awakened by shouts and cheering. She opened her eyes and saw darkness through the hole atop her wickiup. A terrific commotion was taking place in the camp. She strapped on her gun, put on her cowboy hat, and poked her head outside.

Rain poured upon her as everyone swarmed toward the edge of the camp, where several mounted warriors were returning from a raid. The warriors escorted forty horses roped together, plus two stolen wagons full of booty. Some of the women went hysterical at the sight of such tremendous new wealth.

The raid had been led by Delgado, now surrounded by his admiring wives and children. Chief Pinotay approached and Delgado made his report. None of the People had been killed or injured in the raid. Phyllis noticed the brand of the Fourth Cavalry on the horses, and the wagons were filled with U.S. Army bedrolls, ammunition, and equipment.

The warriors dismounted and their women embraced them. Unmarried warriors gazed meaningfully at unmarried maidens because horses could be bartered for brides. Huera sauntered closer to Phyllis, and a condescending expression was on the Apache woman's face. "You do not share our joy, White Eyes girl. That is because you live with us, but you are a White Eyes. Why don't you go home?" Huera laughed derisively.

"I will go home when my man comes back. But why do you want me to leave? What have I ever done to you?"

"Do not think I am a fool. I see how you look at Delgado."

"I look at him the way I look at everybody. I'm not interested in your husband, I assure you."

"Liar."

Phyllis didn't like to be insulted. "Before you said you weren't jealous, but now it sounds as if you are."

Huera scratched at Phyllis's face, but Phyllis uncorked a right hook, connecting with Huera's eye. Huera was stunned for a moment, and Phyllis grabbed Huera's hair,

184

pulling out two handfuls. Huera screeched horribly and wrapped her fingers around Phyllis's throat. Phyllis felt herself being knocked off her feet and she landed on her back, with Huera dropping atop her. The rancher's daughter bucked like a mustang, while digging her fingernails into Huera's wrists, and Huera screeched as red dots appeared beneath Phyllis's fingernails. The women rolled about on the ground as they grappled with each other. Phyllis was about to punch the Apache woman's head through the ground when her arms were grabbed from behind.

Warriors pulled Phyllis away, while others held Huera. Both women glared at each other as they silently swore to continue the battle in another venue. Delgado shouted an order at Huera, who lowered her head. The warriors released her, and she walked in measured steps toward her wickiup. Then Delgado shot a perplexed glance at Phyllis. "Please stop making trouble here."

"She insulted me," Phyllis explained, four vivid scratches on her cheek.

Delgado looked at the bruise on her forehead and the dots of blood erupting from the scratches. "What did you argue about?"

"She thinks that I'm in love with you."

His eyes became cloudy, and the corners of

his mouth turned down. "Women," he muttered. Then he headed toward the wickiup where Huera had gone, ducked inside, and shouted, "Stay away from the White Eyes woman!"

I've just made an enemy for life, Phyllis realized, wiping the blood off her cheek. If she ever comes near me again, she'd better get ready to die.

CHAPTER 7

Marshal Dan Stowe sat in the El Sombrero Saloon, smoking a cheroot and reading a worn old Chicago newspaper that he'd found at the bar. The front page reported the Gold Scandal of '69, which Stowe had read about in detail before, but the El Sombrero had no other printed matter, so he perused the amazing story again.

In an audacious, scurrilous plot, two New York financiers named Jay Gould and Jim Fisk had tried to corner the gold market. They managed to disrupt the finances of the entire civilized world, with disastrous results for American farmers, and would've succeeded in their mad quest for wealth had they not been stopped by President Grant himself, when he ordered the Secretary of the Treasury to dump government gold on the market, depressing the price and ruining the scheme.

After the smoke had cleared, it was discovered that Gould and Fisk had bribed Gold Exchange officials, judges, and politicians of all parties, including the president's brother-in-law! There were even rumors that they'd tried to buy Ulysses S. Grant himself! Numerous bankruptcies and suicides resulted from the nefarious business shenanigans, but did Gould and Fisk go to jail? Not for even one day.

Stowe puffed his cheroot cynically as he considered the vagaries of justice. I'm chasing a man who defended himself in a saloon fight, while Gould and Fisk are still alive, richer than ever, and thumbing their noses at the world. The lawman took a sip of coffee, while keeping one eye on the door. He had a recurring nightmare that an outlaw from his past would hunt him down someday and shoot him in the back.

Then the bat-wing doors were flung open, and Miguelito appeared covered with the dust of the trail. The smile on the midget's face told the story.

"You found her!" Stowe said.

Miguelito sat opposite him, leaned forward, and replied, "She is in an Apache camp, but you could never go yourself. I will take you for another fifty dollars."

"Now you're trying to hold me up, you

little son of a bitch. Our deal was twenty dollars and no more."

"I have been thinking about you, senor. If you offer me twenty dollars to do the dirty work, how much are *you* getting?"

"You're under arrest," Stowe said. "For selling whiskey to the Apaches."

"Prove it," Miguelito replied.

"Let the judge decide." Stowe grabbed the midget by the bandanna around his misshapen neck. "Come with me, half-breed."

Miguelito smiled, showing pointed teeth. "Do not be so excited, amigo. I was only making joke, yes?"

Stowe narrowed his eyes. "How did she look?"

"Very pretty. The chief told me that she and her man found his grandson nearly dead in the desert and saved his life."

Marshal Stowe could smell blossoms in the meadows of Nottingham as he said, "I want to hit the trail by noon."

Duane lay atop the mountain, while the sun neared its zenith in the clear blue sky. Raising himself to a sitting position, he was pleased to note that the storm had stopped and his body was that of a man, not a lion. Neither did he have broken bones or bloody gashes. It was a dream, he realized. But is *this* a dream?

He didn't know what was real anymore. Maybe I can fight a bear, but how do you fight madness? He slapped his palm on the face of the mountain. At least I know this is real, but *how* do I know? In fact, I don't really know *anything*. But who the hell am I, and who's dreaming this dream? He smelled tobacco and spun around. Cucharo sat on the ground, smoking a corncob pipe. Duane leaned forward and gazed into the old man's eyes.

"Start at the beginning," Cucharo said. "Tell me everything."

"I'm so glad to see you," Duane said with a sigh of relief. "I've had a very confusing time."

"That is because you are a White Eyes and fear is your favorite food. I am surprised that you are still here, but tell me — what happened to you?"

"I'm not sure," Duane replied, "but this is the way it seemed. After you left, I drank some cactus water. Then I slept for a while. When I awoke, I got the scare of my life. It seemed that a lion was standing in front of me, and he was in a bad mood. Before I could do anything, he attacked. I thought he was going to kill me, but he disappeared just as we touched. I guess it was a dream."

Cucharo looked at him with exasperation. "You speak of a dream as if it is nothing. You do not understand anything, White Eyes. The lion has given you his power!"

"I don't feel any different."

Cucharo appeared demoralized. "He was trying to tell you something important. Did you try to fight him?"

"I tried to cut his belly with my knife."

Cucharo's features softened. "At least you are not too dumb. What happened next?"

"I saw light at the top of the mountain and thought it was you building a fire. I climbed the mountain, but when I came to the top, I saw a beautiful Apache woman. She was dressed in white buckskin and had white powder on her cheeks. Light seemed to radiate out of her body."

Cucharo appeared to be having a tumultuous inner experience, and Duane wondered if something was wrong with the *di-yin*. Then the old man spoke. "Did she say something?"

"She motioned for me to come closer and then she hugged me. I fell asleep after that, but I remember her guarding me."

Cucharo appeared agitated as he paced back and forth, spat, and kicked a dead branch angrily. Then he turned abruptly toward Duane and hollered, "I have been a *di-yin* all my life, and I have never seen White Painted Woman in a dream! She has shown you special favor, but I do not know why!"

Cucharo shook his head in frustration. "It is hard to understand the way of Yusn, for he is beyond us. But keep going — did you have any more dreams?"

"I slept for a long time, and when I woke up, I was attacked by an Apache warrior whom I'd never seen before. He took me completely by surprise, and we went at it for a long time. Finally I thought I had him, but he just moved to the side. I fell down the mountain and nearly killed myself but ended in a cave with a gold wall, where I found these Apache clothes that you left behind."

The *di-yin* slapped Duane's face hard, and Duane was stunned by the severity of the blow.

"You are so ignorant," Cucharo hissed. "Your grandfather gives you valuable things, but you do not appreciate them. Open your heart, fool. Then you will understand."

Duane was bewildered. "I'm trying, but I still don't know. Why'd my grandfather try to stab me?"

"He was showing his power to you."

"But he almost killed me!"

"Your grandfather would never kill you. How could that be? He gave himself, body to body, so you could see your holy ancestry. You have been a White Eyes long enough.

But stop asking so many questions. Then what happened?"

"I fell asleep again, and when I woke up, I was a lion. I'm not joking, that's just the way I looked. Instead of speaking English, I made lion sounds, and I felt very strong. Just as I was getting used to the idea, all of a sudden I was attacked by a bear. He nearly squeezed me to death, but finally I chewed through his gizzard and killed the son of a bitch. I was covered with his blood and mine, but then it rained and washed me clean. After that, I fell asleep again, and when I woke up, you were here."

Cucharo nodded thoughtfully as he closed his eyes to slits. They sat in silence atop the mountain as breezes whistled past. Then, after a long time, Cucharo spoke. "Everything comes from Yusn," he began. "If I explained Yusn to you, we would be here for a long time. I am not sure that I have the patience, but Yusn has sent you to me and I must try. It will be difficult for you to understand because White Eyes medicine is pitiful. But try to see." Cucharo paused to gather his wits for the ordeal that lay ahead. Then he spread out his arms and intoned: "A long time ago, Yusn made the world. Nobody knows why, and maybe he should not have done it, but he did."

Duane held up his hand. "Wait a minute! Who made Yusn?"

"Yusn always was, and Yusn always will be. No one knows where he came from, because he was always here. After he made the world, he made White Painted Woman, and don't ask me why, because no one can know these things. Anyway, he sent her forth from heaven into the world, and she made her home in a cave in the Sierra Madre Mountains. She had with her a boy named Killer of Enemies, who was her brother."

"Who made him?"

"I told you that Yusn makes everything, and everything returns to Yusn in the end. How can I explain if you keep interrupting me? Where was I? White Painted Woman was in her cave, and she was getting very lonely. One day when she was praying, Yusn said to her, 'When it rains, lie down and spread your legs.' Then it rained and she did as Yusn told her. The water flowed between her legs, and lightning hit her three times. This made her pregnant, don't ask me how. Then Child of Water was born, and when he grew up, he killed all the monsters in the world. That is a big story all in itself, and maybe I will tell it some other time, but the monsters were very dangerous and killed many People. Then one day Yusn called Killer of Enemies and Child of Water to him and laid a gun and a bow and arrow on the ground. Yusn told them to choose, and Killer of Enemies took the gun. That left the bow and arrow for Child of Water. Killer of Enemies became the leader of the White Eyes, and Child of Water became the leader of the People. Too bad Child of Water didn't pick up the gun, but it's too late now. Then Yusn sent the thunder spirits to hunt and gather food for the People, and the People didn't have to do any more work. Everybody was happy, so Yusn decided to bring White Painted Woman and Child of Water into the sky with him. Before they left, they taught the People to be good, brave, and generous.

"Instead the People became lazy, drunk, and full of fighting. It got so bad that the thunder spirits were sickened and returned to the sky. Pretty soon the People were starving, and they prayed to Yusn for help. Finally he forgave them and sent the mountain spirits to teach them how to hunt and gather food themselves. And that is how the world has come to be."

There was silence as Duane let the myth sink in. It made no rational sense, yet he felt deeply moved. "How did you get to be a *diyin?*" he asked.

"It cost me five horses," Cucharo explained. "At the time I was not a good hunter, and I had no woman. So I went to another *di-yin* who had the power of the North Star. I promised him five horses if he would teach me what he knew, and he did."

"What's the power of the North Star?" Duane asked.

"The power of warfare. I became a great warrior and led many good raids." He leaned toward Duane and winked. "I still do, but who is a greater warrior than Lion, who has given you *his* power. You have been greatly blessed, White Eyes."

The *di-yin* placed his hand on Duane's head, and Duane closed his eyes as he received the benediction. He'd been a student of theology for most of his life, and his mind made the connection between the virgin births of Jesus and Child of Water, whereas White Painted Woman was similar to holy Mary, mother of God. The pagan Apache religion didn't seem so pagan, and they had their own strict moral code, too.

"Who was the bear?" Duane asked.

Cucharo opened his eyes wide. "The Bear Monster is worst of all, but you have defeated him, and he will be jealous of you. If you ever see a bear, or even bear tracks, run out of that place right away. But if you see a lion, that is your grandfather. Now you are of the People, and your name is Lion."

Duane felt cat sinews in his muscles. He looked up and saw stars like white dots in the clear blue sky. Something had changed.

The *di-yin* stood before him. "You must never use your power for evil, otherwise it will be taken from you. You must always revere the mountain spirits, for they have taught the People how to live. Now let us hunt an antelope, and we shall eat. I will tell you the story of how Child of Water killed the monsters and then we will return to the camp."

It was night, and a bonfire blazed in the midst of the wickiups as the People danced turbulently to the beat of drums and the pluck of Apache lutes. It was the Property Dance celebrating the influx of new wealth into the tribe, and Phyllis sat with the women at Delgado's fire, trying to make sense of what was happening.

Huera had told her that the Property Dance was a sacred celebration when married and unmarried warriors were permitted to sleep with widows and divorcees without men. But the warriors' wives didn't appear to resent it, and Phyllis couldn't understand their generosity. Perhaps the wives felt sorry for their unmarried sisters, who could enjoy a man on these special occasions and receive presents and favors in addition, while warriors returning from battle could have a hot time.

Phyllis was semirepelled and impossibly excited by the events occurring around her. Conventional Apache prudery was tossed aside as the unmarried women, called *bi-zahn,* danced lewdly, threw their clothes off, and let firelight flash on their bare breasts. Phyllis saw flames of desire in the warriors' eyes as they watched lasciviously, wearing war paint and recently acquired blue army shirts with gold stripes and insignia. The women made suggestive pelvic motions that Phyllis found shocking. She watched in astonishment and horror as a brawny warrior dragged a skinny *bi-zahn* woman into a wickiup. Phyllis heard cries of love as drums pounded incessantly and seminude dancers cavorted everywhere. *Tizwin* flowed freely, with no sheriff to maintain law and order. Phyllis felt frightened, vulnerable, and exposed. But no *bi-zahn* was taken against her will, and indeed all seemed most anxious to fornicate with strange warriors.

Delgado emerged from the desert, accompanied by a middle-aged heavy-breasted *bi-zahn,* the third he'd dragged off so far, and the Property Dance had only just begun. Meanwhile, his four wives were inebriated, fingering pots and pans stolen from the cavalry and chattering about delicacies they intended to cook.

Phyllis felt two eyes burning into her head. She turned toward Delgado sitting nearby, gazing at her with unmistakable silent insinuations. What if he comes over here? she asked herself. Phyllis was no longer a virgin and felt certain womanly needs. She closed her eyes and imagined Delgado ripping her clothes off. My God, what's happening to me! The *tizwin* made her giggle as the Apache lifeway caught her in its sway. Would Duane cut off my nose?

Where is he? she wondered as she gazed at Delgado. He sipped *tizwin* as drums pounded in Phyllis's ears. She felt like dancing naked in the moonlight but knew that she was a Christian, and Christians didn't do these things, as far as she knew. But why not? She saw herself groping naked in Delgado's arms, and her cheeks flushed with emotion. Oh, God, help me before I do something I'll never live down!

Somebody shouted, the drumming stopped suddenly, and the warriors reached for their weapons as a guard burst into the assembly, babbling Apache. Phyllis wasn't fluent in the lingo but gathered that someone important was coming. Warriors moved toward the edge of the camp, and Phyllis joined them with the rest of the wives, while the children scooted down the crevice path, to greet the new-comers.

Cucharo and a tall, lean Apache material-ized out of the night, carrying leather pouches. Phyllis looked at the younger Apache, who bore a certain resemblance to Duane but was more muscular, tense, and ex-otic. My God — it's him! she realized at last.

Cucharo handed the chief a leather bag full of sacred pollen, then bowed to the chief's wife. The *di-yin* folded his arms on his chest and delivered a major oration. Phyllis couldn't decipher every word, but it appeared that Duane had accomplished something im-portant. He appeared alien in his breechcloth and moccasins, the red muslin rag wrapped around his head and paint on his nose and cheeks, as he tossed a pouch to Delgado. Delgado appeared deeply moved, and Phyllis was more confused than ever. What's hap-pened to Duane? she wondered. Everybody's so respectful of him.

The chief, Cucharo, Duane, and Delgado entered the chief's wickiup, and there was si-lence for a few moments. Then the music re-sumed, and dancers re-formed their circle around the fire as tongues of flame licked the sky. Phyllis rose, brushed off her jeans, and strode toward Huera and the other women. "What's going on?"

They peered at her with new interest. "Your man had a great vision," Huera said reverently. "Now he is a *di-yin*. He has been given the power of the Lion, he has killed the Bear Monster, and White Painted Woman has held him in her arms. Cucharo said that his grandfather was from the People. *Enjuh. It is so.*"

Phyllis's skepticism butted against Huera's rock-solid faith. The Apaches saw something in Duane, and even Delgado, who detested White Eyes, had treated him with consideration. Drums pounded, *bi-zahn* women undulated their bodies, and Phyllis was mystified by the latest turn of events. Duane's no *di-yin,* she reassured herself. He's got all these Apaches fooled, probably because he's fooled himself.

The door flap wavered at the chief's wickiup, then Cucharo appeared, followed by Delgado, Duane, and the old chief. In the darkness, Duane had the same high cheekbones as they, his eyes almost Oriental. The men embraced each other, then the chief returned to his wickiup while the others headed in separate directions.

Duane walked directly toward her, and she noticed his lithe Apache gait. Firelight glistened on his long, corded legs, flat stomach, and powerful arms. He appeared more lethal, while war paint heightened his menacing aspect. He came to a stop a few feet in front of her and gazed silently into her eyes. "Come with me."

He grabbed her arm, pulled her to her feet, and their faces were inches apart. She smelled ponderosa pines in his hair, while his eyes struck sparks off hers. Without another word, he lifted her off the ground and carried her toward their wickiup. Drums hammered in their ears, maidens chanted, she touched her lips to his chest, and he lowered her toward the entrance. She crawled inside, but before she could roll onto her back, he was on top of her, tearing at her blouse, his face contorted with desire, and he appeared almost cruel as he stripped her in rough methodical movements.

But somehow it was pleasing, as she lay on the antelope skin, gazing at him in the dimness. He removed his breechcloth and moccasins, then grasped her shoulders and inserted his tongue into her mouth. His hands were strong on her body as maidens chanted love songs around the bonfire and coyotes howled mournfully in far-off caves.

Big Al Thornton sat in his office, smoked a cigar, and looked out the window at the Milky Way blazing across the sky. Where is she now? he wondered.

He couldn't stop thinking about his darling

daughter, whom he believed had died of thirst in the desert. The mere image of her suffering made him weak in his knees. He'd lost twenty pounds, his clothes hung on him, and his expression was grim.

I knew Duane Braddock was trouble the first time I set eyes on him, Big Al thought. He got my daughter killed, and there ain't a damned thing I can do about it. Sometimes Big Al wanted to put a bullet into Duane Braddock's head, although he figured that Duane had been killed, too. He was just a wild-ass kid who wouldn't back down, and my daughter thought he was the best thing that ever happened to Texas. If the Apaches didn't get them, the sun did, or the Comancheros, banditos, renegade miners, or lost, wandering outlaw bands.

Big Al grumbled to himself as he walked down the hall to Phyllis's bedroom. He opened the door, lit her lamp, and gazed sadly at her shelves of books. Her clothes hung in the closet and an old Navaho doll lay on her pillow. Big Al touched the floral bedspread, and a tear came to his eye. Sons of bitches live forever, but my daughter had to die.

It was night on the desert as Marshal Dan Stowe and Miguelito rode along a winding arroyo. They'd been in the saddle since late afternoon, and Miguelito said they'd arrive in the Apache camp sometime tomorrow.

Marshal Stowe sagged in his saddle, dozing lightly, as he let Miguelito lead the way. Sometimes he thought that Miguelito was luring him into a trap where the Apaches would massacre him, steal his horses, and leave his bones to bleach. The most nagging part was that Marshal Stowe didn't have to be there. He could've reported that Duane Braddock disappeared into Mexico, but the lawman had never filed a false report in his life.

He dozed as his horse plodded onward. It reminded him of long night marches during the war and the constant danger from Confederate sharpshooters. Now Honest Abe was dead, General Grant's administration was the most corrupt in American history, and controversy buzzed around General Custer's recent campaigns against the Plains Indians, which some considered massacres.

We were young gods of war, but now we're ordinary people again, Marshal Stowe thought philosophically. I guess glory doesn't last forever, and I should be thankful that I've got a job. If Duane Braddock is living with the Apaches, I'll take him into custody, and if the girl is there, I'll bring her out. And if the Apaches try to kill me, all I can do is go down like a soldier.

CHAPTER 8

The lost detachment wandered across the desert as the sun blasted them unmercifully. They were covered with perspiration, throats parched, eyes hollow, cheeks sunken. A garland of buzzards circled the sky, and purple mountains lined the plain. A mesa stood in the distance like a grotesque monument to a forgotten god.

The detachment was headed in a northerly direction, hoping to find their last water hole, but each man knew it was far away, and they might never reach it. Dazed by the sun, tongues swollen, they fought their way through cactus needles that ripped their clothes and flesh. Every step was agony as they watched for Apaches and prayed for miracles.

Lieutenant Dawes no longer could lie to himself as death lurked straight ahead. They'd become imperiled due to his own heedless folly, false pride, and low jealousy. Weakened by lack of food and water, guilt assailed him as his pants were shredded by thorns, his knees lost their bounce, and his broad shoulders drooped. He placed one foot in front of the other, although he knew that every movement was futile. But a soldier keeps advancing despite illness, wounds, doubts, confusion, and enemy fire.

He looked over his shoulder at cavalry troopers straggling behind him in a column of twos. Bearded, ragged, and demoralized, they wanted to shoot him in the back, and he couldn't blame them. His fancy West Point education hadn't amounted to much in Apache territory, and now he knew how Napoleon felt at Waterloo after Wellington's cavalry split his lines in the victory charge. Not only was he dying of thirst, but he felt like a failure.

He wanted to collapse onto the ground, never to move again, but a West Point officer can't disintegrate in front of his men. He hallucinated the castellated walls and emerald lawns at the renowned military academy on the Hudson. It was a grand charade, with form-fitting uniforms and blaring bands, but it hadn't prepared him for fighting the Apache in the desert of south Texas.

Whatever made me think that I could lead

men in battle? he asked himself dreamily. The desert shimmered before him as Vanessa Fontaine advanced spectrally across the shifting sands. She wore the identical green dress as on the day he'd first seen her outside Gibson's General Store in Shelby. He'd fallen madly in love with her, never suspecting that the golden goddess would lead him to doom in southwest Texas.

"Gawd dammit!" shouted Private Cruikshank behind him. "Maybe I'm a-gonna die — but the son of a bitch who brought me here is a-gonna die first!"

Lieutenant Dawes turned and saw the soldiers arrayed against him. Cruikshank had drawn his service revolver and was pointing it at the middle of Dawes's chest.

Dawes was delirious as he staggered from side to side. He recalled Napoleon stopped by the king's soldiers on the Paris road after returning from his first exile. Lieutenant Dawes raised his trembling sunburnt hands and tore open his shirt, baring his chest. "If you want to shoot your commanding officer in cold blood, here I stand."

A shot rang out, and for an instant Lieutenant Dawes thought he'd been killed. But he was still standing, and no ugly red hole appeared in the middle of his chest. Smoke rose from the barrel of Sergeant Mahoney's gun, who aimed it at the sky. "There'll be no more of that," he said in a deadly tone. "The next shot'll be 'twixt yer goddamned eyes, young private!"

The desert fell silent as the men looked at each other in dismay. All their marching, training, target practice, and spit and polish didn't amount to anything in the Texas desert. Cruikshank mumbled darkly as he holstered his gun. "If it wasn't fer that son of a bitch, we wouldn't be hyar."

All eyes turned to Lieutenant Dawes, who replied in a dry, cracked voice, "We've got to hold together and try to help each other reach safety. It's the only way."

Corporal Hazelwood spat at the ground. "We're finished, and everybody knows it. That fancy-pants bastard brought us, and we oughtta shoot 'im!"

"You're right," Dawes replied. "But if you kill me, you're stuck here anyway. And if the guards had been more vigilant, we'd be fine. I think we should die as comrades in arms, instead of shooting each other in the back like hooligans. We may not be good men, but at least we can be good soldiers."

Weasellike Private Witherspoon said snidely, "I should've deserted while I had the chance."

Lieutenant Dawes thought he'd appeal to

their finer sensibilities. "I think we should bow our heads and ask for God's guidance."

"If there's a God," replied Private Cunningham, a redheaded ex-farmer from Missouri, "He would never've let us in this mess in the first place. We're stove up, and there's no way out."

"I think," Lieutenant Dawes said, "there are some here who still believe with me in the power of prayer. Gather around, men, and let's ask our creator for divine assistance."

They bowed their heads, lips cracked, noses peeling, eyes bloodshot. "Dear God," said Lieutenant Dawes, "have mercy on your poor Christian soldiers."

They stood in silence, thinking of lost loves, squandered dreams, and crushing failures. They knew they were the dregs of the earth, for why else had they joined the frontier army, to fight Apaches instead of becoming carpenters, farmers, mechanics, scriveners, businessmen, or even priests. Each reflected upon the path that had brought them to southwest Texas, where coyotes and buzzards followed at a safe distance, waiting for them to drop.

They heard a cry from Private Duckworth: "Water!" He was their point man, roving far ahead of the main unit, searching for whatever he could find. Their ears perked up, and they heard his parched voice again. "Water!"

They couldn't believe their ears. Was it a false echo from a far-off cave? They looked at each other in alarm, and then, as if driven by a single will, they headed toward Private Duckworth, images of cool trickling liquid on their tongues. They rampaged through clumps of cactus and scatterings of grama grass. "Water!" The voice came closer, and they could see green cottonwood trees in the distance.

"We're saved!" shouted Private Cruikshank.

Lieutenant Dawes believed that God had answered his prayer. It was a sign from heaven, just as God parted the Red Sea for the wandering Israelites. The men began to run, tongues hanging like dogs'. They stumbled over rocks, roots, and gopher holes as they made their way to the oasis in the middle of the desert. Suddenly they'd been given the gift of life!

Lieutenant Dawes tried to contain himself, but his throat was like sand, and his legs moved of their own volition. All he wanted was to bury his face in the water and drink deeply. Then they could hunt meat and become soldiers again. "I told you, boys — we'll get through this if we just hold together!"

They came to cottonwood trees, and the temperature dropped as the water came into view. Grass and shrubs surrounded the hole, interspersed with bare desert sand. Private Duckworth was already on his belly, his face in the water, drinking deeply. The bluecoat soldiers stumbled down the incline, dropped to their knees, lowered their faces into the water, and slaked their leathery throats with ambrosia.

Lieutenant Dawes gulped thirstily. Thank you, God, for your wonderful blessing. You've shown mercy to a sinner, and if we ever make it back to civilization, I'll become a minister of your Holy Word.

He saw himself as a bumbling lecherous fool who'd finally found the truth. I'll preach sermons of piety and redemption, based on my own personal experiences, and deter people from the hellish paths that I myself have trod.

It was the last coherent thought that Lieutenant Dawes had as a rushing sound came to him from the far side of the well. He raised his head and was stunned by the sight of Apaches in war paint bursting out of the ground, with knives, lances, and war clubs in their hands. Sergeant Mahoney shouted the alarm, and Lieutenant Dawes was reaching for his service revolver when an Apache slammed him in the middle of the forehead with a war club. Lieutenant Dawes's skull cracked down the middle, blood seeped out the edges, and he collapsed onto the ground.

The bluecoat soldiers were slaughtered in seconds, their blood flowing in rivulets into the deep dark waters of the well. The Apache renegades stripped away weapons, clothing, Lieutenant Dawes's gold tooth, and everything else of value. They plundered and mutilated like fiends, and their leader was Jamata, the evil sorcerer.

Jamata cut off the officer's penis and stuffed it into his mouth. Then he disemboweled him, guts spilling onto the ground like angry, bloodsoaked snakes. Finally he cut off a patch of the officer's hair as a trophy.

The other renegades did the same. They were the dregs of the Apache nation, and they'd denounced their holy lifeway for rape, murder, and pillage. They'd plotted the route of the soldiers for days, knew the bluecoats would find the water hole, and dug themselves into the ground, to wait patiently for their arrival.

They worked methodically at their gruesome task, until all the soldiers were butchered. Then they gathered up the booty and carried it to the gully where their horses were tethered. They mounted up and retreated into the desert as silently as they'd come. Soon they were gone, and circling buzzards swooped leisurely from the sky for the fabulous fresh meat spread before them. Like gentlemen in black formal suits and orange boots, they settled amid the corpses and dug their beaks into tender body parts.

Gootch had seen it all from a cave cut into a nearby mountain. He was one of a group of scouts spread out across the desert, watching, studying, and waiting for the renegades to show their faces. He knew that good Apaches would be blamed for the bloody deed, more bluecoat soldiers would come to the land, there would be war, and Gootch could see no end to it.

But the war was a long way off. Now his task was to follow the renegades back to their camp, so he could report its location to Chief Pinotay. Extreme caution was required, because the renegades were Apaches, too, with the same knowledge and skills as he. Gootch watched them ride across the rolling desert and waited patiently. He didn't want to get too close, for they might detect his presence.

The flames of vengeance burned hotly within him, for one of his sisters had been killed in the previous massacre. He yearned for the opportunity to slice off Jamata's head.

Meanwhile his cave was silent, dank, and smelled of old coyote manure. Gootch's father had brought him here as a boy, for it was a good observation post. The People knew every water hole, cave, and hiding spot in Arizona, New Mexico, southwest Texas, and Mexico, while the White Eyes wandered around like fools. Gootch couldn't help feeling contempt for the bluecoat soldiers who'd let themselves be slaughtered so easily. The Apache warrior believed that they lacked inner strength, because of the way they raised their children. When a White Eyes baby cried, the grown-ups tried to soothe him, but when an Apache baby was out of sorts, they hung his cradleboard on a tree and let him cry himself out. Gootch thought that the White Eyes spoiled their children, and that's why they grew fragile.

Gootch peeked outside. The renegades were gone, but not their tracks. He crawled out of the cave, heading for a stand of trees where his horse was tethered. "I will track you down, Jamata," he swore beneath his breath. "You will not escape the wrath of the People."

Phyllis ground corn between heavy circular stones. It was hard work, and her arms were getting tired. She wore the standard Apache woman's deerskin blouse, skirt, and boots because her cowboy clothes had been demolished in her tumultuous recent encounter with Duane. Something had happened to him during his time with Cucharo, but he wouldn't tell her the particulars.

Phyllis glanced at nearby women grinding corn. Like them, she was sweaty, tired, in need of a bath, and possessed no underwear. The routine of Apache life was becoming dull grim routine. Sometimes she had the urge to sit on a chair and read a book.

Her bedroom shelves had been full of Lord Byron, Washington Irving, and Keats, among others. Her mother was a former schoolmarm and ordained that Phyllis spend many hours penetrating the minds of great thinkers. Now, as the novelty of Apache life wore off, she missed the intellectual pastime. But Duane had convinced himself that he was an Apache and Yusn had sent him special messages from the great beyond.

Phyllis adored Duane, but there was much in his character that she deplored. He seemed to lack basic common sense, perhaps because he'd been raised in a monastery far from the harsh realities of life. She couldn't understand how the happy-go-lucky cowboy had become an Apache so quickly. He's like a chameleon, but what's his true identity?

Children burst onto the scene, jabbering wildly. Phyllis had lived in the camp long enough to understand what they were saying. The warriors were returning after a successful antelope hunt. The women moved toward the path that led to the camp, to greet their men.

The warriors were already halfway up the ravine, dead antelope lashed head down over their horses' backs. Phyllis spotted Duane, taller than most Apaches, with his six-gun slung low over his breechcloth. The warriors arrived at the top of the mountain, dismounted, and Duane kissed his wife. "I shot a fat one," he said happily. Then he untied the antelope and dumped it at her feet. She stared at it as he led his horse to the corral.

The dead antelope's eyes were open and staring, and a ribbon of blood dribbled from its mouth. Duane had cut his arrow out of the animal's lungs because an Apache warrior doesn't throw good arrows away.

"Duane!" she called out.

He ignored her as he headed toward the corral. She shouted his name again and ran after him. "I want to talk with you!"

He turned around, his features stern as an Apache's. There was something about him that frightened her.

"You may not realize it," she said, "but

216

skinning and cooking an antelope is an enormous job. I didn't mind it when we were in Delgado's household because there wasn't so much to do. But now that you're a warrior yourself, it's getting too much for me."

He didn't smile or say something kind. "I will return you to the White Eyes and find another woman who is not lazy." He stared calmly at her, betraying no emotion.

She looked at him in disbelief as his words struck her like daggers. But she was the daughter of Big Al Thornton and couldn't let herself cry. "I think you've finally gone loco," she said. "You're even speaking English like an Apache."

"I need a woman who can do a woman's work. Maybe it's best if you went home."

"But this is just a game you're playing, Duane. Like the Pecos Kid. If you ever make one of these *real* Apaches mad, they'll skin you alive."

"I will talk to Delgado and find out how to return you to your people."

Phyllis maintained her outward calm. "Is that all I am to you? Somebody to skin the antelope?" Phyllis's vanity was wounded because it appeared that he was dumping her. "What if I don't want to go back?"

"You will become a *bi-zahn,* and no one will bring you antelope meat."

"What if I marry Delgado?" she asked tauntingly.

"What makes you think he wants you?"

"Get him out here, and we'll ask him."

She ran toward the wickiup where Delgado had last entered, and now it was Duane's turn for shock. He didn't want her to marry Delgado because he still loved her madly. But she didn't like the Apache lifeway, and he'd been trying to bluff her into a few more weeks. He felt baffled as she came to a stop in front of the warrior's wickiup. "Delgado!"

A crowd gathered, and children drew closer, their eyes dancing with delight. Old people crawled out of their wickiups, for the day's entertainment was about to begin. The White Eyes were squabbling again, and Delgado was about to be drawn in.

The son of the chief poked his head out of his wickiup and looked at Phyllis. "What do you want, woman?"

"Duane and I aren't going to live together anymore, and I was wondering if I could become one of your wives."

Delgado nearly fell on his face, so astounded was he by the sudden proposal. Apaches muttered among themselves as Phyllis's words were translated for those who spoke no English. Delgado crawled out of his wickiup and drew himself to his full height.

He turned toward Duane and said, "Is this true?"

"She won't butcher the antelope I brought home, and I offered to return her to her father. But she said she'd rather marry you."

Delgado regarded the White Eyes woman through slitted eyes, and he had to admit, in his heart of hearts, that he'd lusted for her since the day they'd met. He tried to smile affably, but it came out awry. "I am sorry, but I do not think it would be right if I married my friend's wife."

"But Duane doesn't want me anymore," Phyllis replied. She turned to her former man. "Tell him the truth."

Duane couldn't admit that he was jealous, but sweet little Phyllis had defeated him yet again. All he could say was "She is lazy, and she is still a White Eyes in her heart. She should go back to her people."

"I don't want to go back," Phyllis insisted. "I want to be Delgado's latest wife."

Delgado shrugged and pretended to be unconcerned. "If she does not want to leave, how can we force her? And if she does not want to live with you, we cannot make her. Maybe I should ask the chief what to do."

Phyllis was insulted by Delgado's disinterest. "What do you want to ask the chief for?" she asked. "I don't want to marry him.

The decision is yours to make."

Delgado sighed as he turned to Duane. "If she becomes a *bi-zahn,* there will be no end of the trouble she makes. All right, I will marry her. I am sure that soon she will want to return to her people and then she will go. I will give you two horses for her."

Duane couldn't admit that he didn't want her to marry Delgado because it would give her the upper hand yet again. I'm supposed to be a mean son of a bitch, but that little cowgirl beats me every time. The mere thought made him angry, and he announced, "She's not worth two horses. I'll take one horse, and it doesn't have to be very good."

Phyllis's calm exterior shattered, and she let out an angry screech. Baring her teeth, extending her fingernails, she ran across the clearing, headed for Duane. He stood slackly, a bored expression on his face, and waited until she came close. Then he plucked her out of the air, turned her over his knee, and proceeded to spank her.

The Apaches exploded with laughter, hugging their sides, jumping up and down. They'd never seen anybody get spanked before and considered it hilarious. Duane slapped her bottom heartily, while she writhed in his lap. Delgado howled until tears came to his eyes, and then his knees became jelly and he had to sit down.

Suddenly a guard appeared, running toward the campsite. He hollered something, and Duane unceremoniously dumped Phyllis off his lap. He drew his six-gun as the Apaches grabbed knives, guns, lances, bows and arrows. The joyful atmosphere transformed suddenly into danger as Gootch rode into the camp at a gallop. He pulled back his reins and shouted in the Apache language. Phyllis had learned enough words to catch the gist of what he was saying. He'd found the hideout of the renegades!

Phyllis was forgotten as Delgado and the other warriors gathered in front of the chief's tent. Duane joined them, along with Cucharo, and they discussed plans for the revenge raid as the women looked on warily from the distance. Phyllis sat beside Huera and asked, "Am I Duane's wife or Delgado's?"

"You are an idiot. Don't you know that the warriors are going on a raid and their success depends upon us? If we are bad, evil will come to the warriors. If we are good, the warriors will win the fight. You will pray with us while the warriors are gone, but first you must skin your antelope."

Huera's order left no room for argument, discussion, or vanity. The warrior queen walked away as Phyllis gazed with distaste at the dead antelope. She pulled out her knife, dropped to her knees, sliced into the animal's flesh around its ankles, and pulled the skin loose. *How did I ever get mixed up with these people?* she asked herself. *What the hell am I doing here?*

The renegade cave was cut into the side of a mountain ten miles from the Apache camp. It could be approached only through a maze of narrow canyons, and enemies had to attack the final fifty yards across a bare rock incline with no cover. Guards were posted night and day, watching for surprise attacks.

The guards peered into the night as the renegade Property Dance was under way, *tizwin* flowing freely and a wild pig roasting over the fire. The renegades had painted their bodies in green, ochre, and vermillion stripes and writhed naked in the light of the fire. Jamata hopped among them, shrieking and giggling happily. In a corner, a couple copulated like dogs. Across the floor, another couple performed a mating act with the man on the bottom and the woman on the top. Everyone was naked. In the open, dancing and committing acts unthinkable in ordinary Apache society. Everything was permitted by Jamata, the more lewd and bloody, the better.

The evil *di-yin* had gathered them from across Apacheria, and their business was theft, murder, and mutilation. Some were sorcerers like Jamata, expelled by their people for nefarious activities. Others had stolen from the People or murdered kinsmen. A few felt cheated by the People, as though their true worth had never been truly appreciated. A few had lost at love and sought revenge among the renegades.

They believed that the old chiefs and *di-yins* were frauds, and the solution was to break all the rules. But the old chiefs and *di-yins* weren't on their minds that night as they barked like foxes and chirped like birds. They all despised the restrictions of the holy lifeway and wanted freedom from Yusn's onerous laws.

The women were as vicious as the men, and the children imps with flashing eyes who liked to torture small creatures for pleasure. Jamata had told them that if you feel something strongly, you must do it no matter what. The renegades squealed with glee as they twisted obscenely in the firelight, brandishing ill-gotten gains and fornicating everywhere.

War ponies galloped through the night as the People's best warriors rode bareback toward the renegades' hideout. The warriors were seminaked, carrying lances, bows, arrows, rifles, and clubs.

Everyone except Duane had known and revered the women who'd been killed, and many of the warriors had been relatives. Their hearts were filled with the lust for the renegades' blood.

The war ponies exploded out of a gully and thundered mightily across a vast basin covered with cactus plants. The renegades had been killing, stealing, and bedeviling the People for too long. The time had come to even the score.

Duane rode in their midst, wearing his breechcloth and moccasin boots, covered with war paint, feeling exhilarated. Nothing he'd ever known could compare with the hellbent-for-leather Apache charge. It was as if their sacred lifeway had entered his blood and bones, and the pious seminary student was gone, along with the lonesome cowboy.

Now he was a warrior, too, his body rippling and strong, finally on the warpath. In addition to weapons, he carried a small bag of sacred pollen for its good influence, but his greatest power was in his Killer of Enemies bandolier, a loosely braided cord sash of two hide strings twisted about each other and draped across his body from the right shoulder to the left side. Only a *di-yin* could make a Killer of Enemies bandolier, and Duane had received his from Cucharo before the raid.

The horses raced across the desert, and Duane felt attuned to every other warrior. He opened his mouth wide and let out his war cry, his voice mingling with the others, as the riders sped onward, headed toward the destruction of the renegades.

Marshal Dan Stowe drowsed in his saddle, drifting in and out of war dreams. Surrounded by desert foliage, with insects buzzing around his hat, he envisioned himself in August of 1864, during a little-remembered battle of the great Civil War.

The Michigan Wolverine Brigade was bivouacking in Chester Gap, taking a well-deserved rest from the war and trying to enjoy a lunch of hardtack and tepid tea, when sentries burst onto the scene with alarming news. Confederate cavalry in substantial numbers were advancing down Front Royal Pike!

It had been an electric moment as all eyes turned to General Custer. The horses were already unsaddled, tents pitched, the food on the fire, but the Boy General never batted an eyelash. He turned calmly to his executive officer and said, "Call the men to horse."

Sergeant Joseph Fought raised the bugle to

his lips, and the battle-hardened Wolverines saddled and bridled their horses in only ten minutes. Skirmishes broke out among forward elements of infantry as General Custer rode to the top of a hill in the vicinity. He leaned on his pommel and studied the advance carefully. It was formed in a column of fours, consisting of a brigade of Rebel horsemen leading huge masses of infantry. Custer galloped back to his men, the battle plan forming in his mind. He ordered his artillery to rain death upon the advancing Confederates and then formed his cavalry in attack formation.

The barrage continued for some time, ripping holes in the Confederate lines, but Fitzhugh Lee's men were brave soldiers and kept moving through cannonballs and canister. When it became clear that artillery alone wouldn't stop the soldiers in gray, Custer ordered the barrage to stop. He took his position at the head of his cavalry squadrons, raised his sword in the air, and ordered the bugler to sound the charge.

The Michigan Wolverines moved toward the valley, and it took a few minutes to reach top speed. Marshal Stowe twitched involuntarily in the saddle as he recalled the enthralling all-out cavalry charge. General Custer galloped far in front, his saber high in the air, his emblematic red scarf trailing in the breeze, as sunlight gleamed off the gold buttons and piping of his fantastical uniform. His voice could be heard to the rear ranks as he shouted hoarsely: "Come on, you Wolverines!"

Flags and guidons fluttered in the air, and men bellowed encouragement to each other as bugle notes sang over the battlefield. The Wolverines galloped over the grass and rockstrewn valley as massed Confederate rifle balls ripped into them. Michigan horses fell, and Michigan men screamed horribly as their arms and legs were blown away, but the bold young commander never swerved in his headlong charge.

Cavalrymen on both sides drew closer, and everyone knew that they might die within the next seconds. Captain Stowe rode ahead of old Troop B, his mustache dark, eyes clear, gut slim, as he braced himself for the ultimate clash. He raised his sword, took a deep breath, and felt a hand on his knee.

He opened his eyes, and it was night on the southwest Texas desert. Miguelito was dismounted beside him. "Riders," said the hunchback midget. "We'd best get off the trail."

Marshal Stowe perked up his ears, couldn't hear anything, but wouldn't question the ears of an Apache. His head reeled with memories of the long-ago battle as he dismounted. He followed the half-breed into the thick brush beside the trail and knelt in the shadows. Miguelito pressed his ear to the ground. "Many horses," he said. "The People go on a raid."

"I wonder how many white folks will be killed," Marshal Stowe replied sardonically. He wanted to smoke, but the light could draw unwelcome attention. The Battle of Crooked Run dissipated into the mists of time, and no longer was he Captain Dan Stowe making history with General Custer and the Michigan Wolverines.

Now he was just a man with a badge and a warrant that he tried to convince himself was worthwhile. Issues were clear-cut during the war, but ambivalence was everywhere now that peace had arrived. Texas had an unpopular scalawag governor put into office by the Union Army. Former slaves had become sheriffs and judges, while former Confederate soldiers worked at menial jobs. Eight hundred thousand men had died on the battlefields of the Civil War to free slaves who would've been turned loose eventually anyway if they'd let history take its course. Marshal Stowe shook his head in chagrin. It was all horseshit, but so interesting while it lasted.

"You are a strange one," said Miguelito,

looking up at him. "You want me to take you to the Apache camp, where they may kill you. And why? To arrest a man? To capture a woman? What are these people to you?"

"It's my job, but you're half Apache and half white. What're you doing here?"

The midget grinned and rubbed his fingers together. *"Dinero."*

It was night in the Apache camp. The women sat around a small fire, chanting prayers in unison as they implored Yusn, White Painted Woman, and the mountain spirits to make their men victorious. Their primordial rhythms rose and fell lugubriously as firelight flickered on their earnest faces.

Phyllis sat among them, joining the simple repetitions, while studying their strange culture. Every Apache woman believed that her behavior would affect the outcome of the battle, an irrational and preposterous notion to Phyllis's mind, yet she could almost *feel* the power of their devotion.

It affected her deeply, for she wasn't always the cold observer that she tried to be. She heard an outpouring of love and concern for the warriors, and it wasn't pure superstition. If a warrior died, who'd hunt for his wife and children? Apache love was based on necessity, not songs and poetry.

She didn't want Duane to be killed on the raid, although she could always return to her family. She believed that she loved Duane deeply, but sometimes she wished for a more mature and stable man, like Delgado. One day Duane wants to be a rancher, next day he's an Apache, and if we ever get to Mexico, maybe he'll become a bullfighter. She wanted to have children, but what kind of father would the Pecos Kid be? Trouble was his middle name, and he didn't have a practical bone in his body. You don't necessarily buy the first horse you ride, Phyllis told herself. I pray to Yusn that Duane doesn't die on the raid, but when he comes back, we'll have a little talk about leaving this place.

The voices of the women droned into the night as they held hands, rocked from side to side, and evoked Apache deities. They knew that their warriors would be approaching the renegade cave soon and then the blood would flow. O mighty Yusn, please send my man back to me whole, otherwise my children will go hungry and the People will die. O Yusn, we call upon you ardently. Please do not turn your heart from the People.

It was silent in the cave, for the Property Dance had ended. The renegade men, women, children, and dogs lay in each other's arms on animal skins strewn on the floor, as faint wisps of smoke arose from ashes in the pit. They were naked, besotted, their bellies full, and sleepy grins spread upon their faces. They'd had a grand time and would tell the story for as long as they lived, passing it down from generation to generation of renegades, as it weaved itself into their warped traditions.

The Property Dance had been a pleasurable experience for everyone except the guards in the desert below. Throughout the night they'd listened to shrieks of delight, drunken ravings, and grunts of passion as they watched for the advent of enemies. But no enemies came, because the cave was far from the main trails that the White Eyes used, while the People didn't visit the canyon often.

Red Claw was one of the guards, twenty years old, the son of Jamata. He felt bitter that he'd been selected to stand guard because he preferred dancing with naked women in the cave. The desert was silent, cold, and dark in the hour before dawn. He sat with his back to a juniper tree, knees in the air, rifle lying beside him. He should be hiding, but he was confident that he'd see or hear an intruder before the intruder caught wind of him.

There would be other Property Dances, and he could play with the women then. Not even his father could ask him to guard two Property Dances in a row. Red Claw was in awe of the mad sorcerer who'd led them across the desert to their new life. Jamata held them together and brought them much booty. The People and the White Eyes were crops that the renegades harvested regularly. Someday Jamata will die, Red Claw reflected as he closed his eyes. And then perhaps I will become chief.

He decided to sleep, for no one would know, and what would it matter? Then he heard a moccasin gently touch the earth behind him. Red Claw opened his eyes as dark shadows swirled above him. He opened his mouth to scream, but a hand clamped over his mouth, while something sharp and terrible pierced his throat. Red Claw coughed as blood spurted from his jugular vein.

The guard fell at Delgado's feet, then more of the People's warriors appeared behind bushes, trees, and clumps of cactus. Ahead was the open incline that led to the cave. The warriors deployed silently, aware that more guards were posted in the cave. Every warrior was prepared to die as they focused on vengeance, glory, and the expression on the faces of their women and children when they returned.

They came to the edge of the vegetation

line, and before them lay the steep rocky slope to the renegades' cave. No orders had to be given, with no pause for rest. One group of warriors with rifles formed to the right, while another group similarly armed positioned themselves to the left. A third group, situated between the other two, would lead the initial charge.

This was the most dangerous task of all, and therefore the most coveted. Duane had convinced Delgado to let him join the vanguard unit, which Delgado would lead. They'd rush the cave, and when guards sounded the alarm, the other warriors would pin down the renegades with arrows and rifle fire. Delgado's warriors would jump over the outside wall and then it would be hand to hand and man to man until one side or the other was vanquished.

The moment had arrived for the blood of the People to be avenged. Delgado raised his hand, pointed to the cave, and leapt forward. Duane and the others followed him, their moccasins making soft brushing sounds against naked rock. They covered twenty yards rapidly, when a head appeared over the top of the hideout. There was a cry, a shot, and the head disappeared. Duane set his lips in a grim line, for the next yards would be the most difficult of all.

The warriors sped up the incline as more renegade heads appeared above the boulders. Shots rang out from the two covering forces, Jamata screamed, and there was bedlam inside the cave. Duane held his war club in his right hand and his knife in the other as he ran swiftly up the side of the mountain. Delgado was the first warrior to reach the boulder barricades, but he didn't slow down and wait for the others to catch up. He hollered his war cry, vaulted over the barrier, and landed inside the cave. Shots reverberated, screams of terror filled the air, and then the other warriors followed him over.

Duane dropped inside the cave amid other warriors, and a scene of unspeakable madness met his eyes. Renegade sorcerers, witches, and imps scrambled for weapons, shrieking eerily. Weakened by excessive food, drink, and forbidden acts, they appeared confused, but they were warriors, too, trained from birth to fight suddenly and without mercy. They grabbed knives, clubs, lances, and anything else they could lay their hands on as they rose to meet their attackers.

A big, burly, completely naked renegade with a scar on his chin ran toward Duane, a knife in his hand. Duane dodged to the side and then swung his war club down. It landed atop the renegade's head, which cracked apart like a rotten egg. The renegade's eyes rolled up and he dropped limply at Duane's feet.

Duane didn't have time to sing a victory song because another renegade appeared before him, wielding a battle lance. He thrust it toward Duane, who batted it to the side with his left forearm and slammed the war club into the renegade's ear. The force of the blow flung the renegade to the ground, where he didn't move.

The cave filled with shots, howls, and the sound of clubs landing upon heads. Duane advanced more deeply into the shadows as dust, gunsmoke, and clouds of ashes billowed all about him. One of the imps ran toward him, a knife in his hand, but Duane stepped backward because he couldn't kill a child. The imp slashed at Duane's legs, hoping to bring him down, but Duane was too fast, dancing from side to side, frustrating the child. The boy lunged desperately, and Duane plucked him out of the air, grabbed him by the neck, and pinned him to the floor. The boy wiggled and struggled like a wildcat, while Duane wondered what to do with him. He couldn't turn him loose, couldn't kill him, and didn't care to spend the rest of the day with him.

A horrible bloodcurdling cry came to his

ears. He looked up and saw a stout Apache woman running toward him, a hatchet in her hand and an expression of fury on her face. Duane turned the boy loose, and the boy jumped to his feet, picked up his knife, and resumed his efforts to hamstring Duane, while his mother sought to bury her hatchet in Duane's brain.

Duane hadn't planned to fight women and children, and all he could do was retreat, trying to avoid slashes and chops. The little boy dived for Duane's calves, but Duane darted easily out of the way. The hatchet zoomed toward his eyebrows, but Duane sprang mightily and landed in the darkness at the rear of the cave. The mother and son murder team came after him but were cut down first by the People's warriors.

It appeared that the struggle was coming to an end. The renegades had been taken by surprise, only a few were still fighting, and it was only a matter of time before they were subdued. Leather bags hung from pegs hammered into the cracks of the stone walls, animal skins covered the floor, and the stench of sweat, garbage, and urine rose to Duane's nostrils. The renegades had renounced their holy lifeway for a filthy existence in a dank, smelly cave.

The sounds of fighting stopped, and Duane

was about to return to fresh air when he saw movement in one of the corners. Under other circumstances, he would've thought his eyes were playing tricks, but his eyes had become more acute since his time on Gold Mountain, and he made out dim outlines of a figure lying on the floor amid piles of animal skins.

"I see you back there," said Duane. "Come out, or I'll go after you."

The figure didn't move, and Duane wondered if it was just animal skins configured like a man. But his sharp eyes perceived something animate beneath leather and fur. He held the knife tightly in his left hand and the war club in his right as he advanced cautiously toward the skins at the rear of the cave. Gingerly, he probed the knife into the rump of the devious individual.

Suddenly the animal skins blew apart, and Duane jumped backward. A naked renegade, the paint on his face blurred weirdly, rose before Duane, a six-gun in his hand. "It is Jamata!" shouted a nearby warrior.

Jamata fired the six-gun, but Duane dived to the side, rolled on the ground, and heard the bullet whiz over his head. He came to his feet and leapt before Jamata could thumb back the hammer for the next shot. Duane crashed into Jamata, driving him backward into the cave. They struggled for possession of the gun, Jamata tried to knee Duane in the groin, and Duane whacked Jamata across the nose with his elbow.

Jamata lost consciousness momentarily, and Duane yanked the six-gun out of the sorcerer's hand. Jamata then pulled a knife from his belt, leapt toward his attacker, and Duane timed him coming in. He smacked Jamata in the face with the heavy hunk of metal, and the sorcerer went reeling backward. Duane aimed the six-gun and thumbed back the hammer as Jamata prepared for another charge. The first cartridge caught Jamata in the center of his chest and burrowed deep into his aorta. The evil one unraveled like a puppet with his strings suddenly removed and flopped onto the ground at Duane's feet. But Duane didn't trust the sorcerer and pumped the remaining five rounds into Jamata's torso as Jamata jerked with the impact of each bullet. The warriors gathered around and looked at the dead renegade chief bleeding on the floor.

There was no time to waste, for no one knew what enemies the shots might attract. The warriors roved through the cave, slitting throats to make certain that the renegades were truly wiped out. Then they heaped everything flammable in the middle of the floor and set it afire. The rags, firewood, and baskets blazed as the warriors ran back to their horses. They mounted up and rode hard toward the first red sliver of dawn as a trail of smoke arose from the mouth of the cave.

CHAPTER 9

The women chanted and fasted into the morning, while Phyllis passed from hunger to numbed stupefaction. There were moments when she caught herself mumbling incoherently. Children watched their mothers solemnly, while old men hovered in the background, recalling lost battles and fallen comrades.

Apache superstition seemed absurd to Phyllis. She could see no linkage between female behavior and warriors on a raid. Yet they believed in the power of prayer, like Christians. *If I ever get out of this, I'll write about my life with them so that people will know the truth.*

She realized that she was talking to herself again, while the others glared at her reproachfully. She stiffened her spine and returned to the steady rhythm. The Apache women felt connected to their men across vast distances, without the walls that the White Eyes constructed. They're a spiritual people, and everything they do has religious significance, Phyllis realized. But women work too hard. She looked at her hands, dark and callused. Her body had hardened, the sun had baked her face, and she had a permanent ache in her back from working animal skins.

They heard the cries of little boys in the direction of the secret path, and the women arose, smiles spreading over their faces. A chill came over Phyllis because she feared that Duane had been killed in the raid. She drifted with the other women toward the edge of the encampment and saw warriors climbing the trail, leading their horses. Phyllis couldn't discern Duane among them, and her heart sank.

The women made a weird ululating sound as the warriors drew closer. It appeared that the raid had been successful as children danced and clapped their hands gleefully. Phyllis spotted Delgado leading the warriors and relief spread over the mountaintop. It appeared that there were no casualties so far, but the warriors looked as if they'd seen the face of hell.

Then, toward the end of the long file, Phyllis spotted Duane. He appeared unharmed, but gravity could be seen in his every move. Phyllis's vision returned to Delgado, and she wondered how one woman could desire two men. If these people knew what was in my mind, they'd burn me at the stake.

The warriors herded their horses into the corral as Phyllis compared Duane and Delgado. When she and Duane first arrived in the Apache camp, a huge gulf had existed between Duane and Delgado, but now they blurred together in her estimation. Somehow Duane had become a warrior, as formidable as any of them. There was something exceptional about him, and she considered him fascinating, but she had to admit that she'd prefer a man with practical habits, not one who thought he was an Apache warrior, the Pecos Kid, and God only knew what else.

Phyllis had liked the novelty of Apache life at first, but now the only thing that made it bearable was Duane. He finished with his horse and walked toward her like a warrior lord. When he drew close, she noticed dark flecks of dried blood on his white breechcloth. The expression in his eyes bore mute testimony to a tremendous ordeal. "Are you all right, Duane?"

He didn't reply and appeared deeply troubled. She placed her arm around his waist and urged him toward their wickiup. Dried blood also showed on the handle of his knife, while his war club carried suspicious stains. Duane had undergone another transformation, she realized, and he reminded her of Confederate soldiers who'd returned home from the war, with the same blank expression in their eyes. Duane and Phyllis crawled inside the wickiup, he wrapped his arms around her and they lay side by side, holding each other tightly.

Duane tried to make sense of what had happened to him. The former acolyte and scholar had busted heads with his war club and emptied his Colt into Jamata. *Thou Shalt Not Kill.*

"Are you sure you're all right?" she asked.

Duane held her closely, feeding off her warmth and strength. The renegades were degraded and degenerate, but what am I? he wondered. Their cave was the Apache Sodom and Gomorrah. "I've killed some people, and I'm not sure what it means."

"If you didn't stop them, they might've killed more women, including *me*. I prayed for you with the other women, and I've been thinking that it's time we left here. We're not Apaches, and this isn't our lifeway."

"We'll talk about it tomorrow," he replied. Their lips touched, because no matter how confused he was, or how irrational the world became, she was his anchor to reality. Together they sank into animal skins, removing each other's clothes.

★ ★ ★

In the middle of the night, Duane awoke with a start. Phyllis lay with her cheek against his shoulder as coyotes howled in the distance. He'd been dreaming about Jamata, the evil sorcerer of the renegades.

What kind of people could become so depraved? he wondered. Why'd they turn their backs on their holy lifeway?

The question burned into the mind of the former seminary student, for it went to the core of evil, original sin, and the devil. It seemed incomprehensible that people wouldn't fear divine retribution. He saw the power of God as a palpable force everywhere and couldn't understand why others didn't recognize what was so obvious to him. The renegades evidently believed that nothing was greater than their own dark appetites. *Woe to you, generation of vipers.* But it's dangerous to think that you're an instrument of God's judgment. The more Duane probed alleys of his mind, the more confused he became. He wanted something to base his life upon but found thin ice instead.

Phyllis made a cooing sound and moved closer to him. Her bare breast jutted against his bare chest, and the troublesome dilemma weakened before the onslaught of her generous warmth. The skin on her back was impossibly smooth. He cupped her breast in his hand.

"What're you doing?" she asked sleepily.

He touched his tongue to her nipple, she placed her hand on the back of his head, a nighthawk squawked as it flew overhead, and insects sang madrigals in the moonlight.

Duane woke up several hours later and heard the ruckus of the Apache camp around him. A column of bright sunlight shone through the smoke hole, utensils clanged, children shouted, and dogs barked. Duane lay on his side, with Phyllis's back snuggled against him. He realized that all was well with the world.

"There's something I want to talk with you about," she said.

She had that nagging tone in her voice, and Duane realized that the tender moment was coming to an end. He was amazed at how she could be warm one moment, cold the next, distracted, concentrated, a creature of many moods, not all pretty. It felt as if their cozy wickiup had become a lawyer's office. "What is it?" he inquired.

"I'd really like to get out of here."

He wanted to explain that there was much the Apaches could teach them, and the lifeway had a beautiful simplicity, but she hadn't responded to those arguments in the past. "Just a few more days," he muttered. "What's your hurry?"

"I've got a pain in my back that won't go away, and we've already been here a month. Look at the lines in my face. Another few years of this, I'll be an old lady! I love you, but I want to go back to Texas."

"I thought we were on our way to Mexico."

"If I know my father, he's hired the best lawyer available. You're probably cleared by now, and I'll bet that the law has forgotten about us. Nobody'll ever convict you for shooting Otis Puckett in self-defense."

"Innocent men have been hung before," he advised her, "and my father was probably one of them. I'm not going back until somebody shows me a piece of paper that says the charges against me have been dropped." He pulled away from her and reached for his breechcloth.

"Where are you going now?"

"To a special ceremony, otherwise the spirits of the dead will haunt us. It's called the Washing of the Weapons."

He believes that primitive nonsense, she thought, watching him beneath hooded eyes as he pulled on his moccasin boots, tied his gun belt, and adjusted his headband. Then he picked up his bloodied war club and knife. "I should be back in time for dinner." He kissed her cheek and crawled out of the wickiup.

Alone, she lay in the darkness, listening to the retreat of his footsteps. It's like being married to a tumbleweed.

The warriors rode to a stream in a nearby canyon and lined up at the bank. All remained mounted except Cucharo, who waded into the whirling waters until he was knee deep. He spread out his arms, looked at the horizon, and chanted a litany of prayers to the mountain spirits. Then he proceeded to wash himself and his weapons, while continuing incantations.

It was a clear day, the sky cloudless. Birds darted from flower to flower, the desert blooming with the promise of summer. Duane sat on his horse near the end of the line, and it reminded him of mass at the monastery in the clouds.

Cucharo sloshed toward Delgado, the first Apache at the beginning of the line. Delgado held out his lance and knife and Cucharo accepted them. The *di-yin* bent, washed the weapons in the stream, and blew upon them, while Delgado intoned his prayer of contrition.

Cucharo passed down the row of warriors, repeating the ceremony with each man, and

Duane couldn't help seeing parallels to confession, holy communion, and baptism. The *di-yin* then splashed toward Duane, who held out his knife and war club. Cucharo lowered them into the cloudy, meandering waters, like Easter mass when the abbot washed the feet of the acolytes. Duane felt deeply moved by Cucharo's devotion as he joined chants for divine forgiveness and understanding. He felt a glow pass from Cucharo's hand to his as he accepted his cleansed weapons. *Forgive me, Father, for I know not what I do.*

Cucharo worked his way to the end of the line. It was a hard job for an old man, but he never faltered, his voice maintaining its steady drone. After absolving the last warrior, Cucharo returned to his horse. He opened a saddlebag, removed the scalp of Jamata, scratched a match on a nearby rock, and brought the flame to the blood-caked black hair. Smoke rose into the air as the hair caught fire. Cucharo watched it burn, his mouth set in a grim line. Then, when the flame licked his fingers, he tossed the scalp into the water, and the eddies carried it away.

It appeared that the ceremony was over. The Apaches pulled away from the stream and headed back to their camp. Duane remembered White Painted Woman, the lion, and his grandfather atop Gold Mountain.

Surely the universe is sanctified, he thought, whether you call him God, Yusn, or Allah.

The warriors returned their horses to the corral, and Duane found Phyllis in front of their wickiup, cooking a stew of antelope meat, roots, and cornmeal. She glowered at him as he approached and began at the identical spot where she'd left off. "Do you think we can leave tomorrow morning?"

"I like it here," he replied. "I wish we didn't have to go."

"I miss my family, and I'm tired of the work. I never realized that you were so selfish."

"You're upset because you've got too much work. Maybe I should marry another woman, to help you."

Her eyes flashed with anger. "So that's it! You just want another woman. Well, I'm not sharing you with anybody!"

"It wouldn't be a real marriage where I'd sleep with her," he explained. "She'd just help you with the work, that's all. Maybe you and she could become friends."

"I'm a Texan, and my father owns a ranch. I don't want to live like an Apache any longer. If you don't come back with me, I'll go myself."

Duane believed that God had ordained her to be his mate for life, but he loved the holy lifeway, too. The decision required a Solomon, but he was only the Pecos Kid. He looked at the swell of her breasts, the curve of her leg, and saw the scale tip slightly in her favor. "All right," he said sullenly. "I'll escort you back to the Bar T, if that's what you want. The federal marshals will probably hang me, but that's the way it goes."

"I don't want you doing anything out of obligation. If you don't love me, have the courage to say so. I'm sure that Delgado would escort me back to safety."

Duane glanced at her sharply. "I said that I'll do it, so forget about Delgado. It's true that I'll miss this place, but you're more important to me than anything else. We can start packing right now."

"If only I could believe that."

"We'll leave first thing in the morning. I was a cowboy once and I can be a cowboy again. If the judge hangs me, I'm sure you'll provide a decent funeral."

"Nobody's going to hang you. You're worried about nothing. I'm certain that my father's lawyer has shot holes through the charges against you."

She was defeating him yet again, and he wondered how he'd gotten into the argument in the first place. The only way to get along with her was to agree with everything she said.

He was about to start packing when the alarm resounded at the edge of the camp.

Duane reached for his rifle and was out of the wickiup in a split second. The warriors carried weapons and were running toward the path that led to the lowlands. Someone was coming, and it looked like trouble. Duane checked the loads in his Colt as Phyllis emerged with her rifle. She and Duane followed the other Apaches and peered down the long rocky incline at two men dressed as cowboys leading their horses upward. One was tall and the other very short.

"It's the midget," Phyllis explained to Duane. "He was here while you were gone with Cucharo. He trades whiskey and guns, and the People seem to respect him quite a lot. Maybe we can go back with him."

"Oh-oh." Duane's Apache vision discerned the tin badge on the vest of the tall White Eyes climbing the ravine. "Here comes John Law."

The marshal was long and lanky, with trailing mustaches and steely eyes, while the midget was a strange mountain elf. The warriors muttered among themselves, unhappy about the newcomer approaching the top of the mountain. Delgado stood in front of the midget and demanded, "Why have you brought the White Eyes here?"

"He is a friend," Miguelito replied. "He has many presents."

Marshal Dan Stowe opened one of his saddlebags, spread a blanket on the ground, and dropped handfuls of cheap trinkets atop it.

"This is for you," Miguelito said. "You do not have to pay. And we have mescal juice to drink."

"What does the tin badge want?"

"Two Americanos," Miguelito replied. "The man is wanted for murder and the woman should be returned to her family."

The Apaches became uneasy, and some glanced nervously at Duane and Phyllis. "Just be calm," Duane whispered softly into her ear. "Maybe he won't recognize us."

The Apaches turned their attention to the trinkets, while Marshal Dan Stowe examined the Apaches. Suddenly Delgado rushed forward, drew his knife, and grabbed the front of Miguelito's shirt. "You should not have brought this White Eyes here — ugly little toad!" He pressed the point of the knife into Miguelito's throat. "You showed him the way to our camp, but you will never betray us again."

Delgado made a sudden motion with his knife and the midget jerked spasmodically. Then the warrior let Miguelito's lifeless body drop to the ground, his throat cut from ear to ear. Marshal Stowe almost drew his gun but knew they'd get him eventually. It was difficult for him to believe that his carefully wrought plans had gone awry so suddenly. Delgado turned toward him, the bloody knife in his hand, "You should not have come here, White Eyes."

"Don't I know you?" Marshal Stowe asked. "I sat at the peace powwow in 1868 . . ."

"I have never seen you before, White Eyes, and I will never see you again." Delgado raised his knife for the death blow, but the former troop commander decided the time had come to take a step backward, yank the Remington, and aim at the middle of Delgado's chest. "Your injun friends will get me in the end," he declared loudly, "but I'll blow a hole through you first!"

Delgado trembled with rage as he gazed down the barrel of the gun. "You will not leave this place alive, White Eyes."

"Maybe not, but if your people kill me, it's not like killing an ordinary farmer or miner. I'm a United States marshal on official government business, and you'll have the United States Army down here in full force. They'll comb every cactus plant in Texas, and if they can't find you in Texas, they'll go to Mexico. You don't think Americans are afraid of

Mexico, do you? There'll be soldiers in this country as far as the eye can see, and you will not escape their vengeance."

There was silence as everyone stared at the badge on his black leather vest. The old chief saw danger in the future for his people and knew that Americans had defeated Mexicans in many battles over the years. "The White Eyes is right," he declared. "There will be bluecoats all over these mountains if we kill him. He can stay overnight without harm, but he must leave in the morning. This is my decision."

"No!" replied Delgado. "If we let him go, he will bring bluecoats to our wickiups!"

"We will move to another mountain, but if we kill this White Eyes, the bluecoats will not rest until we are all dead. I have spoken. *Enjuh.*"

A drop of ruby blood fell from Delgado's knife to the ground as he turned to the White Eyes and translated the decision: "This chief says that you can stay here tonight, but you must leave tomorrow."

Marshal Stowe pointed at Miguelito's corpse. "This man said that the White Eyes man and woman that I'm looking for are in this camp. Where have you hidden them?"

"He lied," Delgado replied. "You should not have paid him, White Eyes."

"I think you're the one who's lying." Marshal Stowe continued to aim his gun at Delgado. "Why are you hiding these outlaws?"

Delgado was becoming furious at the presumption of the White Eyes. "I have told you what this chief has said. But if you make trouble, I will kill you myself."

"I've come in peace," Marshal Dan Stowe replied. Slowly, deliberately, he dropped his gun into its holster. "That's my proof."

Delgado was about to jump when the chief hollered, "No!" Then the chief stepped in front of Delgado. "I am an old man, but I am not afraid of you."

The old man appeared deadly despite his advanced years, and Delgado wouldn't fight his father under any circumstances. Delgado muttered something incomprehensible as he took a step backward. The old chief smiled at Marshal Stowe. "Come with me."

He placed his hand upon the marshal's back and guided him toward his wickiup. The Apaches opened a path while the lawman searched their ranks for Texans. Phyllis lowered her eyes as he passed, and the lawman didn't recognize her as his eyes lingered on hostile warriors carrying death-dealing implements. If they came at him, he'd send a few to the Happy Hunting Ground and then he'd follow.

Marshal Stowe still was trying to recover from the sudden murder of the midget. He'd come to like Miguelito and felt guilty for causing his demise. Miguelito had been butchered like a pig, but death was no stranger to a battle-hardened veteran of the great Civil War.

He'd been in Apache camps before, and this one was relatively small. He glanced at the chief, who examined him thoughtfully. Marshal Stowe attempted a friendly grin, while the chief tried to smile back. They'll probably kill me, Marshal Stowe figured, but nobody lives forever.

Duane and Phyllis returned to their wickiup, sat opposite each other, and looked into each other's eyes. It wasn't necessary to speak the obvious. A federal marshal was on their trail, and a decision had to be made. Duane wished he had something to smoke and a shot of whiskey to help him think.

No longer could he hope that the law had forgotten him. His return to the Bar T was out of the question. He felt sick because he knew that he and Phyllis were coming to a parting of the ways. She'd given him much solace, but he wasn't ready to face a crooked judge. He lowered his eyes and said in a low voice, "I can't ask you to come to Mexico with me, and I'm sure as hell not going back to Texas now."

"We can go to Mexico together," she said in a small voice. "When the charges are dropped, we can come back."

He touched his palm to the side of her cheek and tried to smile. "I appreciate the offer, but we both know that you don't like life on the dodge. You'd always be unhappy, and you'll take it out on me."

"I want a normal life. Is that so bad?"

"Maybe it's time to make a sensible decision for a change." He deepened his voice so that he'd sound authoritative and mature. "The best thing might be for you to go home to your family, and when your father's lawyers clear my name, send me a letter at the post office in Morellos. Then I'll return to the Bar T, we'll get married and spend the rest of our lives together. But I don't trust judges and jailers, and I'll never let them get me in their clutches if I can help it."

She sighed wearily. "I'm afraid that if we separate, I'll never see you again."

"Of course we'll see each other again. We're practically married already."

"You'll find a pretty senorita, or you'll get into more trouble. How can I trust you to come back?"

"I could never forget you, and I'll follow wherever you go."

"I'll bet you said the same thing to Vanessa Fontaine."

He opened his mouth to respond, but his tongue hung in midair as he realized that he *had* made similar statements to Vanessa. It was silent in the wickiup as they stared at each other in the dimness.

"It's decided," he said. "Tomorrow morning you'll go north and I'll go south. This'll be our last night together for a while, so we might as well make the most of it."

Huera sat with Delgado's other wives, weaving wicker jugs out of twined sumac strands. The Apache wife appeared calm as her fingers darted back and forth, but tornadoes agitated her heart. Although she pretended indifference to Phyllis, she was actually extremely jealous of the younger woman. Huera could see that Delgado was infatuated with her pale sickly skin, while Phyllis appeared fascinated with her husband. Huera had seen them gaze at each other across the campfire, but each was afraid to make the first move. Huera knew that one day curiosity would become strong and circumstances congenial. Delgado belongs to me and his other wives. We're not sharing him with the White Eyes bitch.

Huera had resigned herself to losing the battle ultimately, but a new element had just been introduced. The Apache wife gazed across the camp at the White Eyes with the star on his vest. Hmmmm.

Marshal Stowe and the chief smoked the peace pipe together as other warriors drew closer. The lawman offered them tobacco, and soon a large number were blowing smoke at each other. Stowe tried to behave politely but didn't trust Apaches. His right hand never roved far from his Remington, and he was poised to draw and fire. He knew that Apaches preferred sneak attacks to full frontal battle.

Women scuttled among them, throwing chopped roots and chunks of meat into a big cast-iron pot suspended over the fire. On the other side of the circle, Delgado accepted the pipe, filled his mouth with pungent smoke, and scrutinized the lawman. If he makes one hostile motion, Marshal Stowe thought, I'll drill him.

If it weren't for that two-thousand-dollar bribe, I wouldn't even be here, he reflected wryly. He remembered when Big Al Thornton had stuffed the first payment into his shirt pocket. I should've given it back because now he thinks I'm just another crooked lawman, and maybe I am.

He wondered what had happened to Phyllis Thornton and Duane Braddock. Maybe the Apaches killed them, or they're in Morellos, looking for a job. Perhaps I've missed them, but if I get out of this hellhole alive, I'll track them down yet.

The sun sank toward the mountains in the distance as more warriors joined the group, while others departed to their wickiups. Marshal Stowe felt the need to relieve himself but had no idea where to go. "Where's the latrine?" he asked Delgado.

Delgado pointed behind him with his thumb. Marshal Stowe rose, hitched up his gun belt, and headed in the direction indicated. Something told him that a few warriors might slit his throat in the darkness, so he held his right hand near the walnut grip of his Remington. Darkness descended on the mountaintop as his eyes scanned for scorpions, rattlesnakes, and gopher holes. The camp was surrounded by higher mountains, rendering it invisible to the outside world. He hoped it didn't become his burial ground.

He found the latrine, a big smelly hole. On his way back to the camp, he paused to roll a cigarette. A twig crackled behind him and he dropped the match, drew his Remington, and spun around. It was an Apache woman standing behind a chokecherry bush. "I want to speak with you," she said softly.

He looked both ways, certain the ambush had come. Aiming his gun at her, he drew closer. "What's on your mind?"

"I will tell you where the White Eyes are, if you give me some tobacco."

Duane and Phyllis lay naked in each other's arms, as the fragrance of cooking drifted into their wickiup. "I've changed my mind," she said. "I think I'll go to Mexico with you because I can't give you up so easily."

"We don't have any money," he reminded her. "You'll be miserable, and you'll make me miserable. It's better for you to go home and let me know when the charges are dropped. As soon as I receive your letter, I'll be on my way to the Bar T. We'll have a big wedding and invite everybody in Texas. During the war, some husbands and wives didn't see each other for five years. If we can't tolerate a few months apart, we shouldn't be together at all."

Footsteps approached, and Duane heard the clank of spurs. He reached for his Colt as he heard the voice of Marshal Stowe above them. "I know you're in there, Braddock! Come out with your hands up, or I'll start shooting!"

Duane and Phyllis stared at each other as

their worst fear came true. "A woman's in here," he replied.

"You'd better come out, too, Miss Phyllis. I was talking with your father a few weeks ago, and he's damn worried about you."

Duane wondered whether to open fire in the direction of the voice, but he might hit one of the People by mistake. Meanwhile Phyllis hastily donned her buckskin clothes as she tried to figure out who had betrayed them. "I'll take care of this," she said.

She crawled out the door, and the marshal sat cross-legged in front of her, six-gun in hand. A crowd of Apaches had formed in the distance, watching curiously. "Are you Phyllis Thornton?"

"Am I wanted for anything?"

"Not as far as I know, but *he* is." The lawman pointed his Remington at the wickiup. "Come on out, Braddock."

Phyllis tugged on the lawman's sleeve. "Why don't you let him go? He hasn't done anything wrong."

"Got to arrest him, ma'am. Sorry." Marshal Dan Stowe returned his attention to the wickiup. "I'll bring you in dead or alive, Braddock. It doesn't make a damn to me either way."

"Don't shoot," Duane replied. "I'm coming out."

"Throw your gun in front of you."

A Colt flew out of the wickiup, followed by Duane's Bowie knife. A deeply tanned hand appeared, followed by a red bandanna. The lawman's eyes widened at the sight of a bronzed Apache kneeling in front of him.

"Are you Braddock?"

"I don't suppose it concerns you that I'm innocent."

Marshal Stowe held his gun steady. "Not in the least."

He didn't see anything coming. One moment he was aiming his Remington at Duane's nose and the next moment he was thrown to the ground, one of Duane's hands clamped around his throat and the blade of Duane's knife probed his jugular vein.

"Don't move," Duane said, "or I'll kill you."

Marshal Stowe struggled to breathe. "You kill me, you'll have every federal marshal west of the Missouri after your ass."

"If I kill you," Duane replied, "your body will never be found. For all the law knows, a rattlesnake got you. Phyllis, take his weapons and boots."

"Not my boots!" the marshal protested.

Phyllis collected a derringer, a large knife, and a smaller one hidden in his fine San Antone boots. The Apaches laughed as she removed them from his feet.

"Let's talk sense, Braddock," the lawman pleaded. "From what folks say, you're an innocent man. The judge'll turn you loose eventually, but if you kill me, you'll hang."

"I'm not going to kill you, although it's what you deserve." Duane removed his knife from the lawman's throat and rose to his feet. Marshal Stowe pushed himself up, brushed off his pants, and said, "What now?"

"Take Miss Phyllis back to her father and mother first thing in the morning, but I'm going in another direction because I don't trust your judges."

Marshal Stowe couldn't believe his good fortune. I'm going to London! He saw himself strolling along Bond Street, dressed in a frock coat, twirling an ebony cane. "I can't bring you in against your will," Marshal Stowe conceded. "I just tried it, and you could've killed me."

"Try it again, and next time I will."

After dinner, Marshal Stowe sat at a big fire with the other Apaches. He'd given the chief the keg of mescal, and it was making steady rounds as women and children watched fearfully from the distance. When the barrel came back to the lawman, he took a few more gulps. He had no weapons, was barefoot, but good luck had invigorated him. I'm on my way to

Piccadilly Circus, if I can just get out of this place alive.

His eyes searched among the warriors, but he couldn't find Duane among them. The marshal didn't know what to make of the young outlaw's superhuman speed and strength. He's probably alone with the girl, and they're saying good-bye.

The lawman touched the warrant in his shirt pocket. He'd sworn to uphold the law, and there could be no shilly-shallying. As long as this warrant is in effect, I've got to do my duty. He'd expected to find a stoved-up cowboy on the dodge, but Duane Braddock had become an Apache! And sweet Miss Phyllis Thornton must be one hot little pistol, the lawman mused.

He noticed the Apaches becoming uncoordinated, and an argument broke out on the other side of the fire. He questioned the sense of bringing mescal to an Apache hideout, but it had seemed a good idea at the time. No telling what might happen if they went loco. He'd heard stories of Indians committing massacres and orgies while under the influence of demon liquor.

Something struck his back. They were his boots, and the Pecos Kid stood a few yards behind him.

"I want to talk with you," Duane said.

Marshal Stowe pulled boots over socks filled with holes. "What's on your mind?"

"Come with me."

Duane headed toward the edge of the encampment as the jittery marshal followed at his heels. "What about my gun?"

"You'll get it back when you leave."

"If those Apaches keep drinking, maybe they won't let me leave."

"Have a seat."

They dropped to cross-legged positions opposite each other as insects sang in thickets around them. Duane peered into the marshal's eyes. "Somebody told you that Phyllis and I were here. Who was he?"

"I'm not telling you, and I don't care if you pull out my fingernails. I'm not one of those lawmen who takes the easy way out. Now see here, Braddock, we don't know each other, but let me give you some advice. If you run away now, it'll be considered an admission of guilt. But if you come back to Shelby with me, it'll be looked upon favorably by the judge. I promise to testify on your behalf, and I'm sure the judge'll let you go."

"I don't trust you, I'm an innocent man, and nobody's locking me up."

"All the witnesses said you were innocent, but Lieutenant Dawes doesn't like you and wouldn't withdraw his charge when I suggested that he should."

Duane spat into the dirt. "All you damned government officials are alike. The fancypants lieutenant wouldn't withdraw his humbug charge, and you won't look the other way."

"Wouldn't be much of a lawman if I broke the law myself."

Marshal Stowe opened his cigar case, and one cheroot lay inside. He'd been saving it for a special occasion, but he held out the case to Duane. Duane removed the cheroot, scraped a match to life, and puffed fine Virginia burly.

"I spoke with Big Al Thornton," the lawman began, "and he's hired a lawyer to work on your case. If they challenge the warrant, it'll probably be quashed. The most respected folks in Shelby say you're innocent, and the lieutenant's wife was one of your strongest supporters. She begged me not to shoot you, by the way. It's none of my business, but I'd say that she's still in love with you."

Duane's eyes narrowed with anger at the mere reference to the former Miss Vanessa Fontaine, while Marshal Stowe took a few moments to study the man who'd inspired such love and hate. "I'll be honest with you, Kid. Until this warrant is voided, I'll keep coming after you. You got the drop on me today, but maybe next time I'll get the drop on you. I know where you're headed, and I'll find you sooner or later. Why don't you surrender and make it easy on the both of us?"

"I've got my reasons, and my mind is made up. By the way, you ever hear of an outlaw named Joe Braddock?"

The marshal smiled triumphantly. "I was waiting for you to ask that. You're damned right I heard of him. After I was issued your warrant back in San Antone, I thought the name was familiar. I looked it up in our files and found some old wanted posters for an outlaw named Joe Braddock. He got hung in this territory back in '54, and they say he was boss of the Polka Dot Gang."

This was the first official information that Duane had ever received about his father's past, but he recovered his composure quickly. "What's the Polka Dot Gang?"

"They stole a little here, rustled a little there, shot a few people, burned down a few places — you know what I'm saying, Kid. Outlaws."

"Somebody told me once that my father was killed in a range war."

"The Polka Dots claimed they were Mexican War veterans running a ranch, but they hit up against a big combine from the east."

"What if the combine bought the sheriff?"

"What if the Polka Dots were stone-cold killers? You ever heard of Quantrill's Raiders? They claimed to be Confederate soldiers but were the worst band of outlaws this country has ever seen. They used to burn down entire towns."

"Some say I'm an outlaw, too, but I never killed except in self-defense. Then I ran into a lying son-of-a-bitch newspaper reporter, and he named me the Pecos Kid. Next thing I knew, a fancy-pants cavalry officer arrested me for a crime I didn't commit, and now I'm an owlhoot."

"Come back to Shelby with me and stand trial like a man. If that lieutenant isn't careful, he's liable to end up washing pots and pans at some lonely outpost in northern Montana."

Duane shook his head defiantly. "They'll believe the lieutenant before they believe me, and maybe the judge is a friend of his. They hung my father, but by Christ, they're not going to hang me. After Big Al Thornton's lawyer gets me off the hook, *then* I'll come back. Miss Phyllis and I'll get married, and we'll send you an invitation."

"There's something you don't understand, my friend. Once I drop off Miss Phyllis, I'm coming after you. It's nothing personal, but

I've got this warrant in my pocket — and it's my job."

"Why can't you wait for the lawyer to clear me? What's your hurry?"

"Somebody has to stand up for the law, otherwise the whole world'll go to hell. I'm a lawman, not a priest, and I've got a warrant for your arrest. I'm bringing you in — it's as simple as that."

Duane looked him in the eye. "Let me give *you* some advice, Marshal. If you crowd me, I'll have to kill you. I'm not saying that as a threat, but it'll happen."

The lawman winked. "Not if I kill you first."

Phyllis sat in front of her wickiup, becoming more furious with every passing minute. An Apache had betrayed them, and she thought she knew who it was: Huera. Delgado's wife was jealous of her because of her flirtation with Delgado. Huera was the only Apache with a motive for betrayal, and Phyllis had suffered no disagreements with anyone else.

I should ride away and forget these people, Phyllis counseled herself. Nothing good can come from a fight between Huera and me. But I can't run away with my tail between my legs.

She gazed at Huera gathered with Delgado's other wives around the fire, while Delgado sat the warriors before the chief's wickiup. Huera thinks she's defeated me, but she's wrong, Phyllis thought as she dusted off her voluminous buckskin skirt and prepared for the encounter. She knew that she should stay where she was, keep her mouth shut, and be a good girl, but she was the daughter of one of the toughest men in southwest Texas.

Delgado's wives were dining on roast turkey, their lips and fingers greasy, as Phyllis approached. Huera heard Phyllis coming and turned, a drumstick in her hand. Phyllis grabbed Huera's hair, punched her in the mouth, and Huera went sprawling backward toward the fire. She singed her backside, let out a screech, reached for her knife, and leapt to her feet. "White Eyes girl, I am going to kill you."

The quarrel had taken a twist that Phyllis hadn't foreseen, and she knew from dressing animals that it didn't take much to spill guts. Before Phyllis could draw her Colt, Huera darted forward, slashing at Phyllis's pretty face. Phyllis's first impulse was to run for her life, but she gritted her teeth, grabbed Huera's wrist in midair, twisted, and pushed Huera off balance. Huera fell to the ground, Phyllis landed on top of her and sank her fingernails into Huera's right wrist, but Huera's left fist was free and she rammed it into Phyllis's mouth.

Phyllis had never taken a punch before and tasted blood on her lip. When her vision cleared, Huera stood in front of her, waving her knife from side to side. "I have always hated you, and now I am going to cut your head off."

Huera charged, raising her arm for the knife blow that would disfigure the White Eyes girl. All Phyllis could do was try to grab Huera's wrist again, and if she missed, it would be steel in her guts. Then, suddenly, a darkness came upon Huera as her hand was stopped in midair. Delgado held her firmly in his grasp and pried the knife from her hand. "What is the matter with you, woman?"

"Leave me alone!"

Phyllis declared, "She told the lawman that Duane and I were here."

Delgado looked at Marshal Stowe standing at the edge of the crowd. "That is so, tin badge?"

"No," Marshal Stowe lied.

Delgado grabbed his wife's blouse. He was half-drunk, his eyes bloodshot, tongue thick. "Tell me the truth, woman! Did you talk to the lawman?"

Huera couldn't look her husband in the

eyes and neither could she respond. Delgado swore beneath his breath. "Go to your wickiup."

Huera walked away, holding her head high. She'd been publicly humiliated and tried to hide it with Apache bravado. Then Delgado turned toward Phyllis and placed his fists on his hips. "You will leave here in the morning."

"I'd leave right now if I could," she replied. "I know that you hate me because I'm a White Eyes." She was about to return to her wickiup when she bumped into Duane.

He saw the trickle of blood at the corner of her mouth. "What happened to you?"

She pushed him away and headed for the shelter. Delgado staggered toward Duane and placed his arm around Duane's shoulders. "The women were fighting like bitches in heat, but it is over now. Come, let us drink firewater together."

Duane joined the warriors at the fire, and the keg was thrust into his hands. He raised the spigot to his lips, and the mescal tasted dusky and devilish as it rolled over his tongue. It was smoother than the usual white lightning and sweeter than *tizwin*. Duane gazed into writhing flames and saw mountain spirits dancing merrily. A length of wood popped while orange sparks shot into the sky.

"My woman and I must leave here," Duane

said to Delgado. "My woman will go with the tin badge to her father's house, and I'll head for Mexico. I wish I could stay, but I love my woman more."

"I understand," Delgado said. "Everything I do, I do for my women — but they never appreciate nothing, and they make me loco. I will miss you."

"I'd never leave here if it weren't for my woman."

"Miguelito betrayed us." Delgado rubbed his fingers together. "White Eyes do anything for money."

"There's something that I want to tell you before I leave, Delgado. You must make peace with the White Eyes, otherwise the White Eyes will wipe you out. They are much more numerous that the People, and their weapons are better than yours."

Delgado scowled. "If we go to the reservation, you will starve us. The blankets you give will be full of holes, and the soldiers will insult our chiefs. It is better to die a warrior than live as a rat. There can be no peace between the People and the White Eyes." Then Delgado's features softened, and he smiled, "But you are a strange White Eyes, and your woman is very beautiful. Maybe one day our paths will cross again."

Stars splattered the sky overhead and the

full moon smiled. Duane glanced at the other warriors and felt one of them . . . almost. Then he gazed at the fire and saw his Apache grandfather smiling at him. *"Enjuh,"* the old warrior said. "It is good."

CHAPTER 10

It was morning as Duane led his horses toward the chief's wickiup. He wasn't anxious to leave the People, but the time had come for another dodge. The tribe had congregated for farewell ceremonies, the fire burned in front of the wickiup, and the great man was flanked by Delgado, Gootch, and a few other senior warriors. Phyllis stood to the side, while Marshal Dan Stowe hovered in the background, hand near his Remington.

Duane came to a halt in front of the chief and bowed his head. "I must go," he said, "but I will never forget my time with the People."

"The Lion never stays in one place long, but you will always be my son, and our blood is your blood."

Duane felt the old man's strong, gnarled hands clasping his. He didn't know what to

276

add, so he stepped to the side and landed in front of Delgado.

"Good-bye, my brother," Duane said. "I am sure we will meet again someday."

"We will hunt antelope together," Delgado replied, "and drink *tizwin*."

Duane was giving up the precious lifeway, but it was the price he had to pay for his ladylove. His eyes roved the tawny desert beauty whom he'd held in his arms only hours before. "I don't know how I'll get along without you," he said as he embraced her one last time.

"It'll be the happiest day of my life when you ride up to my front door, Duane."

They touched lips lightly, and Duane had the premonition that he'd never see his child bride again. They separated, tears rolled down her cheeks; they'd spent the most intense moments of their young lives together, but the time had come to say adios. Duane felt melancholy, but a warrior can't let anything show. He looked at Marshal Dan Stowe and said, "You'd better take care of her."

"It's not too late to change your mind," Marshal Stowe replied. "Come back with me and I'll guarantee your safety."

"You can't even guarantee your own safety, lawman."

"You can hide wherever you want, but I'll

find you. We'll have a showdown someday — mark my words."

"Up to you," Duane replied.

There was nothing more to say, and no reason to linger. Duane summoned his will, climbed onto his horse's back, wheeled the animal toward Mexico, and found Cucharo standing in front of him. The old *di-yin* raised his hands and Duane bent to clasp them. "I'll never forget you, Cucharo. You've taught me the most important lessons of my life."

"May the mountain spirits smile upon the Lion. I have placed some food in your saddle-bags, for Mexico is a long way."

Duane took one last look at the camp and knew that it would disappear soon. The People would never return now that the White Eyes knew its location. He turned to Phyllis, and his eyes became misty. He knew that if he hesitated, he'd never be able to leave her and the judge would hang him high.

He prodded his horse, and the animal clomped away from the camp. Duane's next task was to wait for Phyllis's letter in Morellos, but he dreaded returning to the land of the White Eyes. His body would become soft, he'd waste time in saloons, and what if her letter never came? He remembered the look in her eyes when they'd kissed for the last time. *Good-bye forever, my love.*

The prospect of sleeping without her made him gloomy as he rode along. Ahead lay labyrinthine canyons, but Duane knew the terrain like the palm of his hand. He had no doubts about his ability to survive in the desert but didn't know how he'd get along without Phyllis. The camp was barely out of sight, but he felt homesick for his wife-to-be and his little wickiup.

Unfortunately, the law was on his trail. He needed to put as much distance between him and Marshal Stowe as possible because the lawman obviously was a fanatic. And Duane had to admit that there were some practices of the People that he couldn't abide. If Phyllis ever had twins, he could never kill one of them, and he didn't believe that a warrior had the right to cut off his wife's nose.

He rode steadily throughout the morning and came to a stream at midday. He let his horse drink as he watched the desert cautiously, rifle in his hands. Then he drank from his canteen, refilled it in the stream, and continued to watch for unusual movement. An Apache never lingers near water, the most dangerous gathering spot of all.

He nudged his horse's withers as the animal crossed the stream. Cold water kissed Duane's moccasins, and he realized that he had to find some regular clothes. If the White

Eyes see me like this, they'll try to kill me. But where can I get some clothes? I have no money and nothing to trade.

He stopped for a meal in the shade of a cottonwood tree, then searched through the saddlebags for dried mescal, nuts, and roots that he'd packed. A small deerskin pouch lay on top — the gift Cucharo had mentioned. Duane lifted it and was surprised by how much it weighed. He upended the pouch, and the pupils of his eyes expanded as three solid gold nuggets spilled onto his palm.

Must be worth a lot of money, he figured, astonished by the sight of so much wealth. Gold was sacred to the Apaches, yet Cucharo had given it to him. They're not as savage as we think, Duane realized. Babies die in big cities, too, from starvation, rat bites, and diseased milk. We kill them on a wider scale, but nobody gets blood on his hands. I guess evil depends on what side of the peace pipe you're sitting on.

Marshal Stowe and Phyllis rode blindfolded among Delgado and three other Apache warriors, but knew they were headed in a northerly direction through thorns that clawed their legs. The air was thick with the aroma of flowers, and the morning sun warmed their clothes.

Phyllis thought of the Bar T and was anxious to see her mother and father again. Soon her life would be normal, and she wouldn't have to rub animal skins, but she was worried about Duane. She imagined him in his Apache getup, traveling alone across the vastness of the desert. How could I let him go? she wondered.

"Are you all right?" asked Marshal Stowe affably.

"I've been thinking about Duane," she admitted.

"Too bad he doesn't trust the law, but he believes his father was hung unjustly, though he doesn't know a damn thing about it. Duane Braddock'll never settle down until he shoots the man or men who hung his father."

"You're wrong. Duane said he'd come back to me, and we'll get married before long. He's a man of his word, and I believe him."

"It's always good to be a little suspicious, missy. Ever heard of Vanessa Dawes? I'm sure he made promises to her, too. It's interesting — the former Miss Fontaine threw her reputation out the window when she ran off with him, and you risked jail to spring him from that army camp. I can't help wondering about Braddock, because no woman ever went three steps out of the way for me. He doesn't seem so great, but I don't have the eyes of a woman. What is it that makes you love him?"

Phyllis shrugged. "I'm sure there are women who wouldn't look twice at Duane Braddock."

"Haven't met one yet," replied Marshal Stowe.

Duane lay on his belly as he peered through pronghorn cactus leaves at two miners panning for gold in a creek. Their small stained canvas tent sat nearby, while half of a butchered mule deer hung from a tree. Both kept their rifles handy in case an Apache happened by.

Duane didn't dare ride close to the miners because they'd open fire. So he'd hobbled his horse a mile away and traversed the rest of the distance silently on foot. There were a fat miner with a long black beard and a skinny miner with pockmarks visible beneath sparse red whiskers. Duane thumbed back the hammer of his Colt and said, "Don't move, or I'll shoot."

The two miners dropped their pans in alarm, and their eyes became as big as their tin dinner plates. They glanced at each other, and then at their nearby rifles.

"Don't try it," Duane said as he rose from the green desert foliage, his Colt aimed at them. "But maybe we can do business to-gether." He held up a gold nugget.

They ogled it, licking their lips in anticipa-tion. It was what they'd been panning for, and an English-speaking Apache had just shown up with the biggest lump of gold they'd ever seen!

"Where'd you git that?" asked Fatty.

"I'll give you half of it for a shirt and a pair of pants."

"Hell, that's the best deal I ever heard. Come on back to the tent. My name's O'Neil, and my partner is Perez. Who might you be?"

Duane didn't reply as he kept his Colt moving back and forth between them. They arrived at the tent, and O'Neil ducked inside. "When you come out," Duane said, "make sure your hands're empty."

"I ain't lookin' fer no trouble," replied O'Neil. "Where'd you say you found that nugget?"

Duane kept his mouth shut, but Perez grinned and showed empty gums. "Must be a helluva strike, eh, amigo?"

A pair of blue jeans flew out the front door of the tent, followed by a red-and-black-checkered shirt. Then O'Neil appeared, a big grin on his face. "Are you an Apache or a white man?"

Duane held up the nugget. "Chop this in half."

"Right over here." O'Neil pointed to an ax in the stump near the stream. "Must be one helluva strike. Want some firewater?"

Duane picked up the clothes, then followed the miners to the stump. They signaled to each other with their eyes, so he kept his distance, with his finger firm on the trigger. He tossed the nugget to O'Neil, who brought it close to his beady eyes. "You must be a-sittin' on a fortune. How come yer a-wearin' that injun outfit?"

"Don't have much time," Duane replied, indicating the stump with the barrel of his gun.

"Yes, sir." O'Neil glanced at Perez, who took a few steps to the side, and let his hands hang loose. Duane studied them with his sharp Apache eyes. O'Neil placed the nugget atop the stump, then raised the ax over his head. He aimed, and then suddenly pivoted, hurling the ax at Duane.

Duane's six-gun fired the moment the ax left O'Neil's hand, then Duane ducked. The ax flew over his head, while O'Neil was knocked backward by force of the bullet. Duane whirled as Perez reached for his six-gun. Duane's Colt fired again, and a red dot appeared on Perez's shirt. The miner dropped to his knees and then collapsed onto his face. Smoke billowed across the campsite as Duane picked the nugget off the stump. The miners could've taken half, but had died for it all.

Duane returned the yellow metal to its leather pouch, then roved the campsite. He took cans of beans, a fork, a spoon, a box of matches, two Colts, two Sharps rifles, and all available ammunition. The booty went into a burlap bag, which he threw over his shoulder. Buzzards squawked happily high in the sky as Duane retreated into the desert and in seconds was gone.

It was midafternoon, and scouts had been coming and going all day. Marshal Stowe and Phyllis couldn't see them, but could hear hoofbeats and exchanges in the Apache language. The prisoners still were blindfolded, with no idea of their surroundings. It was their second day on the trail.

Phyllis felt wretched now that Duane was gone. She wondered where he was and whether he was still alive. It was a long way to Mexico, and she wondered how much he'd really learned of the Apache lifeway. What is it about Duane that puts other men off? she wondered. She became aware of the air becoming cooler, and the horses came to a stop.

"Climb down," said Delgado.

Phyllis lowered herself to the ground and smelled Delgado opposite her as he untied her blindfold. Her eyeballs were seared by a sudden burst of light, then a water hole came into view, surrounded by desert flowers. Marshal Stowe stood beside her, towering in the air, rubbing his eyes. "Where are we?"

"Many bluecoat soldiers are headed this way," Delgado said, "and we will leave you now. You may fire your guns a few times, to attract their attention."

Delgado and Phyllis looked meaningfully into each other's eyes. They'd come to the fork in the road. Both wondered what might've happened if the right opportunity presented itself, but it hadn't.

"You've been very kind," she said haltingly. She wanted to invite him to the Bar T for dinner, but her father would blow his head off.

"You are very pretty," he admitted. "I will miss you."

He turned abruptly, embarrassed by what he'd said, and faced Marshal Dan Stowe. "Do not try to find us again, White Eyes. Because next time we will kill you."

Delgado issued a curt order to the warriors. They returned to their horses, climbed into their saddles, and paused. Delgado sat atop his mount and gazed at Phyllis one last time. Then he wheeled away from her, and the horses broke into a trot. Phyllis listened to their receding hoofbeats as they vanished into the desert.

She looked around at the water hole. It was strange to be alone in the desert with a man she barely knew. Marshal Stowe led his horse to the water, then knelt beside the hole, filled his hat with water, and drank out of it.

Phyllis lay on her belly and lowered her lips to the water. It was cool and sweet on her tongue, with the faint taste of alkali. She wiped her lips with the back of her hand and glanced at Marshal Stowe. There was something about him that she didn't like. Maybe he was too self-righteous, or perhaps it was his long, skinny nose.

"If those savages told the truth about the cavalry, your worries are over," he said gaily. "You can go back to your father, and you'll never have to worry your pretty head about Indians anymore."

"What about you?" she asked.

He tapped the document inside his shirt pocket. "I've still got a warrant for the Pecos Kid, and I'm going after him."

"But you know he's innocent!"

"I'm not the judge, and neither are you."

"Why can't you wait until the warrant is

overturned? What's your hurry?"

"Some people always look for the easy way out."

"If I wanted the easy way out, I never would've run away with Duane."

"But you're not running away with him now."

His words struck her like bullets because they were true — she'd abandoned her man. "If it weren't for you, I'd probably still be with him."

"So you say."

Phyllis felt confused by conflicting emotions. She loved Duane but hated life on the dodge. Back and forth it went in her mind, like a pendulum in a grandfather clock. "There are so many outlaws in Texas — why're you making Duane special?"

"If I had a warrant for somebody else, I'd go after him just as quickly."

"You know what I think?" she asked. "You're jealous of Duane because all the women like him. That's what it sounded like when you were talking about him before."

"Maybe so, but until that warrant is withdrawn, I'll stay on his trail."

"Duane's got eyes in the back of his head, and when he draws his Colt, he doesn't miss."

"I wouldn't have it any other way," Marshal Stowe replied. "That's what makes it interesting." His eyes were blank and cold in the wan afternoon light.

"I think you're a little loco."

Marshal Stowe thought her a spoiled brat, while she considered him a sanctimonious bastard. They were glowing disapproval at each other, when they were startled by the sound of a voice. "Haalooooo."

Stowe drew his Remington and turned toward a white man in buckskins advancing on the trail, while two Apaches in blue army shirts followed him. "My name's Krandall," said the white man. "I'm a scout for the Fourth Cavalry. Who might you be?"

"Marshal Dan Stowe, and this is Miss Phyllis Thornton."

"You got to be crazy, wanderin' around in Apache territory like this. And this is yer squaw, ya say?"

"I'm not a squaw," Phyllis replied, "and the Apaches treated me very well."

Krandall had long brown muttonchop whiskers, and buckskin fringe hung from his arms and legs. He stared at her Apache clothes and asked, "What you say yer name was?"

"Phyllis Thornton."

"Related to Big Al Thornton back in Shelby?"

"My father."

The scout became more respectful. "The main detachment'll be hyar any minute, ma'am." He said something in Apache, and the two warriors moved toward the well. Krandall took off his hat and wiped his forehead with the back of his arm. "What the hell you doin' out hyar anyways?"

"I'm on official business," Marshal Stowe replied. "Miss Phyllis was living with some Apaches, and that's where we ran into each other."

Krandall appeared impressed with the strange news as the rattle and clamor of cavalry could be heard approaching in the distance. Phyllis realized that her ordeal was coming to an end. She looked at her Apache clothes and they appeared foreign to her. I'm a fright, she thought, touching her hand to her tangled hair.

The first rank of the detachment came into view, beneath the guidon of the Fourth Cavalry. They were led by their commander, gold shoulder straps gleaming through the afternoon haze, his gray wide-brimmed hat slanted low over his eyes. He sat ramrod straight in his saddle as he raised his hand in the air. His horse slowed, and a cloud of dust arose among the dusty, sweaty soldiers. They were in rotten moods as they fingered their weapons and searched for Apaches.

Krandall reported to the captain: "I found these two folks, sir. He's a federal marshal, and she's the daughter of Big Al Thornton."

"I've met your father," said the captain, stepping down from his saddle. He was forty years old and appeared constructed from steel rods. "My name's Turner, and I met you when you were a little girl, after I first came to this territory. I've heard about your recent antics, missy. It seems that you've got yourself into a little trouble."

Phyllis didn't know how to reply, but Marshal Stowe performed the task for her. "She was on the dodge with an outlaw named Duane Braddock, but I found her in an Apache village and brought her out. Braddock is on his way to Morellos, and if I can borrow one of your fresh horses, maybe I can catch him."

"I was in Shelby only five days ago," Captain Turner replied, "and Duane Braddock is all they were talking about. They said he's innocent, and now I'm looking for Lieutenant Dawes. He and his detachment have disappeared on a scout through this area. You haven't seen them, have you?"

A chill came over Phyllis as she remembered the Property Dance. "No, I never saw him," she replied.

Marshal Stowe noticed her reaction. "Neither have I, but the Apaches had a load of army horses in their corral and lots of army equipment lying around. Wouldn't be surprised if they bushwhacked them."

"Goddamned savages," Captain Turner replied. "Texas won't be safe until every one is dead."

Phyllis recalled praying around the fire with the women on the night of the revenge raid. It hurt her to think that the People could be massacred by the Fourth Cavalry. Meanwhile, Marshal Stowe selected a fresh strawberry roan and two troopers saddled the animal.

Captain Turner stood next to Phyllis and appraised her with concern in his eyes. "You look a little peaked, missy. We'll stay here a spell and water the horses. Living with the Apaches must've been quite an experience." The officer chuckled as he raised the canteen to his cracked lips.

Marshal Stowe rode the strawberry roan toward them. "Guess I'll be moving on," he said to Captain Turner. "Thanks for the horse, and good day to you, Miss Phyllis. When you see your father, tell him I hope to visit soon."

"You're a cruel man," she replied.

"The law is cruel, ma'am. I hope you have a safe trip home." He laughed oddly as he urged the horse forward.

The animal took a few steps and burst into a lope. It kicked up clods of dirt, and soon the lawman was gone.

"He's liable to ride into a nest of hornets at the rate he's going," Captain Turner said. "And besides, everybody knows that his warrant is a joke. Texas judges are crooked, but not so crooked that they'd hang an innocent man."

"It's happened before," she told him.

"I don't think Mister Braddock has got anything to worry about if he shot Otis Puckett. You and he'll get together again someday, missy. Now where's that goddamned mess sergeant of mine? I could use a cup of coffee."

Captain Turner marched off in search of his cook, while Phyllis sat a short distance from the well. Soldiers set up tents for the night as she gazed in the direction Marshal Stowe had ridden. I hate that man, she admitted.

She was feeling worse about her separation from Duane. Something told her that she'd made a mistake. He needed me, but I didn't have the courage to go on the dodge. And I missed my family like a little girl. Yet if I stayed with him, there would've been trouble — no doubt about it. Duane Braddock draws it like a magnet, and I've never known it to fail. Do I want to *die* for him?

Duane Braddock arrived in Morellos at high noon two days later. He rode down the main street and passed thick-walled adobe buildings jammed side by side. Horses carried riders or pulled wagons alongside him, and he looked about warily, uncomfortable in the miner clothes that were far too big. He wore no hat, and his long black hair was held in position by his red Apache headband. Ahead was a sign that said GUNSMITH.

Duane angled his horse in that direction. Men sat in the shadows beneath the eaves of saloons and stores, and he knew they were watching the new face in town. He climbed down from the saddle, threw his saddlebags over his shoulder, picked up the sack of weapons, and carried them into the gunsmith's shop.

The man behind the counter wore glasses and was reading a newspaper. "What can I do for you?"

"I've got some guns to sell."

Duane poured the weapons out of the sack, and the proprietor looked them over carefully. He asked no questions, not even the name of the person he was confronting. "I'll give you seventy-five dollars for the lot."

Duane held out his hand, and the proprietor dropped the coins in it. "Where can I buy a hat?"

"Down the street on the left."

Duane saw a wagonful of something covered with a tarpaulin creaking down the center of the street, and he wondered what was being hidden. He'd never been in a border town before but knew they contained dangerous men on the dodge from all directions. He walked along the dirt sidewalk, passed El Sombrero Saloon, and came to Buckley's General Store.

Inside, a middle-aged woman was working behind the counter. "Can I help you, sir?" She was serious, mid-thirties, with a wedding band.

"I need some clothes."

She looked at his Apache headband and then peered at his Apache moccasins. "My God," she whispered, turning pale.

"Have you got a black hat with a wide brim, a high crown, and a neck strap?"

She gingerly wrapped a tape measure around his head, then took down a box and removed the lid. Inside was a big black cowboy hat influenced by the Mexican sombrero. "I also need a pair of jeans and a shirt."

She searched among the shelves, while he removed his silver concho hatband from his saddlebags. He tied it around his new hat as the woman laid out shirts and jeans on the counter. He selected black jeans, a red shirt, and a black bandanna. She showed him the dressing room, where he changed clothes.

"You speak English very well," she said.

"So do you."

He stood in front of the mirror, and the Pecos Kid looked back at him, black hat slanted low over his eyes, conchos flashing, gun belt slung low and tied down. "How much?"

He paid the woman, slung the saddlebags over his shoulders, returned to his horse, waited for a wagonload of animal skins to pass, and backed his horse into the street. Phyllis had stolen the animal from her father's ranch, and he was spooked by his abrupt return to civilization. "Take it easy, boy," Duane said, patting his black mane. "This isn't a picnic for me, either."

The horse didn't know what to think as his big luminous eyes roved back and forth. He'd been leading an easy life as one of Big Al Thorton's favorite mounts, and then, before he knew what happened, people were shooting at him. Next thing he knew, he was living with Apaches who ran their horses until they dropped and then ate them. Now he was on the dodge again in a town that reeked of danger.

They came to Sullivan's Stable, and Steve the cow horse walked through the big front door. Inside were rows of brothers and sisters in stalls, the fragrance of hay, oats, and manure permeating the air. A man in his mid-twenties, wearing a smudged white hat, stepped out of the shadows. "Help you, sir?"

"I'd like to leave my horse for a few days."

"Put 'im in any empty stall. What's yer name?"

Duane hesitated, because he didn't want to say.

The stable man grinned. "Give me any name, so I'll know who owns that horse."

"Smith."

"I've already got six Smiths. Can't you think of somethin' a li'l different?"

"Butterfield."

"There was a fast hand once name of Butterfield. But he'd be a lot older'n you, if he's still alive."

"What's the best hotel in town?"

"The McAllister."

Duane left the stable and made his way down the street, passing saloons, a barbershop, a lawyer's office, and then the bank. He slowed as he recalled his gold nuggets. They were too big to spend, and he'd have to trade them for dollars. He pushed open the bank door, and a teller in a green visor was seated behind the cage. "Help you, sir?"

Duane took out the leather bag and spilled the nuggets onto the counter. "I'd like to sell these."

The teller's eyes widened. "The manager handles gold transactions personally."

The teller sped toward the back corridor as Duane examined the shellacked wooden interior of the bank. How can anybody feel safe with his money in this place? he wondered. A robber could walk through the door and hold it up with no trouble at all. Then the manager appeared, wearing a thin black mustache and suave manners. The teller pointed to the gold nuggets, and the manager knitted his brows as he picked one up. "I'll have to assay them," he said.

Duane followed the manager to an office at the end of the hall. The sign on the desk said BABCOCK. The manager sat in his chair, took out a scale, and lined up bottles of chemicals. Then he proceeded to apply scientific tests to the nuggets. "Where'd you get them?" he asked pleasantly.

"Somebody gave them to me."

"He must've been a very good friend."

"The best."

"You'll have to give me your name, for my records."

"Joe Butterfield."

298

The banker weighed the nuggets. "The best I can do is nine hundred and fifty dollars."

"It's a deal."

"That's a lot of money to carry around. It might be prudent to invest such a sum. We have numerous interesting opportunities available in this very area. How'd you like to buy a saloon?"

Duane was surprised. "You can buy a whole *saloon* for nine hundred and fifty dollars?"

"Depends on the saloon."

"Let me think that one over."

Duane stuffed the money into his boot and left the bank. "I guess I'm rich," he muttered. He wondered what to buy first and decided on a good meal. A few doors down, he found the Red Rooster Saloon. He pushed open the bat-wing doors, stepped into the shadows, and checked the crowd. A Mexican with a wide sombrero sat in a corner, cleaning his fingernails with a knife. Two cowboys and three vaqueros played poker, deeply intent on their cards, a mound of coins piled in the middle of the table. There was the usual crowd of drunkards at the bar, and waitresses in low-cut blouses carried food and drink along the narrow aisles.

Duane found a table and sat facing the door, his hand near his Colt. Maybe I should bury the money, but what if a gopher digs it up? He was approached by a waitress in her late twenties, with black hair and two teeth missing, one on top and one on the bottom. "Where'd you blow in from?" she asked saucily.

"Give me a steak with all the trimmings and a mug of beer. Have you got any tobacco and paper?"

She looked him up and down. "I got anything you want."

"I'm not arguing with you."

She appeared uncomfortable, blushed, and launched herself toward the chop counter. Duane pulled the brim of his hat lower over his eyes and examined his companions once more. The men looked like they could steal your stockings without removing your boots, while the ladies were the kind who'd do anything for a dollar. The saloon was dingy and squalid, a far cry from the clean air at the top of Gold Mountain. Duane missed Cucharo, Delgado, the old chief Pinotay, and even Gootch, but most of all he missed his woman.

He felt incomplete without her, as if his kidney or liver were missing. He wasn't sure that he'd see her again because anything could happen in Texas. He couldn't help wondering if she and Delgado had finally got together, because many times he'd noticed them looking at each other with desire in their eyes. Perhaps they'd surrendered to their natural inclinations now that I'm not there to watch them. It's not as if she's still a virgin, he thought dourly. For all I know, she's flirting with Delgado at this very moment.

His eyes scanned the saloon relentlessly because a fight could break out at any moment. He'd seen it happen time and again, and usually he'd ended up in the middle. From now on, I'm staying out of fights, and I don't care what they say about me. I'll take me a little vacation in this town, and I'm sure I can find something to do.

The waitress returned with a steak platter and a foaming mug of beer. She placed them before him, told him the price, and he paid. "Is there a library in this town?" he asked.

"No, but do you know how to read?"

"I went to school for most of my life. How about you?"

"I can read a little, but I never read a whole book. Is it hard to learn?"

"Not at all."

"If I pay you, would you give me readin' lessons?"

"I don't plan to be in town very long."

Duane didn't realize that she wanted more than mere reading lessons, but he only had eyes for Phyllis Thornton. He dug into his steak, thinking of the hot kisses and mad embraces in their cozy little wickiup. There'd been moments when he thought they'd tear each other's skin off. He still carried a scar from one of her neck bites.

He felt excited at the mere thought of her, but she was far away, and his bed would be cold that night. He frowned morbidly as he sliced into his slab of beef. First good-looking man that comes along, she'll be on him like a dog on a bone.

The Fourth Cavalry rattled and clanked across the desert, while morale plummeted. The Apache scouts had found the spot where the raiding party had stolen Lieutenant Dawes's horses, and now they were following the trail of the lost detachment as it proceeded in a northerly direction.

Phyllis rode beside Captain Turner at the head of the formation, and behind them came the bugler and trooper carrying the colors of the Fourth Cavalry. Phyllis dreaded what lay ahead because there was no way that Lieutenant Dawes's soldiers could survive without horses in this remote corner of Apacheria.

Phyllis had met Lieutenant Dawes once, and the West Pointer had been impressive in his immaculately tailored uniform. It was difficult to believe that such a cultured and sophisticated man could die violently in a barren, remote wasteland.

The scouts appeared among the cactus, led by Krandall in his stained and smudged buckskins. Phyllis could see the weight of death on their faces. Krandall saluted Captain Turner. "They're up ahead, sir."

The detachment rumbled onward, as word traveled back through the ranks. Evidently Lieutenant Dawes had led his small detachment into deepest Apacheria, and the results had been disastrous. "This might be a little hard for you to take, Miss Phyllis," said Captain Turner out of the corner of his mouth.

"Don't worry about me," she replied staunchly, for she'd heard about massacres all her life, although she'd never actually seen one. She gritted her teeth and hardened her heart, for it wouldn't do to faint among the soldiers. They had enough to do without taking care of a sickly woman.

"There they are," said Captain Turner deep in his throat.

At first Phyllis thought she was seeing bleached branches lying among the bushes and cactus spines, but then she realized they were human bones! Her eyes fell on a skull severed from its body. Its eyes huge, black, and staring endlessly at the sky. Arms and legs were chopped from torsos, skulls cracked in two, and everything had been picked clean by buzzards, ravens, crows, and rodents. Phyllis caught a vision of Apaches attacking suddenly, transforming the desert into a slaughterhouse of cavalry troopers. But now it was over, the troopers had gone to their just rewards, and the desert had returned to its cruel splendor.

The men set to work digging graves as Phyllis sat alone with her canteen in the shadow of a cottonwood tree. The final shred of her innocence dissolved in the killing ground before her. Elegant and dashing Lieutenant Dawes was a bunch of bones somewhere out there.

Meanwhile, Captain Turner fulminated at the edge of the clearing as he paced back and forth. "General Sheridan ought to send a thousand men down here and clean the redskinned bastards out once and for all! Boys, one of these days we'll run into 'em, and we'll make 'em wish they were never born!"

Marshal Dan Stowe looked at the buzzards circling in the sky, dipping to earth and rising again. It appeared that a feast was taking place straight ahead, and he wondered whether to see what it was or circle around.

He was passing through territory that had never been surveyed and didn't know exactly where he was. His crude map said Turkey

Creek was up ahead, and he needed to water his horse. He held his gun in his right hand, but it wouldn't help against an arrow shot silently from behind a poinsettia bush. He knew that he should travel at night and sleep during the day, but he didn't want the Pecos Kid to get away.

Sometimes he wondered what was wrong with him because all he had to do was collect his remaining nineteen hundred dollars from Big Al Thornton and head for Westminster Abbey, Parliament, and Stratford-upon-Avon. This doesn't make sense, Marshal Stowe told himself. If the Pecos Kid is innocent, maybe I should forget about him.

The lawman's much-vaunted honor seemed a charade in the boiling desert. What's Duane Braddock to me, and what am I to him? I'll just say he disappeared, and perhaps Prince Albert will invite me to tea. I might even settle in London and fall in love with a duchess. He remembered the famous lines by Sir Walter Raleigh:

Now what is love? I pray thee, tell.
It is that fountain and that well
Where pleasure and repentance dwell.
It is perhaps that sauncing bell
That tolls all into heaven or hell:
And this is love, as I hear tell.

The beautiful lines evaporated in his mind as he drew closer to a small mining camp. Buzzards cackled as they ripped flesh from two forms sprawled on the ground. The stench struck Marshal Stowe's nostrils, reminding him of battlefields covered with rotting corpses.

He fired his gun into the buzzards; they screeched angrily, spread mammoth wings, and leapt into the air. Marshal Stowe pinched his nose as he urged his horse closer. He noticed steel pots, clothes, boots, and the ax and realized that Apaches hadn't killed them, because Apaches would've stolen everything in sight. And they sure as hell didn't kill each other. Marshal Stowe examined the half-eaten corpses with the cold eyes of a frontline officer but couldn't discern what had done them in.

The lawman examined the scene of the crime as his horse drank from the creek. Inside the tent he found blankets, buffalo skins, more clothing, canned food, tobacco, and whiskey. But he couldn't find rifles, pistols, or cartridges.

He tried to reconstruct what had happened. Someone had evidently killed the miners, stolen their weapons, and taken any gold lying around. If the Apaches didn't do it, who did? There was no trace of a third miner, and

Turkey Creek wasn't exactly a crossroads of the world.

But Marshal Stowe knew of one person who'd been headed this way. Did the Kid do it? he wondered. He studied the ground, but the tracks were blurred, and he didn't have the eyes of an Apache. What if nice, polite Duane Braddock was the cold-blooded killer that Lieutenant Dawes suspected? Marshal Stowe scratched his chin in thought. It wouldn't be the first time that one man was right, and everybody else wrong.

CHAPTER 11

A stout man wearing a blond beard and a green visor sat behind the counter in the Morellos Post Office, reading an old *Harper's Magazine.* "Sir?" asked a voice.

The postal clerk glanced up and saw silver conchos gleaming atop a black cowboy hat. "What can I do fer ye?"

"Any letters for Duane Braddock?"

The postal clerk shook his head.

Duane strolled out of the post office. It had only been five days since he'd seen Phyllis, but he couldn't help hoping that her letter would be waiting for him. There was nothing to do in Morellos except drink yourself to death, unless somebody shot you first. He hadn't had one solid night of sleep since he'd arrived because carousing, shooting, and singing went on twenty-four hours a day. It was a wide-open town, with one sheriff trying unsuccessfully to keep the lid on.

The soles had worn through both of his Apache moccasin boots, and Duane didn't have his woman to repair them. He crossed the street to Buckley's General Store and found the same pleasingly plump lady working behind the counter, displaying a bolt of cloth for the perusal of a Mexican grand-mother. "What can I do for you today?" the proprietress asked Duane.

"Pair of boots."

"Have a seat and take off the ones you're wearing. I'll be with you in a few minutes."

Duane looked at articles of men's and women's clothing hanging from the rafters amid crates, boxes, and advertisements showing fashionable ladies and gentlemen strutting about a city. The proprietress cut a few yards of cloth from the bolt, and Duane pegged her at mid-thirties, efficient, business-like, an excellent advertisement for her wares. She spends her life pushing the merchandise, he realized.

After the Mexican woman departed, the proprietress approached Duane with two sheets of paper and a pencil. "Place your feet on these."

She knelt before him and traced the out-lines of his feet on the paper. Color came to her face, and she appeared flustered as she re-turned to her position behind the counter.

"Are you part Apache?"

"My grandfather was an Apache. Do you own this place?"

"Are you planning to rob me?"

"I was watching while you were waiting on the Mexican woman, and I wondered who you were."

"My name's Arlene Buckley, and yes, I own this place. I'm alone here because my husband was killed by Apaches three years ago." A chill came over the store as she opened a book that showed pictures of boots. "It takes four weeks, and you'll have to pay half down."

Duane reached for the money and tried to smile. *Maybe I should shut up about my Apache grandfather.*

"The cavalry's a-comin'!"

Big Al Thornton perked up his ears at the sound of the guard's voice. It was afternoon at the Bar T, he was working in the office, and most of his cowboys were riding the range. Grateful for the excuse to leave his desk, he put on his big cowboy hat, stuck a cigar into his mouth, and lit it. Then he made his way to the front porch, where he found his wife looking at a cloud of dust in the distance.

It wasn't unusual for the cavalry to stop by the Bar T on its scouts through the area. The officers knew that they could water their horses, and Big Al always had a bottle of whiskey for the men in the ranks. Big Al placed his arm around his wife's shoulder because they'd grown closer since their daughter had disappeared. Phyllis was an emptiness in their hearts that would never be filled.

The detachment rode closer, and Big Al spotted Captain Turner riding in front with the guidon. Apache scouts protected his flanks, while a squaw rode alongside Turner. Big Al and Martha walked side by side down the incline as the detachment rumbled into the yard between the barn and the main ranch house.

Captain Turner touched his finger to the brim of his hat. "Howdy, Mister and Mrs. Thornton. Thought I'd bring you a little present."

Big Al and his wife looked at each other in mystification. Why would Captain Turner bring them a present? They turned toward him, while he was looking at the squaw. The squaw smiled faintly, and Big Al's cigar fell out of his mouth. "It can't be," he whispered.

"But it is," replied Phyllis as she climbed down from the saddle.

Her parents looked at her in astonishment. It was Phyllis, brown as an Apache, wearing

Apache clothes, a bead necklace around her throat, a little taller, and more filled out in the bosom. They stared at each other for a few moments, then Phyllis rushed into her father's and mother's arms.

Marshal Stowe rode down the main street of Morellos, examining faces on both sides of the street. It was late afternoon, and he hoped that he'd see Duane Braddock before Braddock noticed him. He came to the stable, stepped down from the saddle, and waited for the man to shuffle closer.

"I'd like to leave my horse here."

"Pick any stall you want, Marshal."

Marshal Stowe leaned closer and winked. "I'm looking for a man about this tall" — he held his hand at Duane's approximate height — "eighteen years old, black hair, looks like an Apache."

"That could describe half the men in town."

Marshal Stowe reached into his pocket and took out a five-dollar coin. "He arrived within the last week."

"I don't remember anything about any-thing."

Marshal Stowe flipped the coin at the stable man. "Take care of my horse and give him all the oats he wants."

Marshal Stowe ambled out of the stable, saddlebags slung over his shoulder. The first thing he saw was El Sombrero Saloon across the street. He dodged a crowd of Mexican vaqueros riding past, entered the saloon, and all eyes turned toward the tin badge. Three men lowered their hat brims over their faces, and one cowboy fled out the back door. Marshal Stowe stepped up to the bar, where the bartender was waiting, a bottle of whiskey and a glass in his hand. The lawman nodded, and the bartender filled the glass halfway.

"Where's your gunsmith?" Marshal Stowe asked.

"On the other side of the street."

The marshal tossed the whiskey down his throat, exhaled loudly, and threw coins on the bar. Then he crossed the street and came to the gunsmith's shop. Two customers stood at the counter while the gunsmith tried to sell them a used John Adams revolver. "Can I help you, Marshal?"

"I'll wait until you're finished."

Marshal Stowe stood to the side of the window and looked into the street. He had a lawman's hunch that Braddock might stroll past at any moment and then the fun would begin. Marshal Stowe loved the moment of arrest when the outlaw realized that the long arm of the law had finally caught up with him.

Sometimes they reached for their guns, but Marshal Stowe was careful to get into position first. He didn't want a face-to-face shootout with a fast hand.

The customers bought the John Adams revolver and departed. "If you want a good gun," the proprietor said to Marshal Stowe, "that's what I'm in business for."

"Has a man been here within the past few days, about eighteen years old, trying to sell a batch of guns and rifles?"

"A lot of people pass through this place."

"He looks like an Apache, with black hair and dark complexion. But he might be wearing white man's clothes. He's about this tall, and he's got the kind of face that girls like."

"I don't remember every galoot what comes in here."

Marshal Stowe grabbed the front of the gunsmith's shirt. "He's killed eight people that I know about, and he'll probably kill more. I'm going to ask you one last time. Did he come here?"

The gunsmith replied softly, "He sold me some guns and rifles, then went across the street to Buckley's General Store. That's all I know."

Marshal Stowe recrossed the street, dodging a stagecoach arriving from Chihuahua. He found the general store, where a buxom middle-aged woman waited on customers. "Anything wrong, Marshal?"

"May I speak with you alone, ma'am?"

"I'll be right back, ladies." Mrs. Buckley appeared alarmed as she led the lawman to her parlor.

"I'm looking for a man about eighteen, this tall, black hair, and he's part Apache. I heard that he came here."

Her face paled. "What's he done?" she asked weakly.

"Murder and robbery. Do you know where I can find him?"

"I knew there was something dangerous about him, but what makes you think *I* know where he lives?"

"Maybe he mentioned where he's staying."

"There's only one place in this town: The McAllister Hotel."

"If you see the man I'm talking about, please don't mention this conversation."

Marshal Stowe moved swiftly down the sidewalk, his nose sniffing like a bloodhound. The Kid was in town, and the time had come to take him into custody. The former troop commander made his way to the sheriff's office and found the door locked. Marshal Stowe cursed his luck as he lit a cheroot. But he knew that small-town sheriffs often were called away to robberies and murders in the surrounding area. Marshal Stowe realized that the Pecos Kid might leave town suddenly, and there was no time to lose.

"Son of a bitch," he muttered as he trudged down the block to the hotel. He wished he had somebody to watch the back door, but it wouldn't be the first time he'd arrested a man on his own. He entered the hotel, and all eyes followed him as he approached the front desk. "Do you have a guest named Duane Braddock?"

"Never heard of him."

"He might be using another name. He's about this tall, black hair, eighteen years old, decent-looking."

The desk clerk shrugged. "Hard to say."

Marshal Stowe grabbed a fistful of shirt. "You know everybody in this hotel and what they had for breakfast. Braddock's part Apache, and he's a cold-blooded killer."

"Never heard of him."

"You're under arrest for obstructing justice. Let's go to jail."

"Who'll watch the hotel? I'll be fired!"

"What room is he in?"

The clerk appeared defeated. "Room one-oh-six."

"Is he there right now?"

"He comes and goes all the time, and

sometimes uses the back entrance."

"I'll bet he does," Marshal Stowe replied as he drew his gun. It reminded him of cavalry charges during the war as he plunged into the network of corridors. He knew that he might be killed in the next few minutes, but the murdered miners clinched it for the lawman. They were working hard, trying to extract gold from the ground, when the Pecos Kid shot them in cold blood and left them for the buzzards. From now on it's him or me.

Marshal Stowe approached the room on his tiptoes. He stood with his back to the wall, reached around, and banged the heel of his hand on the door. "This is Marshal Dan Stowe. Open the door, or I'm coming in after you."

There was silence. Marshal Stowe imagined the Pecos Kid trying to climb out the window. The lawman aimed his gun at the lock, pulled the trigger, and the corridor rocked with the explosion. Smoke billowed around him as he kicked the door open. The window was locked, bed unmade, washbasin turned upside down. There was no closet, and the Pecos Kid wasn't hiding underneath the bed.

Where the hell is he? the lawman wondered. If he hasn't left town, he's probably in a saloon. He held the Remington in his right hand as he backtracked through the corridors. The gang in the lobby watched him curiously as he passed, and a crowd of curious on-lookers had gathered outside. Word was spreading rapidly through town. John Law had arrived and he was looking for somebody named Duane Braddock.

Marshal Stowe held his gun tightly as he marched to the First Savings Bank of Mo-rellos. Three customers were lined up in front of the teller.

"You can't go back there, sir!"

"Official government business," Marshal Stowe replied as he opened the gate. He crossed behind the teller, knocked on the door at the end of the corridor, and turned the knob. The manager sat behind his desk, his eyes widened in alarm, and he reached for the gun in his top drawer, but his hand froze when he saw the tin badge.

"I'm Marshal Dan Stowe, and this is an of-ficial investigation. Has anybody brought you gold nuggets within the past week?"

"It's our policy not to divulge the business of our clients."

"You're under arrest for receiving stolen gold and for being an accomplice to murder." Marshal Stowe aimed the gun at him. "Please come with me."

The bank manager blanched. "What murder!"

"The murder of two miners back in the desert. Let's go."

"Wait a minute. All I did was buy the nuggets. He didn't tell me that they were stolen."

"Which way did he go?"

"I didn't notice."

Marshal Dan Stowe walked out of the bank and headed for El Sombrero Saloon. His plan was to visit every drinking establishment in town until he found Braddock. He carried the Remington ready in his right hand as he entered El Sombrero, dodged out of the light, and examined the crew before him.

They were the usual wary bunch of drunkards, desperadoes, and fools, but he couldn't find the Pecos Kid among them. He backed out of the saloon, walked a few doors down, entered the Black Cat Saloon, put his back to the wall, and studied the patrons, but no Duane Braddock materialized. Then he proceeded to investigate the remaining saloons in town, while the crowd followed at a safe distance. It looked like a shootout was in the offing, and bets were made with odds heavily in favor of the lawman.

Marshal Stowe couldn't find Braddock in the next three saloons, and the last stop was the Wheel of Fortune Saloon. There was no place else where Braddock could be, and the lawman was ready for a showdown. But no Apache-looking cowboy drew his Colt as Stowe threaded among the tables, placed his foot on the rail, and leaned toward the man in the apron. "Double whiskey."

The bartender filled the glass, then Marshal Stowe carried it to a table against the left wall. He sat heavily, pushed back the brim of his hat, and sighed. *Where's that little son of a bitch?*

He tried to think strategically as he sipped whiskey. *He's headed deeper into Mexico, but I'll follow him to Patagonia if I have to.* No longer was there doubt in Marshal Stowe's mind, and gone were considerations of Trafalgar Square at sunset. The Pecos Kid killed the miners, stole their gold, and took their weapons — no doubt about it. *He'd fooled the good folks in Shelby, but he didn't fool Lieutenant Dawes and he's not fooling me.*

He swallowed more whiskey, which settled him down. He realized that he'd been running around Morellos like a madman, without any clear plan. *I wonder where he'll turn up next?* The best way to outthink an outlaw was to analyze all that was known about him. Marshal Stone noticed saloon patrons glancing at him nervously and realized that the town was worried about his next move. I'm liable to start a riot if I keep on this way.

He relaxed in his chair and continued to drink whiskey. *If I were Duane Braddock where'd I go?* The bastard son of an outlaw and an unknown prostitute had been orphaned at an early age, raised in a monastery, and started screwing everything in sight as soon as he returned to the world. Everybody, even Lieutenant Dawes, had said he was a charmer, and he put on a big show of being religious.

Marshal Stowe sat straighter in his chair as a new thought occurred to him. His brow wrinkled with thought, he wiped his mouth with the back of his hand, and his pinched nose twitched with the excitement of the chase. *Why didn't I think of it before?*

He rose, gun still in hand. Everyone watched the lawman cross the floor, spurs jangling with every step. Outside, housewives looked through their windows at the commotion in the street. Marshal Stowe felt enlivened by the prospect of a dramatic arrest. "You folks'd better stay out of the way," he said in the booming voice of a former troop commander. "There might be gunplay."

He aimed the Remington straight ahead as he walked along the sidewalk, followed by the crowd at a safe distance. He knew that he might make a mistake and they'd laugh at him afterward, but he believed that if you understood an outlaw's mind, you've got him beat. The lawman turned onto another street and made his way toward the outskirts of town. He came to a scattering of adobe homes surrounding a large white adobe church with a steeple and a big cross on the front door. The sign said IGLESIA DE SANTA MARIA.

Marshal Stowe glanced behind him, where townspeople hid in alleys or behind buildings. There was nothing to wait for, and Marshal Stowe believed in the old military adage that surprise was the most important element of attack. He ascended the stairs, opened the front door of the church, aimed the gun straight ahead, and a wave of incense struck his nostrils.

He saw Christ crucified on the wall behind the altar, while candles burned before a crudely carved and painted statue of Mary. A young man with black hair and a red shirt knelt in a pew, his head bowed in prayer. "Put your hands up, Kid. You're under arrest."

Duane's heart stumbled at the sound of the lawman's voice. He was in the midst of mild religious ecstasies and suddenly had been placed in custody? Dazed, confused, his vision of paradise fading, he dived to the floor.

Marshal Stowe pulled the trigger as the back of the pew exploded above Duane's head. Duane drew his gun, thumbed back the trigger, and tried to recover his equilibrium. He'd been saying Hail Marys, and now his life was endangered yet again.

Marshal Stowe ducked behind the back pew and held his Remington ready to fire. "Throw your gun into the middle of the aisle, Kid. Make it easy on yourself."

"Leave me alone, Marshal. I've got no beef with you."

"I've got a warrant for your arrest, and I found those two miners you killed on Turkey Creek. I have reason to believe you've stolen their gold, and by Christ, you're not getting away with it."

"The gold was mine, not theirs. The Apaches gave it to me, and the miners tried to kill me for it."

"Isn't it strange how everybody's trying to kill you? You can tell it to the judge, but in the meanwhile, put your hands up and move into the center of the aisle, or I'm coming after you."

There was silence for a moment, then Duane said, "If you come after me, I'll kill you."

"So be it," replied the former troop commander.

Duane didn't want to kill a lawman, so he had to plot a way out of the church. There was a back door, the front door, and some windows. If I make a run for it, he'll shoot me down, but if I stay put, time is on his side. He heard creaking as the marshal crawled across the back of the church. Stowe's plan was to maneuver around, then advance down the far aisle until he came to the pew where Duane was hiding. Once in position, he'd take quick aim and fire. The Pecos Kid was boxed in, like shooting a duck in a barrel.

But the Pecos Kid possessed precise Apache hearing and could hear every movement that the lawman made. It didn't take long to figure out the lawman's plan, so Duane aimed his gun straight down the pew. As soon as he saw the lawman's head, he'd blow it off. "You're making a mistake, Marshal! The charges against me'll never stand, and you'll die for nothing!"

Marshal Stowe refused to reply because he didn't want to give his position away. He had no idea that Duane's ears located every touch of his pants on the floorboards. The lawman held his breath as he crept beside a painted statue of Saint Jude, with a golden flame erupting out of the deity's head.

"Listen to me, Marshal," Duane pleaded. "I've shot people who've tried to kill me first, but I never looked for trouble in my life. If I shoot you, your blood will be on your own hands, not mine."

Marshal Stowe thought of the Battle of Crooked Run as he inched forward. Duty, honor, country, he told himself. He passed the long pews, and a statue of Saint Joseph looked at him mournfully. The marshal knew that the next few yards would be the trickiest, but it was the same way at Chester Gap, and the Michigan Wolverine Brigade had carried the day.

"I can hear where you are," Duane said levelly. "You're trying to catch me from the side, but I'll plug you, I swear it. I'll give you the money from the nuggets or anything else you want, you self-righteous son of a bitch, but don't make me kill you, too."

"It's too late, Braddock," Marshal Stowe replied. "The miners are dead, and nobody's bringing them back. It's the same with the folks you shot in Shelby. You've got everybody fooled with your pretty face, but you never fooled Lieutenant Dawes and you're not fooling me!"

Marshal Stowe leapt forward and swung his Remington across the pews at the young man crouching before him. It was the last image the lawman ever saw as his mind thought, I've got him.

A bullet smacked the lawman in the chest and threw him back against the statue of Saint Jude, which rocked from side to side. The church filled with gunsmoke as Marshal Stowe struggled to hold his Remington steady, but his knees gave out. He went crashing to the floor, worked to catch his breath, but his throat and lungs filled with clots of blood. He wanted to raise his gun but instead saw his old cavalry saber clutched tightly in his hand. "Forward . . . you Wolverines . . ." he whispered as he pitched onto his face. He didn't move as a pool of blood widened around him.

Duane rose, his gun still aimed at the fallen lawman. He sidestepped across the pew, knelt beside his adversary, and the full implications dawned upon him. I've killed a federal marshal, and I've got to get out of town immediately, but where should I go? He felt drunk, although he'd touched no whiskey that day. Less than five minutes ago he'd been deep in communion with the Mother of God and now he'd killed again. He turned toward the altar, where Christ gasped on the cross, blood flowing down his face from the crown of thorns. Duane crossed himself and said, "Father in heaven, forgive me."

He had no time for Hail Marys, Our Fathers, and Glory Bes. Marshal Stowe wasn't the only lawman in Texas, and they tended to back each other. Duane headed toward the rear door of the church, opened a crack, and saw townspeople lurking behind woodpiles and sheds, potential witnesses for the prosecution, but they had to catch him first.

He headed for the hotel, fighting the rising ocean of panic. The posse could show up at any moment, so he held his Colt straight ahead, ready for anything. He tried to think of where to go, knew nothing about Mexico, but Texas was no longer a viable option for the Pecos Kid.

He came to the hotel. The lobby was empty, and the clerk had deserted his post behind the desk. Duane marched to his room, gathered his belongings, and made sure his rifle was loaded. Then he tossed the saddlebags over his shoulder. He returned to the lobby cautiously, the Colt aimed straight ahead, but no one was there. Peering out the door, he saw a clear path to the stable. For all he knew, sharpshooters were on the roofs of nearby buildings, but all he could do was make a run for it.

He pulled his hat tightly on his head, took a deep breath, and dashed across the street, expecting a bullet to plow through his brain at any moment, but no one tried to stop him, and he landed in the stable. The next step was to find his spooked chestnut stallion. Duane heard a footstep behind him, rolled out, and aimed his Colt at the stable man, who smiled graciously as he raised empty dirty hands. "Can I help you, sir?"

"Where's my horse?"

The stable man led Duane down the stalls, while Duane watched him carefully. "Don't try anything funny," Duane said. "Don't make me shoot you like I shot that damn fool marshal."

"Din't figger he'd live long. He was in too much of a hurry."

The stable man saddled Duane's horse as Duane looked warily out the front door. The street appeared deserted, but maybe sharpshooters were moving into position behind windows on Main Street. The stable man brought Steve, who was twitching with the prospect of more danger. Duane stood in front of him, grabbed the bridle with both hands, and looked into his eyes. "Now listen to me, Steve. When we leave here, we've got to go at a fast gallop because somebody might shoot at us. It won't be much fun, but you'd better put every ounce of strength you've got into it, understand?"

The horse nodded his head up and down, and Duane wondered if the animal was talking with him as he flung his saddlebags over the beast's mighty haunches. Then Duane climbed into the saddle, jammed his rifle into its scabbard, and touched his heels to Steve's flanks. The horse eagerly bounded toward the light, while Duane held his Colt ready in his right hand. Townspeople watched fearfully from behind windows and through alleys as horse and rider charged onto Main Street. Duane pulled the reins toward the south, Steve raised his front hooves high, and then raced headlong down the street, while Duane crouched low in his saddle, shooting his Colt in the air to warn anybody who tried to stop him. Steve pounded steadily onward as cactus and juniper revealed themselves straight ahead. Townspeople craned their necks around corners and out of windows as they watched the handsome young killer recede into the desert, sunlight gleaming off his silver concho hatband. He looked back once, fired a final shot at the sky, and cried, "Adios, amigos!"

And thus the Pecos Kid departed for sunny Mexico.

CHAPTER 12

The bearded young stagecoach driver held the door for Mrs. Vanessa Dawes, who was attired in a black dress, hat, and veil. Her luggage had been loaded on the coach, and the time had come for her departure from Shelby. She took one last look at the residents who'd come to see her off and the scattered ramshackle buildings that dared call itself a town. She'd already said her farewells, and the only thing to do was climb aboard. "Thank you," she said softly to the driver as she stepped into the cramped interior of the coach.

It smelled of tobacco, whiskey, and perfume, and she saw a traveling salesman with a toothy grin and big ears sitting near the window. He made room for her, and she smiled in gratitude as she dropped daintily beside him. She gazed out the window at the townspeople waving and blew them a kiss, like a visiting dignitary. The driver climbed onto his perch, grabbed the reins, and pushed the brake forward. "Giddyup."

Harnesses creaked, horses' hooves struck the ground, and the stagecoach lurched forward. Vanessa looked at the shacks passing her window as her mind filled with jumbled memories. She'd come to town on the arm of one man, married another, and now was a widow. She didn't know whether to laugh or cry.

The stagecoach approached rows of canvas army tents at the edge of town, and she remembered the afternoon when Captain Turner had visited her out of the blue. He'd told her that her husband, Lieutenant Clayton Dawes, had been killed in action against the Apaches and was buried in an unmarked mass grave somewhere near the Mexican border.

"Are you a native of this area?" asked the salesman with a wet grin.

"If you don't mind, I'd rather not talk about it."

The salesman tipped his hat. "Sorry."

People deferred to ladies in black veils, and Vanessa planned to make the most of it during her stagecoach ride. A tall, lanky cowboy sat opposite her, fast asleep, mouth hanging open, a bottle of whiskey lying like a baby in his lap. To his left sat an elderly man who looked like a judge, banker, or politician. On the other side of the cowboy slept a young girl with pale skin, in a gingham dress, and she had the shopworn look of a working girl. Young love, Vanessa mused cynically.

She still didn't know what to think about the sudden demise of the late Lieutenant Dawes. They'd been together such a brief time, they barely knew each other. Now she was on her way to Austin, to confer with a lawyer on matters pertaining to her inheritance. The lieutenant had accumulated a fair sum during his lifetime, thanks to a bequest from his grandfather plus his own intelligent investments over the years. She'd also get a widow's pension from the army, and she'd never have to sing in another saloon for the rest of her life.

The stagecoach rumbled onto the desert, followed by its cavalry escort. Vanessa leaned back in her seat and closed her eyes. It was going to be a long trip, but soon she'd be rich again. She'd always known, even during her darkest hours, that she'd prevail. When the money was hers, she'd return to South Carolina and buy the old family plantation.

She saw herself on the wide veranda of her ancestral home, entertaining guests as in the days before the War of Northern Aggression.

She'd invite the cream of Charleston society, and the last of the scalawags would be thrown out of office by then, she was certain. Yes, the South will rise again, and I'll rise with her.

Her distinguished guests would dance into the night, tables would groan with rare delicacies, and the band would play fine old Dixie tunes, but something was missing from the dream, and she didn't quite know what it was. Occasionally she caught glimpses of a tall young man in black jeans, a black shirt, and a black hat with silver conchos strolling among the revelers, an insouciant smile on his face, his eyes a-twinkle with mischief. She'd heard that he was wanted for killing a federal marshal in a rough border town and was riding hard for Mexico when last seen. She thought of him alone in the desert, running like a hunted animal against all the odds. No matter how hard she tried, she couldn't forget his cowboy grace and theological speculations. Sleep well, my darling boy, she whispered softly. Perhaps someday our paths will cross again.

Mr. Simmons sat at the counter of the post office in Morellos and looked at the pile of letters spread before him. The shipment had just arrived on the stage from Fort Stockton, and it was time to sort the envelopes. Mechanically, he picked them up and placed them in their appropriate slots. It wasn't a bad life, though sometimes he got headaches from reading too much fine print.

He came to an envelope that said:

DUANE BRADDOCK
General Delivery
Morellos, Texas

The address was written in a woman's hand, and the envelope carried the faint trace of perfume, and was postmarked Shelby. Simmons dropped the envelope into the box that contained other letters addressed in the same handwriting to Duane Braddock, General Delivery. The postmaster was tempted to open them but had controlled his curiosity thus far. I guess I'll have to send 'em back someday, he thought philosophically. The Pecos Kid don't live here no more, and it don't look like he's a-comin' back.

Big Al Thornton awakened in the night due to faint sobs down the hall, as his daughter cried herself to sleep yet again. He stared at the ceiling and frowned because all his vast holdings — ranch, herd, and wealth — couldn't buy happiness for the person he loved most.

He figured that she'd get over Duane Braddock after a while, but weeks passed and she didn't seem to be pulling out of her sorrow. She usually held up fine during the day but wept pathetically into her pillow every night. Big Al ground his teeth in frustration. He'd rather get skinned alive by Apaches than hear his daughter cry.

A fancy lawyer had quashed all proceedings initiated by the late Lieutenant Dawes, but now the Pecos Kid was in new trouble. He'd killed a federal marshal in Morellos, and American officials were negotiating with Mexico about sending the Fourth Cavalry after him.

He's probably livin' in a cave with coyotes and rattlesnakes, but one day he'll get lonely and that's when they'll catch him. I thought he was a-gonna be my son-in-law, but he'll end up with a rope necktie, if they don't shoot him first. It's a damn shame 'cause he was a good, hard-workin' cowboy.

LP
F
BOD
Bodine, Jack
Apache moon

C. 1

AUG	2003		